Friends Forever?

As tears dribble down my face, my mind is racing. Claude, Fleur and I have hung out together since, like, Day 1 of Blackwell School. Ever since the gangly blonde chick and the little prim black girl with her hair in bunches sat down beside me in Year 7 French. We're like sisters. We're a team. We live our lives together! If they're sad, I'm sad. If I'm sad, well, they try to sort things out for me. And, sure, we've had bust-ups before, but that's just because sometimes we can all be extra-specially infuriatingly annoying! Like when Fleur falls in love with a different aftershave-drenched drongo every ten minutes. Or when Claude gets all swell-headed about her straight-A grades. Or when I forget birthdays or turn up late for stuff. Or, say, when Claude and Fleur post pictures of me all over the Internet, taken at a sleepover, asleep with my mouth open, wearing Blu-Tack devil horns. Oh, how I laughed.

But we always make friends in the end. Don't we?

OTHER BOOKS YOU MAY ENJOY:

Guitar Girl	Sarra Manning
How My Private, Personal Journal Became a Best-Seller	Julia DeVillers
I Was a Non-Blonde Cheerleader	Kieran Scott
Keeping the Moon	Sarah Dessen
LBD: It's a Girl Thing	Grace Dent
LBD: Live & Fabulous!	Grace Dent
Rules of the Road	Joan Bauer
Squashed	Joan Bauer
The Truth About Forever	Sarah Dessen
24 Girls in 7 Days	Alex Bradley

LBD

Friends Forever!

by
grace dent

C.4

speak

An Imprint of Penguin Group (USA) Inc.

SPEAK
Published by the Penguin Group
Penguin Group (USA) Inc., 345 Hudson Street, New York, New York 10014, U.S.A.
Penguin Group (Canada), 90 Eglinton Avenue East, Suite 700, Toronto, Ontario, Canada M4P 2Y3
(a division of Pearson Penguin Canada Inc.)
Penguin Books Ltd, 80 Strand, London WC2R 0RL, England
Penguin Ireland, 25 St Stephen's Green, Dublin 2, Ireland (a division of Penguin Books Ltd)
Penguin Group (Australia), 250 Camberwell Road, Camberwell, Victoria 3124, Australia
(a division of Pearson Australia Group Pty Ltd)
Penguin Books India Pvt Ltd, 11 Community Centre,
Panchsheel Park, New Delhi - 110 017, India
Penguin Group (NZ), 67 Apollo Drive, Mairangi Bay, Auckland 1311, New Zealand
(a division of Pearson New Zealand Ltd)
Penguin Books (South Africa) (Pty) Ltd, 24 Sturdee Avenue,
Rosebank, Johannesburg 2196, South Africa

Registered Offices: Penguin Books Ltd, 80 Strand, London WC2R 0RL, England

Published in Great Britain in 2006 by Puffin UK, London.
First published in the United States of America by G. P. Putnam's Sons,
a division of Penguin Young Readers Group, 2006
Published by Speak, an imprint of Penguin Group (USA) Inc., 2007

1 3 5 7 9 10 8 6 4 2

THE LIBRARY OF CONGRESS HAS CATALOGED THE G. P. PUTNAM'S SONS EDITION AS FOLLOWS:
Dent, Grace. LBD : friends forever / by Grace Dent. p. cm. Summary: Now sixteen years old,
Ronnie, Fleur, and Claude try to repair an unexpected rift in their friendship by getting summer
waitressing jobs together at a seaside resort. [1. Friendship—Fiction. 2. Waiters and waitresses—
Fiction. 3. High schools—Fiction. 4. Schools—Fiction.
5. England—Fiction.] I. Title. PZ7.D4345Lam 2006 [Fic]—dc22 2005023963
ISBN 0-399-24189-2 (hc)

Speak ISBN 978-0-14-240831-5

Designed by Gina DiMassi and Katrina Damkoehler.
Text set in Wilke Roman.
Printed in the United States of America

To **jon wilkinson**.

contents

1. she treats this house
   like a hotel — 1

2. three—the magic number — 24

3. a good turnout — 57

4. thumbs-up — 98

5. cometh the mailman — 127

6. booty camp — 156

7. more tea, cressida? — 176

8. booty quake — 211

9. the morning after — 253

Chapter 1

she treats this house like a hotel

Bang! Bang! Bang!

Three abrupt knocks on my bedroom door, then I'm invaded by the sleep police.

"Ronnie? *Ronnnnnnie?* Are you under there?" my mother quacks, lifting up a corner of the duvet, letting cold air surge over my limbs.

She knows how much that annoys me.

"Ronnie! Helllllloooo?! Earth calling Veronica Ripperton? Wake up!"

"Gnnnngnn! Go away!" I groan, whipping the quilt back from her and wrapping myself up like a sausage roll.

"Ugh! What do you *do* in this room?" she says sniffily, flinging back the curtains so the morning sunlight scorches my face. "How can you make a room so messy!"

I lie very still, praying for her to leave.

"You'll have rats in here before long," continues Mum, picking up a half-eaten chocolate chip muffin discarded on my desk. "Rats, I tell you! With big tails and sharp teeth! Well, not that rats would put up with this mess," she mutters under her breath.

"Uggghhh," I groan, hiding my face in the pillow.

"Ronnie! Can you hear me? What's this? What's going on here?" Mum says.

I sit up in bed, rubbing my eyes. Mum's peering at the front of my iMac like it's an extraterrestrial. "The front of this thing is flashing! Is it on? You'll start a fire in here! Why do you always leave things switched on?"

"Don't touch it," I mumble, watching Mum jabbing the power button, probably crashing the computer and corrupting all the files. "It's in sleep mode."

"Sleep mode! Pghhh!" she mutters. "You're in sleep mode, you lazy lump! Get up!"

"Gnngnn . . . ," I grumble, catching sight of myself in the mirror with pointy morning hair and a pillow crease down my face. "What is wrong with you? Are you a complete freak?"

I look at my bedside clock. It's 7:58 A.M.

"Ha!" Mum snorts. "What's wrong with me? What's wrong with you, more like?! You lie in your pit all day, then gawp at TV and play bass guitar all night long. Your body clock's upside down! You hardly see the sun. It's like living with a bat!"

"Ugh!" I groan, hiding my face under the covers again. "Look, you insane old goat! My last GCSE exam was on Wednesday. Two days ago! And I studied really hard for them too! And I'm not back at school till September. I've nothing to get up for!"

"Oh, there's *plenty* to get up for, young lady!" Mum hoots, clearly elated that I'm rising to her bait. "When I was sixteen years old, I'd be up with the lark on a glorious June morning like this. I'd be making breakfast and doing housework, really helping my mother out!"

"Oh, pur-lease," I groan.

"And you can start by minding Seth for me while I go to the wholesaler's. I'll be gone two hours," Mum twitters, poking me a bit. "Oh, c'mon, Ronnie, please? He's dying for you to play with him. He's been so miserable since he caught that tummy bug."

"Is he still projectile pooing?" I frown.

"Mmm . . . no, that seems to have cleared up," Mum sniggers. "But, y'know, best wear something wipeable, just to be safe."

"Euuuh!" I grimace, swinging my legs out of bed.

Mother has won again. *She always wins.*

"Hey, and when I get home . . . ," Mum says, "I'll help you fill out that waitressing application form for the Wacky Warehouse."

"Er, pardon?" I splutter. "I'm not working at a Wac . . ."

"It'll teach you the value of money!" Mum snaps back. "You're not freeloading off me and your dad until September."

"Huh! I *know* the value of money, thank you!" I say, beginning to raise my voice. "Listen, Mother, I am *not* working in a Wacky Warehouse! I'm not mopping up the ice cream and vomit at children's birthday parties! Cynthia Morris from Blackwell School had a Saturday job there, and they made her dress up in a squirrel costume and jump up and down on a mini trampoline playing the bongos for six hours a day. I'm not that wacky!"

Mum just rolls her eyes at me, then heads for the door. "Well, you better start feeling wacky soon, Lady Muck," she snaps crossly. "Or you're working downstairs with me as the

Fantastic Voyage's dishwasher. I'm not paying an extra body while you laze about up here!"

"What? Aaaagh!" I howl, imagining the prospect of nine weeks trapped in the basement of our family pub, unblocking hair from the waste disposal and gutting fish. "That is so unfair!"

"Veronica, life isn't fair," clips my mother. "Now, I want you up, dressed and in the den, frolicking with an incontinent toddler in ten minutes. Or else! Oh, and if you're bored, I've left notes about other chores on the fridge."

"I'm not going to be your slave for the summer!" I yell, getting angrier by the second. "And I won't work at the Wacky Warehouse either! I'd rather die! In fact, I'm going to fling myself out of my bedroom window . . . straight after breakfast."

"Mmm . . . don't do that, sweetheart," Mum says dryly, opening my bedroom door. "You'll make a terrible mess."

Mum trots out, smashing the door shut behind her. I've been awake less than forty-five seconds and we've already had our first bust-up. This is impressive, even by our standards.

"But this was meant to be . . . ," I yell as she clomps away down the landing, "my summer break!"

I strip off my nightgown, pulling on a hoodie and some baggy jeans, dragging my long auburn hair into a pink bobble, pausing to look at a photograph on my noticeboard. It's a picture of me, Fleur Swan and Claudette Cassiera, or Les Bambinos Dangereuses, as we're universally known, taken last summer when we had a fabulous adventure at the Astlebury Music Festival. Spike Saunders and tons of other bands played. The whole thing totally rocked. In the photo, I'm grinning like a demented hobbit, my arms wrapped around my two friends' shoulders. Fleur, as ever, looks fabulously, nauseatingly pretty. Blonde hair, perfect skin, big blue eyes, she's doing her typical "rabbit ears" trick behind my head. Next to her, Claude's goofing about, pulling one of her daftest faces. We look so happy.

I let out a long sigh. I really have got nothing to get up for today.

"Les Bambinos Dangereuses," I mutter, reaching my fingers out and touching Claude's ebony cheek, "what on earth has happened to us?"

radio ripperton

"Ah! You're up!" Dad chuckles, looking at his watch for comic effect. "Good afternoon."

It's 9:15 A.M. and Lawrence "Loz" Ripperton is on the sofa upstairs at the Fantastic Voyage, having a quiet half hour before his bartending duties begin.

"Oh, don't you start," I groan, sitting on the sofa, grabbing the remote and flicking on MTV, which is showing a rerun of last year's Big Beach Booty Quake party in Destiny Bay. On the TV, Big Doggy the rapper is performing on stage while hunks in trunks and a zillion perfect girls in thong bikinis quake their booties to a ragga beat.

I take a slurp of my coffee. Dad peers at the screen, which is full of undulating flesh, making a face that indicates he'd be outraged if he had the energy, before carrying on with his sports section.

"I've just been frog-marched out of bed by Attila the Mum," I grumble.

"Ah yes," smiles Dad, nodding toward the bedroom next door where Mum's dressing. "She's in fine form this morning, isn't she?"

My father accepts my mother's ruthless dictatorship with exceptional good grace. It's almost as if he enjoys his day being spelled out for him in yellow Post-it notes. He stays here through choice! I'd be gone tomorrow if I had any other option.

"Wonnie! Wonnie . . . Beawblooooo!!" burbles Seth, my seventeen-month-old brother, crawling toward me with a grin. "Wonnie!" he gargles again, attempting to stand up, but somehow pirouetting and falling headfirst toward the coffee table.

"Whooooah there, little fella!" I gasp, leaping up to grab him. "God, Dad, can't we get him a crash helmet or something?"

"Wonniebeawblue?" repeats Seth, wrapping his tiny arms around me.

I kiss the top of his little blond head, inhaling that great baby smell. "Beawblue?" I repeat, finding it impossible to stay cross.

"Ahhh," says Dad, who's a pro at translating baby babble. "He means the *Bear in the Big Blue House* DVD. Don't you, Sunny Jim?"

"Beablah!" Seth gurgles.

"Er, the one with the colors and shapes and stuff?" I ask. "Does he understand that?"

"I don't know," Dad announces solemnly. "But he's silent when it's on, Veronica. That's enough for me."

"Good point," I say as Seth wriggles around in his powder-blue baby suit, desperate to be put down on the floor.

"Beaw-tance!" Seth says rather forcefully. "Tance!"

"Oh, yeah," Dad adds. "He only likes the first six minutes, when the big hairy fella dances. He gets grouchy after that and wants it rewound."

"Tance!" Seth squeals excitedly.

A stripe of brown goo is beginning to ooze from the back of his suit. Dad spots this, quickly rustling his newspaper in front of his face.

"That's chocolate sauce . . . right?" I groan.

"Yeah, right," Dad says dryly.

Right that instant, my mobile phone starts squeaking and shuddering on the coffee table, playing a polyphonic version of Carmella Dupris's latest hit "KrazyGirl." That's the ring tone I've assigned to Fleur! Hurray!

The screen fills with a jpeg of a beautiful blond girl wearing a stripey T-shirt and a powder-pink beret, marred somewhat by the chopstick jammed firmly up each nostril.

"Oh, yeah, that reminds me," Dad says distractedly. "Your phone's been ringing for the last two hours. Me and Mum tried to open it. But we couldn't find the bit to talk into. It's all *Star Trek* to us, those things."

"Why didn't you wake me?" I fume.

"Ronnie, you're not a morning person," Dad says, chuckling. "I leave the wake-up calls to your mother. She's braver than me."

I wrinkle my nose at him, then press "answer."

"Fleur!" I say. "All right, babe? What are you doing?"

"Hey, Ronnie!" Fleur giggles. "Guess where I am?"

"Dunno," I say.

"Give you a clue," Fleur says, sounding excited. "I've just bought that fabulous cerise polka-dot bikini. This month's 'hot buy' in June's *Elle Girl* magazine!"

"Er, you're on High Street?" I guess. "Or the Westland Park Shopping Mall?"

Fleur giggles a bit more. "I'm at Emerald Green Shopping City! I'm in It's a Girl's World at Emerald Green Shopping City!"

"Emerald . . . Green! Emerald Green Shopping City!" I say, feeling rather rattled. "Fleur, that's, like, two hundred miles away."

"I know," she laughs.

"Who are you with?" I say suspiciously.

"I'm, er . . . all alone," Fleur says, sounding a little less jubilant now. "Dad was driving down really early for the Motor Show at the Exhibition Center nearby. I only found out last night, so I nabbed a lift."

"Oh," I say. "That's . . . er, cool."

"Yeah, sort of," says Fleur. "On the downside, Paddy's bent my ear for two hundred miles about getting a summer job. Apparently I need 'direction in my life.' "

"Gnnnngnn . . . don't even go there," I groan.

There's a small awkward silence.

Why didn't she ask me to go?

Emerald Green Shopping City, aside from being literally a "city of shopping," is home to Britain's flagship It's a Girl's World store. IGW totally rocks! It's the LBD's own personal mecca, to which we're always planning a pilgrimage. As well as six whole floors of amazing clothes and accessories, the store runs daily catwalk shows and features its own TV station broadcasting on huge banks of plasma TVs. You can book personal shoppers who'll make you look like a pop star, plus there's a sweets shop, a nail bar, hair boutique and a *floor* devoted to sunglasses, hair clips and hats. There's also an entire basement of customized antique and retro designer clothes. (It's Claude's favorite floor. Last Christmas she found an amazing black sixties Mod dress for £20!)

"Hey, Ronnie," Fleur says, sounding slightly lonely. "I'm standing at the bottom of the ground floor escalator."

"Where the Million Dollar Models scouts always are?" I say, grabbing the DVD remote control and pressing "play." Seth's eyes light up as the dancing bear fills the screen.

"Yeah," Fleur says. "This is where they found Devan Davies, the Joop girl. No luck for me today, though."

"It'll happen one day," I tell her.

"Hope so," Fleur sighs.

There's that sad, awkward silence again.

I know the LBD have been having some major problems recently, but this has got way out of hand now. Fleur going to Emerald Park without us just seems so final.

The LBD *always* go to Emerald Park together! Ever since Year 7, when we got our first proper allowances.

"Are you okay?" Fleur asks sheepishly.

I'm trying to swallow my feelings, but the words just flood out. "No . . . I'm not really, Fleur!" I say. "Why didn't you call me to go with you? I've got Girl's World vouchers to spend!"

"I called you this morning," Fleur argues. "Three times! Your folks kept picking the phone up, but they couldn't work out what bit to speak into."

"Oh God," I groan, clutching my head.

"And then they couldn't hang it up," Fleur says. "I could hear them chatting to each other for ages."

"What about?" I gasp.

"Errr . . . nothing really," Fleur says. "But, er, did you know your mum's nipples are almost back to normal after breast-feeding?"

"Shut. Up," I grimace. "You're kidding me?"

"Er, no," Fleur says. "You might want to go through your phone's memory and check out who else Radio Ripperton has been broadcasting to."

"I'm going to kill them," I say quite seriously. My parents will not be satisfied until I literally die of shame. I'd happily divorce them.

"Well, whatever, Fleur," I continue huffily. "You didn't try that hard to reach me. Did you? You could have rung me last night."

"Pgggh . . . well maybe I didn't feel like ringing you last night, okay?" Fleur snaps back. "I thought that you'd be round at . . . ," Fleur begins to say something, then stops herself. "I thought you'd be too busy."

She means Claude. She won't even say her name.

"I was playing bass guitar in my bedroom like a right Billy-No-Mates all last night, Fleur!" I yell. "I reckon Claude was on her own too."

"Doubt it," Fleur hisses. "She'll be with her new best friend!"

"Oh, for God's sake," I say. "This is soooo stupid! We could have all gone to Emerald Park together today. We could be in the food court slurping milk shakes and checking out the passing hotties right now!"

"I've slurped my last milk shake with Claudette Cassiera," Fleur scoffs. "Claude and I are over, Ronnie. She's out of my life now. I feel much better for it too!"

"Don't be daft, Fleur," I say. "Look, let's have an LBD meeting tonight at my place. Let's talk about this."

"What?!" Fleur says. "After her behavior?! I'd rather kiss the cat's bum."

"This isn't all Claude's fault, y'know," I begin to argue.

"Oh, go on, stick up for her. Like you always do!" Fleur says, sounding like she's almost blubbering. "Look, why don't you all just be friends together this summer? I'll find something else to do."

"Like what?!"

"Like . . . like whatever I want," she says firmly. "See ya, Ronnie."

And then the phone goes dead.

I slump back on the sofa.

What on earth do I do now? Tell Claude? Call Fleur back? I feel sick.

Dad puts down his newspaper gently. "What's going on there?" he says.

"Nothing," I say, chucking my phone and folding my arms.

"Oh, right," Dad says. "Doesn't sound like nothing."

I stare ahead at the TV.

"You girls had a bust-up?" Dad says.

"No, we're fine," I say, clearly fibbing my head off.

"What's it about?" he says. "Lads?"

I scowl at him.

"Knew it," Dad says. "It's always lads."

"It's not lads," I grump.

"That's all you ladies ever row about," Dad says, trying to cheer me up. "Cuh, I've had a few young chickadees cat-fighting over me in my time, I'll tell you that for nothing," he says, miming straightening his invisible tie.

Who's he kidding? His face looks like it was knitted by his mum.

"It's not about lads," I say.

"Well, it's something . . . I saw Claude yesterday night walking up Lacy Road. She looked like a wet weekend."

"You saw Claude?" I say, my eyes widening. "Which way was she going? At what time?"

"Er . . . back to her mum's, I s'pose," Dad says. "Six-ish?"

"Hmmmph," I say. Claude hasn't returned my calls for days.

"I can always count on little Claude for a smile and wave," continues Dad, "but she didn't even see me. Had her head down. She looked really miserable."

A tear forms in the corner of my eye. I bat it away. Dad sticks his big arm around me.

"Awww, come on, Ronnie! Give us a clue, eh?" he says. "I'm not as useless as I look. I bet I can help."

"You can't, Dad," I say quietly. "No one can. It's all a big mess."

"But what . . . I mean, where . . . ?" Dad begins. "Isn't there . . . ?"

My lips simply become tighter. Dad knows from long experience that there's no point in questioning me further.

As tears dribble down my face, my mind is racing. Claude, Fleur and I have hung out together since, like, Day 1 of

Blackwell School. Ever since the gangly blonde chick and the little prim black girl with her hair in bunches sat down beside me in Year 7 French. We're like sisters. We're a team. We live our lives together! If they're sad, I'm sad. If I'm sad, well, they try to sort things out for me. And, sure, we've had bust-ups before, but that's just because sometimes we can all be extra-specially infuriatingly annoying! Like when Fleur falls in love with a different aftershave-drenched drongo every ten minutes. Or when Claude gets all swell-headed about her straight-A grades. Or when I forget birthdays or turn up late for stuff. Or, say, when Claude and Fleur post pictures of me all over the Internet, taken at a sleepover, asleep with my mouth open, wearing Blu-Tack devil horns. Oh, how I laughed.

But we always make friends in the end. Don't we?

"C'mon, precious," Dad says. "Dry your eyes. Look, are you sure you can't give me a clue what's up?"

"Maybe later, eh?" I sniff, wiping tears down my hoodie sleeve.

"Okay," Dad whispers. "Leave you to it. For now."

not an octopus

Suddenly, Mum appears in the doorway, freshly painted lipstick denoting her imminent exit.

"Ah, good girl. You're up!" she smiles, picking up her car keys. "Huh, Loz, I'm going to make that wholesaler's life hell this morning! Eight items missing on the last order. Eight! I'm not leaving his office until I get at least forty percent off next week's invoice."

"Good luck, my little tinderbox," Dad nods. "Go easy on him, won't you?"

"Not likely," says Mum, making a googly face at Seth, then turning to me.

"You can cope with him, can't you, darling?"

"Mmm," I say. I've had enough flipping practice.

"Word of advice, though, Ronnie," Mum says, blotting her lipstick on a beer invoice. "You need to watch him every single second these days. He's smarter than he looks. He found a staple gun at your aunty Susan's yesterday and tried to pierce her cat's ears."

Seth smiles at us all and waves his hands. He's the epitome of cute.

"She's not wrong, Ron," nods Dad sagely. "I like to think of him as the face of evil."

"Uh-huh," I sigh.

Mum peers at me awhile longer, eyeing me up and down.

"You're, erm . . . ," she says, pointing at my baggy hoodie and jeans, "not going out dressed like that, are you?"

Oh God.

"I'm not going anywhere," I tut. "I'm looking after your son."

"Oooh, that time already? Must fly," Dad announces. He's such a chicken. Last month, after one of me and Mum's screaming bust-ups, I found him two hours later, sitting in the beer cellar, wearing his Discman and reading the *Sporting Post*.

"Loz! I need you—don't go anywhere," Mum commands, turning again to me. "It's just those shapeless jeans, Ronnie. They do nothing for your figure! And that hooded top makes you look like a painter and decorator."

"Oh, leave me alone," I moan. "What do you know about what people my age wear?"

This is a foolish thing to say. My mother is an authority on absolutely everything.

"Well, I saw Nicole Jones, your aunty Susan's goddaughter, in Asda yesterday and she looked absolutely gorgeous!"

"Oh, for God's sake . . ."

"She was wearing a peach cardigan, and a fresh white tailored blouse and fitted black trousers. She looked immaculate! Her mother must be so proud of her."

"Nicole Jones is a complete buttmunch, Mother," I fume, glaring at my mother. "She competes with her brother in Scottish country dancing competitions! She eats school lunch with an imaginary friend! She collects thimbles!"

"Well, at least she makes the best of herself," Mum drones, "not like you and your bunch."

"Oh, here we go," I say. I am not in the mood to discuss the LBD.

"There's you, off to paint the Forth Road Bridge, there's Claude, who looks like a little old granny most of the time in those old moth-eaten dresses . . . oooh, and as for that Fleur Swan, well, she had jeans on so tight the other day, I could see the outline of her . . . well, I won't say! Poor Paddy Swan, he must be absolutely driven to despair with her!"

"Whatever," I sigh.

"C'mon, play nice now, ladies," Dad says, trying to move past Mum. Mum frowns at us both, picking up her cardigan and throwing it around her shoulders. She walks across and stares out the living room window for a few seconds, letting out a

15

long sigh. Then she turns to me again. She looks pretty anxious about something.

"What's up now?" I tut.

"Oh, nothing. It's just your nan," Mum says. "She called last night. She's not sounding too good."

"Really?" I say, feeling guilty because I've not visited for almost two months. "What's up with her?"

"Well, she just sounds confused, y'know?" Mum says quietly, sounding more angry at life now. "She was wittering on about police chases and drug raids near her house." Mum rolls her eyes, biting her lip slightly. "She's getting herself worked up again."

"Oh, dear," I say. I think Nan's going a bit bonkers.

"I called the local police to double-check," says Mum, "but they said that there hasn't been a disturbance in her post code for more than four months. They don't know what she's talking about."

Mum's eyes go a little glassy.

"Maybe she's getting mixed up with something on TV," I say. "You know she loves cop dramas."

"Well, either way, it's not good, is it?" Mum says. "Everyone forgets she has a heart condition. She's eighty-two, you know?"

"Mmm," I say.

"If you were any sort of granddaughter," Mum says, switching on the moan again, "you'd go and see her. It's only an hour away on the train. She'd love to see you . . ."

As my mother drones on and on, I switch to "white noise" in my head and block her out. But now that I think about it, I'd love to see my nan. She never gives me a hard time. In fact, the dafter I dress, the more she likes it. And she bakes her own cakes too.

She might even know what to do about the LBD. She's pretty sussed for an old lady.

"Okay," I interrupt. "I'll go this afternoon."

"'Where's Ronnie?' That's what she always asks," Mum twitters, oblivious. "But oh no, you can't spare the time for an old woman, can you? Unless it's your birthday and she's got her hand in her purse—"

"Mother! I'll go this afternoon!" I yell. "I'll get the two-thirty train and I'll be in her kitchen eating scones and reminiscing about Princess Diana's lovely wedding dress by four. Is that okay?!"

Mum stares at me, slightly dumbfounded.

Dad gives me a "nice one" wink.

"Today?" she repeats.

"Today!" I say, flaring my nostrils. "Try and stop me."

"Well . . . okay then!" Mum says, turning on her heel and heading for the door. "All I need is a bit of help!" she shouts as she stomps down the stairs. "I've only got one pair of hands to do everything! I'm not an octopus, y'know. I'm not a flipping octopus!"

In the living room, Dad and I are left staring at each other in utter bemusement.

"She's not an octopus, y'know?" says Dad mock seriously. "I'm glad we got that one cleared up."

"Hmmm," I say.

"How long before school starts again?" asks Dad, wincing as Seth toddles over smelling distinctly like an explosion in a bum factory.

"Nine weeks," I say, holding my nose.

thunder and lightning

Because pheasants are on the track just outside Chipping Tanbury, the 2:30 Mainline Clipper service to Little Chipping is delayed by approximately forty-eight minutes. Actually, this might have been "peasants on the track"—the Mainline Trains announcer had a dreadful mucus problem.

Whatever, the delay allots me a nice lengthy space of dead time to sit on a cold metallic bench beside a railway track and think about my future without the LBD. I've got a specific iPod play list of angry songs for when life is beginning to make me commit murder, so I cue up "Another Homicide" by Psycho Killa, a blistering 3:20 rap ditty involving plenty of bad language and mild glorification of violence, then sit staring at the tracks, brooding about my own personal misfortune.

I am utterly bereft.

The train pulls into the station and I jump off. I wander miserably down Little Chipping's sleepy main street, past the post office and the dressmaker's boutique, past the Village Hall where Nan has her Tuesday Club meetings, past the kids' swing park, turning right into Dewers Drive, where Nan lives at number eleven. The white paintwork on Nan's terraced house seems a touch tatty now that Granddad's not around to climb ladders with a paintbrush every other day, although Nan's rosebushes, dotted all over her small front garden, look typically fabulous. As the tiny gate snaps closed behind me, I ring Nan's bell.

Bbbbbbbbbbbbbbbbbbbbrrrrrrrrrrrrrrrrrrrr!

I pause for a minute. Total silence.

Mum promised me Nan would be in.

Bbbbbbbbbbbbbbbbbbbbrrrrrrrrrrrrrrrrrrrr!

Inside I hear the tapping of a walking stick. "Helloooo!" a little voice shouts. "Who is it?!"

"It's me, Nan!" I smile. "It's Ronnie!"

"I'm very content with my gas supplier!" Nan shouts. "None today, thanking you kindly!"

"It's Ronnie," I repeat, giggling. "Your granddaughter!"

Total silence. Has she gone?

"Nan! It's Ronnie. Let me in!" I say, ringing the bell again. More silence.

"Ronnie?! Oooh, Veronica! It's you!" Nan shouts eventually, chuckling wildly. "Hang on!"

A multitude of keys are jangled, locks turned and bolts undone before the door flies open, revealing Leticia Warton, aka Nan, in her full Nan glory. Mischievous smile, large brown reading spectacles that make her eyes ginormous, snow-white tightly permed hair, wearing her trademark blue-and-lavender floral shift dress with a gold brooch, slightly hidden by a pink housecoat, a brown walking stick firmly in one hand. Every time I see Nan, the fairies appear to have stolen a little more of her away. She's simply not the huge stout woman I think I'm going to visit.

"Good afternoon to you! Come inside!" Nan says excitedly as I kiss her powdery cheek. "They've almost got him! Come on!"

"What?" I say as Nan vanishes down the hallway, moving surprisingly speedily for a woman supposedly crippled with rheumatoid arthritis.

"The man they're chasing!" shouts Nan, beckoning me into the kitchen. "The man with the gun! He's a drug dealer, you know?"

Oh, no. Please God, not today, I think. Trust her to choose the day I'm here alone to go totally crazy. What do I do now? What would Claude do?

"Nan," I say, moving gingerly into the kitchen behind her, "there isn't a man with a gun. Let's just sit down, shall we? I'll put the kettle on."

"Shh," Nan says, walking over to a mysterious black radio on the kitchen table and fiddling with the dials. "I'm listening."

"All points are on full alert, Sarge," a voice says anxiously on the radio. "We have one IC1 male. Armed. Repeat, armed! Approaching Harpingdon. Do you read me?"

"Nan . . . what's that!?" I say, staring at the hissing contraption.

"One second," Nan says, putting a finger to her lips.

"Nan, is that a police scanner?" I say in disbelief. "Are you listening to police broadcasts?"

"Go on! Get him!" Nan shouts at the scanner. "Block him off at Junction Fourteen. If he gets past the Harpingdon bypass, you've lost him!"

"Nan, where did you get that thing?" I shout over the racket.

"Tango Delta 435, are you receiving? He's out of the car and on foot! We've got him covered, Sarge," says a voice on the box. "Unit 234 is closing on him . . . he's making the arrest."

"Hurray!" shouts Nan, clapping her hands. "They're so much faster than those numskulls on *The Shield*."

"Nan, where did you get that scanner?" I repeat firmly.

"What, this thing?" Nan says, turning off the machine. "Miriam from church's son Tony gave me it."

"Tony Crossgate?" I moan. "Nan! He's totally shady."

"Nonsense!" laughs Nan. "He's a lovely young man. He's just so madly keen on electronics—his bedroom's full of them. He keeps all his extra stuff in Miriam's garden shed."

"Extra *stolen* stuff," I mutter.

"You see," Nan says, "I was at Miriam's last Tuesday having my hair set and Tony said that seeing as I was one of his favorite old ladies, I could have a police scanner or one of those DNA whatchamacallits."

"DVD players," I say, trying not to laugh.

"That's the fellows!" laughs Nan, putting two tea bags into the teapot. "Why, what's up? Am I in trouble again?"

"No," I say, smiling. "Not really . . . I'm relieved. Mum thought you were going cra . . ."

I stop myself. Nan rolls her eyes.

"Yes, yes, I'm aware everyone thinks I'm losing my marbles," she smirks. "Nobody listens to me properly! I told Magda about Tony's scanner. She just kept telling me to calm down. She's always been the same, that girl. Bossy. Never listens."

"Hmmm," I say.

"Veronica," Nan continues, pouring boiling water into the pot, "I'm not ready for the funny farm yet."

"Sorry, Nan," I mutter, blushing.

"Anyhow, petal, take a seat," she says, pouring the tea. "I want to hear all your news. Exams . . . they're over?"

"Yeah," I sigh.

"Well, that'll be a relief, then?" Nan twinkles. "A-levels next, eh? Then, off to university? How exciting!"

"Mmm, s'pose," I say. I've never actually agreed that I'm going to university. Mum might have. I certainly haven't.

"So, what's the plan for the summer?" she says. "I bet you and those pals of yours, Claudette and Fleur, have got some high jinks in order to celebrate, haven't you?"

"Mmm, not really," I mumble, feeling a little choked.

"Oh?" Nan says, looking surprised. "No summer adventure? You went off to that pop music festival last year, didn't you?"

"Astlebury," I sigh.

Nan pushes some strong brown tea in front of me. "Well, then, what about that . . . Jimi Steele?" she asks. "That good-looking fellow of yours? How's he doing?"

"We split up," I say firmly. "For good this time. It's all got a bit, er, messy. He's, erm, with someone else now."

"Crikey!" says Nan. "Well . . . good riddance to him! Never liked him anyhow. Or his silly skateboard."

I try to smile, but there's a lump in my throat.

Nan looks at me anxiously. "Dewdrop," she says, passing me the sugar, "you're really far too young to be wearing a sad expression like that. Whatever is the matter?"

I really want to tell Nan, but it's complicated. "I don't know where to begin," I mutter.

Nan looks concerned. She stands up and hobbles over to her pantry cupboard. "Well, I have an idea," she says. "You start right at the beginning. I'm going to make some fruit scones. You talk, I'll bake. Then if I can't solve your problem, at least we'll have lovely scones to eat."

I look at her, with a small smile growing on my face. "Mmm . . . but have you got any black treacle?" I ask, raising an eyebrow. Nan bakes the most amazing light, fluffy fruit scones, which she always serves fresh from the oven with clotted cream and black treacle, or Thunder and Lightning, as she calls it. They're the most delicious things on the entire planet.

"A whole tin of it," winks Nan. "Do we have a deal?"

"Okay," I say, taking a deep breath to begin.

Chapter 2

three—the magic number

Last autumn, returning to Blackwell after summer break was really cool.

Not only was everyone still gossiping about the LBD's amazing adventure at Astlebury Music Festival, where we'd been hanging out with the stars and getting our faces all over the tabloid newspaper standing with our close personal showbiz buddy, "Duke of Pop" Spike Saunders, but this term was very special indeed.

The LBD would be Year 11 babes!

Utterly mature. I'd been yearning for this moment since Year 7. Now, the only Blackwell inmates able to look down on us would be the Year 12/13 crowd (including obnoxious bully Panama Goodyear and her perfect-skinned android disciples Abigail Munro and Leeza Palmer), but thankfully they rarely left their A-level common room anyhow. It was the Year 11s who ruled the school!

As Year 11 chicks, we could breeze into lunch on any sitting we desired—no more eating leftover knobbly chicken nuggets that look like deep-fried mice. Yak! And we could use Blackwell's posh "Senior School" doorway, which sliced up to *five minutes* off some journeys.

Best of all, we were now entitled to proper wooden seats during Blackwell assemblies. Marvelous. On freezing mornings, the LBD would grab seats in the very back row, in the corner by the radiator. While Mr. McGraw, our clinically depressed headmaster, droned on and on about "school pride," I'd snooze, Fleur would do homework and Claude would knit a variety of bobble hats for unfortunate associates. Claude's romance with Damon, an apprentice electrician she met at Astlebury, had taken a serious nosedive since she'd presented him with one of her legendary knitted bobble monstrosities. Sadly, this didn't prevent Claude from knitting Spike Saunders one too, just in case he felt chilly on his stadium tour of Latin America. Spike sent us a card to say he'd received it, but although we checked *Red Hot Celebs* magazine every week, we'd never spotted him with it on.

A further super-cool thing about Blackwell this term were the Golden Anniversary celebrations. Okay, this sounded potentially dull, but bizarrely, McGraw had green-lighted a few fab events "to commemorate fifty years of Blackwell at the heart of the community." In fact, taking place in the first week back at school was a charity nonuniform day, aka "Fancy Friday." As long as pupils paid £3 each, we could wear whatever we pleased—fancy, fashionable or funny! Neat, eh?

"Why doesn't the LBD dress exactly the same?" Claude said, giggling. "Like triplets! That would freak people right out. Teachers always say we're like three peas in a pod."

"Oh. My. God! Excellent idea," agreed Fleur, flapping her hands. (Fleur Swan loves dressing up. She once appeared at Liam Gelding's birthday party dressed as an Egyptian belly dancer, claiming she thought it was "fancy dress." She then boogied all night in a gold bikini while everyone else was dressed normally.)

"But people will laugh at us," I worried. "Especially Panama and—"

"Oh, who cares?" butted in Claude. "Let them laugh!"

"She'll just be jealous, because we'll look so hot," Fleur said.

Quickly it was agreed. Friday was going to be Triplet Day. Immediately, Claude started arguing for a "sexy ninja fighting squad" look, while Fleur began planning a "Parisian babe" feel. After a lot of squabbling and shopping we agreed on three black-and-white stripey long-sleeved T-shirts, three black pleated mini-kilts, black high heels, black opaque tights and the perfect finishing touch—powder-pink berets worn at a jaunty angle.

Naturally, Triplet Day was a massive triumph.

Jimi, my Year 13 skater boyfriend, said he'd never seen me look so totally babelicious. He wrapped me in his arms and said he'd never been so proud to be seen with me in the whole two years we'd been together.

And when the LBD appeared at Blackwell that Friday arm-in-arm, sashaying down the main corridor, kids were hanging out of windows whooping and hollering. It was so great! I didn't even flinch when Panama cornered me in the dining hall to inform me that "saggy-chested dumpy girls" such as myself should avoid horizontal stripes and skirts above the shin. And okay, sadly, we didn't win the Fancy Friday prize. But that was because Year 9's Darius Carver painted himself turquoise, festooned himself in plastic wrap and tampons and came as an interplanetary life-form.

But who cares, because the LBD still appeared in the *Local Daily Mercury* under the headline "Triple Trouble at Blackwell's Golden Celebrations!" This made Magda, Paddy and Gloria, Claude's mum, extra happy because they could call all their friends and bore their pants off.

"That was a grand photo of you!" Nan says, laughing as she sifts flour into a white mixing bowl.
"Hmmm . . . ," I say. "Well, Fleur looked better in it than me."
"Nonsense!" Nan tuts. "She's not a classic beauty like you are."

Triplet Day turned into Triplet Weekend.

I hadn't laughed so much in ages. That Friday night we wore our berets and T-shirts to the noodle bar Shanghai Shanghai, then afterward we had a sleepover at Fleur's. (Fleur's parents had just bought her a "facts of life" book called *Your Body, Yourself.* Oh my Lord! We had no idea so many unpleasant yeast- and fungus-related things could occur on your bodily parts! Yeucccch!) On Sunday we hit Westland Mall to suss out the fresh fall collections arriving at Top Shop, Morgan and River Island. Of course, that went out of the window when Fleur spotted Baz Kauffman, a Year 12 from Chasterton School, and persuaded the LBD to stalk him around Marks and Spencer snapping telephone pictures of him buying underpants!

At that point in my life, one Sunday last September, I don't think I'd ever been so happy. With life. With Jimi. With the way I looked. With my friends. Being part of the LBD absolutely rocked.

the new girl

But then, the following Monday, just after registration, we were in form room drooling over a surf hunk centerfold in *Bliss* magazine, when the door swung open and the doom-meister general Mr. McGraw swept in. Standing meekly in his shadow was a tiny, elfin, decidedly beautiful young girl, with long golden hair hanging loose over her shoulders and a blunt fringe chopped just at her eye line. The girl's powdery-pale complexion, doll-pink cheeks and cherubic pout were slightly beguiling. Her long floaty gray skirt, nipped at her tiny waist, a blue cashmere jersey, expensive crocheted tights and black pumps with crisscrossed ribbons were a spurious nod toward the Blackwell uniform.

She had a touch of Cinderella about her. The entire room was silenced by her prettiness.

"Well, helloooo, missy!" leered Liam Gelding as the rest of the boys stared in wonderment.

"Now then, listen here, Class Eleven-B," sighed McGraw, holding aloft a skeletal hand, "I need your full attention. I have with me here today Miss Cressida Sleeth. Everybody say hello to Cressida."

"Hello," Cressida said coyly, twinkling her hand with a slight jangle of thin silver bracelets.

"Hello, Cressida," chorused the class.

"Isn't that a hobbit name?" Fleur said quietly.

"It's Shakespearean," whispered Claude.

"Now class," McGraw continued, "Cressida will be joining Eleven-B for the duration of Year Eleven. And as you must be aware, this will be a difficult time to begin a new school what with the GCSEs drawing closer, so I expressly want you all to be especially philanthropic to her."

"He means 'kind,' " Claude whispered to Liam.

"Oh, I'll be kind to her, don't worry," Liam said, shuffling uncomfortably in his chair. Claude tutted.

Cressida surveyed us all angelically, her eyes like two large, clear gray pools.

"Now, Claudette Cassiera," McGraw said, putting both hands on Claude's desk, "I've examined your files. You and Cressida share seven classes in common: geography, Latin, chemistry, biology, et cetera. So would you be so good as to help the new recruit settle in?"

"Er . . . no problem, Mr. McGraw!" Claude said, bristling with pride.

"You'd better take a seat," Fleur said with a wink, pulling back the spare end-of-row chair beside the LBD and patting it.

A new person! How exciting! I thought, giving Cressida my best nonscary grin.

"Thank you," Cressida said, sitting her teensy-tiny bum down. She smelled of fresh flowers and beeswax hand soap.

"Where've you come from?" Claude whispered.

"Windsor," Cressida said.

"Wow! The Queen has a castle there, doesn't she?" said Fleur.

"Yes, we lived about a mile from there," said Cressida a touch sadly.

"What brings you here?" Claude asked.

"My dad's the new head of chemical research at Farquar, Lime and Young Pharmaceuticals," she said. "Have you heard of it?"

"Yeah," I said. "It's pretty famous. In fact, it sometimes accidentally sprays white dust over the nearby village and the residents break out in a rash . . ."

Claude and Fleur shot me withering looks.

"Anyway," I said, shutting up, "welcome to Blackwell!"

"I'm Claude, that's Ronnie, and that's Fleur!" Claude explained.

Cressida smiled, gazing around the room at the shabby decor and disheveled pupils, then fixing her eyes upon us again. "Cressida Sleeth," she said, looking like a little otherworldly princess. "Lovely to meet you."

I didn't have much to do with Cressida at first.

During study hall she'd perch serenely beside Claude on the end of the row, reading kooky books with titles like *How to Channel Your Life Happier!* or *The Karma Conundrum.* Occasionally she'd talk about the ponies she'd left behind in Windsor, or her strong belief in guardian angels, or her endless string of allergies (wheat, pets, dairy, strong sunshine, etc.). I thought she was a bit freaky, albeit in a harmless way. Because her previous school in Windsor didn't follow exactly the same GCSE curriculum as Blackwell, Cressida spent most of her free time in the library doing catch-up study sessions. Of course,

Claude, being the huge boffin she is, began joining her some lunchtimes just for fun.

The weeks whizzed past, and by mid-October the LBD were lost under a mountain of school projects. Suddenly I had a GCSE music project to compose, a mock French oral exam to prepare, a thousand-word Buddhism paper to draft for religion and two creative writing assignments!

"Why do we never have fun anymore?" moaned Jimi when I refused to go over to his house midweek to watch DVDs. I'd been seeing Jimi for almost two and a half years and loved him more than life itself. But things had been getting kind of strained lately.

"I *can't* have fun!" I yelled. "My mother won't let me! I have to study two hours a night or my allowance is getting cut off. She's threatening to buy my clothes for me. Do you want a girl-friend who looks like a thirty-six-year-old woman?"

"Oh, whatever," Jimi sighed. "I'll give Suzette and Aaron a call, see if they want to do some geography homework."

"Okay," I said. "See you at school tomorrow?"

"Maybe," he sulked.

I wasn't lying. Not only was my mother adamant that I was going to pass these exams, but I was on very shaky ground with her over Jimi. Earlier that month she'd caught me coming home from Jimi's with a love bite on my neck and my T-shirt on back-ward.

Oh my God. She was livid beyond belief. It all got totally heavy. We had a big embarrassing talk, and she warned me that any more "behavior" like that and she'd ensure that I'd never see Jimi Steele again. I screamed at her that I hated her. And why did she have me anyway if she quite clearly hated young people? And I bawled that I was leaving home as soon as I could anyway. But once I'd calmed down, I'd decided that my best plan if I wanted to keep Jimi was to start studying. Hard. So that's what I did.

And that's why I missed what was happening right under my nose.

the thin lady sings

"Guess where I'm going on Friday night?" Fleur cooed last November as we sat in my room composing an "original piece" for our music GCSE.

Two whole months we'd been slaving away. Depressingly, all we'd captured on DAT so far was me playing a plinky-plonky jazz bass line while Fleur improvised lyrically in a free-form operatic style. Fleur thought it sounded "really crazy and edgy."

It didn't, by the way. It sounded like a drunk woman being bundled into a police car while someone attacked my bass guitar with pliers. It was so awful it could have been played by the British Army to disorient enemy troops.

"Dunno," I said, retuning a bass string. "Where y'going?"

"Cressida's house!" Fleur smiled. "Cressida's mum's going to give me a Reiki healing session. For free!"

"Really?" I said, trying not to sound weirded out. "That's, er, cool. Do you need healing?"

"Well, Cressida says that I have a very heavy aura," Fleur said. "It might be because of my inner sadness over my breakup with Spencer."

"With who?" I asked. Fleur's boyfriends tend to change quickly.

"Spencer Pickett!" she said. "Half-grown goatee? Ate a lot of Oreos? Rode a very small child's bike everywhere?"

"Oh *him*," I shuddered. "You need to be healed over him?"

"Awww . . . he was quite nice, y'know, Ronnie?" Fleur argued. "He had a good heart, y'know? I could have really fallen in love with him. Well . . . if that judge hadn't put that antisocial behavior order on him so he couldn't visit our side of town."

"What a spoilsport," I muttered dryly.

"I know!" tutted Fleur. "He only smashed up one bus shelter. Well, two. Okay, three if you count the big SPENNY he spray-painted on the one on Holmacres Drive."

"Hmmm. Yes, he was quite the guerrilla artist," I muttered. "So you're having Reiki over Spencer then?"

"Well, Cressida's not entirely sure," Fleur said. "It could be a past-life scarring issue I need help with."

"Past-life scarring?" I said, trying to keep a straight face.

"Yes!" said Fleur. "Cressida says she gets the feeling I've lived before as one of Cleopatra's ladies-in-waiting! Isn't that freaky?"

"Hmmm," I said, putting down the guitar. "Well, what's freakier, I reckon, is how no one ever seems to have a past life working in a pie shop. Or as a public toilet attendant! Do nonglamorous people never get reborn?"

Fleur's face dropped. She usually laughs at my jokes. "Well, I'm really psyched about it anyhow," she muttered.

"Oh . . . well," I said quickly, realizing I'd somehow hurt her. "I'm sure it'll feel amazing!"

"I know!" Fleur said, brightening a little. "And I'll get to see

Cressida's house too! It's one of those big new ones on Larkrise Manor, down the road from Panama Goodyear's mansion. Apparently Cressida has the entire basement all to herself! And they've got a hot tub too, so I'm taking my bikini."

"Cool," I smiled, feeling slightly rattled inside.

I couldn't quite get my head around this whole Cressida business. I mean, okay, it wasn't strange that Claude was studying with her—they had seven classes in common—but now Fleur was warming to her too! It was really unsettling. These days, whenever Claude, Fleur and Cressida came back from biology (a subject I was too thick to take) they always had a side-splitting story or a new-age tip to discuss. Or worst of all, a private joke they'd invented when I wasn't there.

But when I tried to be friends with Cressida, she just wasn't interested.

I tried inviting her to sit with me in German, the only class we had together, but she said she suffered migraines if she didn't sit near the board. I offered to study vocab with her, but she said she didn't need my help. But weirdest of all, whenever Cressida and I had to walk anywhere together, she'd say absolutely nothing at all.

Not a word.

So I'd yadder away, making jokes and telling stories, feeling stupider and more flippant by the second, trying to fill the silence. Eventually Cressida would finish these little agonizing one-on-ones by turning to me, forcing a smile and saying something like, "You're very funny, aren't you, Ronnie? You're simply always the clown. It must be soooo exhausting being you."

What the hell did that mean?!

The second we rejoined Claude and Fleur, she'd be charm personified, wowing them with tales of crystals and hot stone therapy.

Was I just being paranoid?

Maybe I was so pathetic and needy I just couldn't cope sharing the LBD with anyone? Let's face it: I couldn't even handle Fleur visiting another girl's house for a healing session! Ugh! How freakish and clingy was that?

I vowed right then to try harder to be friends with Cressida Sleeth.

bad vibes

It was a fortnight later, early last December, and the LBD were gathered in HQ, Fleur's bedroom, to discuss some ultra-hot topics, namely:

a) Jimi Steele being really distant and buttmunchy lately. Fleur reckoned he had Asperger's syndrome.

b) Claude's mum's boss, Mr. Rayner, running away to Bermuda with his twenty-seven-year-old big-boobed legal assistant, leaving Gloria Cassiera out of a job. And . . .

c) Fleur's new boyfriend, Thurston Barron, who was turning out to have very wandering hands and spent most dates, it seemed, trying to knead Fleur's boobs into one big central one. Not nice. He had to go.

So, with all this business to deal with, why were we talking about Cressida?

"Hang on! What do you mean, I give out negative energy to Cressida?" I fumed as Fleur and Claude gazed at me sympathetically.

"Mmm, well, she wasn't really specific," Fleur mused. "Something to do with your chakras being out of alignment."

"Oh, for the love of God," I sighed, feeling my cheeks flush with anger.

"Hey, hang on, Ron, you're taking this all wrong. Cressida wasn't being bitchy," Claude reassured me. "She wants us all to be friends. She just has a few issues with the, er, darker side of your aura."

"Darker side of my aura? But I've been really nice to her!" I said vehemently. "I'm always nice to her."

Why was I defending myself to my two best friends?

"Awww, Ronnie, chill out," Fleur laughed, leaping over and giving me a hug. "We're not getting at you. It's not that big a deal."

"That's right, Ronnie," whispered Claude, grabbing my hand. "Don't get upset. It's just that, well, you have to admit Cressida must be lonely spending every lunch hour studying in the library."

"And when we invited her to eat with us," continued Fleur, "she said . . . well, she said she didn't want to increase the bad vibes."

"There aren't any bad vibes!" I said.

"We know," said Fleur. "It's just a silly misunderstanding."

"Y'know what Cressida's like—she's just really sensitive," Claude said rather fondly. "Let me talk to her."

One week later, with our "silly misunderstanding" ironed out, the LBD swept into Blackwell's lunch hall with Cressida Sleeth tottering daintily in our wake. Claude and Fleur were soooo happy. We had truly been honored, in their eyes. They didn't raise an eyebrow when Cressida rejected 99 percent of the food offered because of her lacto intolerance, wheat allergies or vegetarian beliefs. Or when she bitched at Dolly the dinner lady about the "seventy-two different pesticides on a nonorganic apple," or moved us from our usual LBD lunch table by the window because direct sunlight made her "sneezy." She even began telling us how her dad worked alongside Panama Goodyear's father at the pharmaceutical factory and that she'd started playing tennis with her!

"Wow! We'll get all the insider gossip on Panama and her gang," laughed Fleur. "It'll be like having a double agent!"

"How cool is that?" beamed Claude, who I'd never had down as prize chump before.

As Fleur yaddered excitedly about the invites she'd bagged for all four of us to Miles Boon's birthday party, I pushed mashed potato around my plate, trying to appear chock-full of happy-happy-joy-joy vibes. This worked at first, but when the conversation flipped over to Cressida and Claude's jam-packed study schedule, I started to feel rather hot and nauseated.

Because things suddenly became crystal clear.

Fleur Swan was one of the most beautiful, well-known girls

at Blackwell School (after Panama Goodyear, of course, who is stunning yet clinically evil). Claudette Cassiera was the brainiest, most dedicated GCSE coach a pupil like Cressida could desire.

Of course Ms. Sleeth wanted to hang with them both.

But what did I have to offer?

Nothing.

Suddenly I was on very shaky ground.

I was being phased out.

"Well, she sounds like a right manipulative little madam!" Nan says, throwing handfuls of plump sultanas into the mixing bowl. "There's one around every corner, unfortunately. What happened next?"

"It got worse," I say. "Much worse."

the witch

February came around way too quickly.

Now, you could barely go five minutes at Blackwell without a teacher bumming your life out with a GCSE reminder.

Thankfully, however, *Mistress Minny III: The Witches of Philadelphia* was finally hitting cinemas that Friday the 13th, and the LBD had a big girlie night out planned. Claude just loves *Mistress Minny*. She has read all the books ten times over and lurks about on the web message boards analyzing subplots and symbolism. What a geek! She even harangued Fleur and me to dress up like Mistress Minny for the screening! Luckily, we presented a united front against the plan, although Claude still wore a green pointy nose and stick-on face boils for the ticket line. She looked really funny.

It felt just like old times, just me, Claude and Fleur. Yet annoyingly, just as we were finding our seats in the dark, a dismally familiar voice shattered my good mood.

"Sorry I'm late, ladies," Cressida Sleeth announced. "Dad was late home from the factory, so I had to beg a lift from . . . er, the girl down the road. . . . Hey, Claude, *loving* the nose!"

"Cressy!" Fleur and Claude said, laughing and giving her hugs and air kisses. They'd started air kissing lately. It made me queasy.

"Cressida," I said, nodding acknowledgment.

"Hey, Ron! Fabby jeans," said Cressida, pointing at my new indigo hipsters before kissing the nothingness past both of my ears.

My skin crawled.

It seemed there was nothing I could do to stop Cressida from infiltrating the LBD . . . well, without me simply looking insane. Worse still, Cressida was finding out more private, personal bambino business every day.

She knew that the Cassieras were broke and getting really worried about it.

She knew that Jimi and I kept arguing about the fact that I wouldn't lie to Mum and sleep over at his house.

She knew Fleur had been getting overly freaky with Baz Kauffman from Chasterton School and had taken to perusing *Your Body, Yourself* lately with a worried expression.

She'd even been shown that shameful home movie of the

LBD, in our underwear, performing various hits from *Moulin Rouge*, filmed during Fleur's birthday slumber party. That *Moulin Rouge* tape needed to be burned, not shown to Cressida Flipping Sleeth!

My instinct shouted that letting Cressida so close was a mistake.

During the film, Fleur was her typical hyperactive self. She yaddered incessantly on her mobile phone, began an interschool popcorn battle with some lads from Lymewell Academy, shouted out plot spoilers . . . and probably worst of all, right at the most touching, serious part of the film, let out a long squeaky bottom explosion, before shouting, "Oooh, Ronnie Ripperton! That stinks!" The entire theater erupted in laughter. I could have strangled her!

As we filed out of the multiplex afterward, Baz Kauffman sped up in his VW Golf, wearing sunglasses at night and too much hair wax for my taste, blaring bad 200-beats-per-minute happy hard-core music through his sunroof. He looked ridiculous, but Fleur still climbed inside the car, begging us to cover for her until 9:30 P.M.

Claude and I just rolled our eyes and nodded.

"C'mon, girls," smiled Claude, linking arms with me and Cressida. "Let's go and get coffee at Ruby's Cafe."

"Great!" smiled Cressida.

"You okay, Ronnie?" asked Claude.

"Fine," I said. Cressida put her head down, stifling a smile. We walked in silence.

About ten minutes farther down the road, Cressida eventually spoke. "Fleur was a live wire tonight, wasn't she?" she said matter-of-factly. "That usherette was so angry when she spilled her Pepsi!"

"Oh, that's our Fleur for you," chuckled Claude fondly. "Acts like a chimpanzee in public. We're constantly embarrassed by her, eh, Ronnie?"

"Hmmm," I said.

Cressida smiled and said nothing. "So that was Baz?" she asked. "The one she's been snogging?"

"Mmm . . . yeah, think so. Looked like him," said Claude, distracted by her watch. "She's got a different lad slobbering after her every week. She's probably lost track herself by now. Hey, anyway, come on—Ruby only serves until 9 P.M."

"But are the smoothies and cakes organic?" asked Cressida.

"Not sure," said Claude. "We can ask."

I watched as they wandered off, giggling merrily.

round one

The following day, Saturday, I didn't hear a word from the LBD. I assumed everyone was working on GCSE projects, what with the deadlines being near. But by Sunday night when Fleur ignored my third totally hilarious text message, I decided to call.

"Yes," Fleur said rather oddly.

"All right, babe?" I chirped. "Why's your phone off? You okay?"

"I'm fine," she clipped.

"Er . . . been busy?"

"Just studying," she said. Fleur sounded angry. "Oh, and Cressida popped by with a biology textbook for me last night. We made brownies together."

"Right," I said. There was an awkward silence. "You sound weird, Fleur, what's up?"

"Nothing," said Fleur. "Gotta go."

"Fleur!" I shouted. "Tell me what's up!"

"Hmmm . . . well, okay then!" Fleur said, taking a deep breath. "I just think that if you and Claude find me such an embarrassment in public, then I won't come out with you ever again!"

"Eh?" I said.

"So I act like a chimpanzee, do I?" she yelled. "Well, thank you very much! Some friend you are. At least I'm not uptight and paranoid like you!"

"But, I . . . ," I stuttered.

"And I've just phoned Miss Claudette 'acts like a forty-year-old woman' Cassiera and given her a few home truths about herself too!"

"Oh God," I groaned.

"And FYI, I'm not such a cheap tart that I can't even remember who my current boyfriend is!" shouted Fleur.

"Fleur!" I yelled. "That's not what—"

"I can't believe you'd both slag me off like that," said Fleur, her voice crackling into raw tears.

"Cressida told you all this, didn't she?" I screamed. "Well, what a shock! Fleur, you have to listen to me about Cressida—"

"Cressida *accidentally* told me a little bit of it," sniffled Fleur.

"And don't you start blaming this on her just because you've never liked her. Don't turn this back onto her!"

"Fleur, it wasn't like that!" I protested, but on the other end of the line I could hear the usually brash, fearless Fleur Iris Swan sobbing her heart out.

And that's when things started to go downhill.

Silences, gossiping, arguments, mistrust.

It took me two hours to calm Fleur down and explain the perfectly innocent context in which Claude had made those silly remarks. Claude was pretty upset too, especially as Fleur had called her "tedious" and "big-headed."

By midnight, we were all cool again. But I was determined to hear Cressida Sleeth's explanation for this.

showdown

That Monday, I spent my entire German class drilling holes in the back of Cressida's head with my eyes. When the lunch bell sounded, I let Frau Chalmers and the other pupils file out before cornering Ms. Sleeth in the classroom all alone.

"Right, you little tofu-munching freak," I began. "I want a word with you!"

Cressida lifted her gaze and smiled at me serenely. "Darling, I don't speak to you, remember?" she said, shooing me away with her tiny hand. "You're the dull one."

I have to say, that sort of floored me. Turning on one ribboned pump, Cressida made for the door.

"Oh? Erm, right! You admit that, do you?" I yelled, following after her, grabbing her hair and yanking her blonde tresses backward. "You've tried pushing me out. Now you want Fleur and Claude at loggerheads! What are you getting out of this . . . you total weirdo?"

Cressida stopped in her tracks and smirked. "Well, at the moment, sweetheart, I'm being taken to all the best parties by Fleur and I'm getting my geography and history homework done for me by Claude. While you . . . well, let's see." Cressida placed one finger to the corner of her mouth to ponder. "Oh, yes, you're getting cheated on by Jimi Steele with Suzette Laws because she doesn't squeal like a pig every time he puts his hand up her T-shirt. Ha ha ha!"

"What?" I said, my face crumbling.

"Oh, sorry!" said Cressida patronizingly. "Didn't you know that? Me and my big mouth! You should play tennis with Panama—she knows all the best gossip."

"You . . . evil cow!" I shouted as Cressida sped out of the room heading for the Year 11 lockers with me on her trail. "You won't get away with this, Frodo!" I yelled. "I'll die stopping you!"

"Lay one grubby unmanicured finger on me again and my daddy will sue you," Cressida laughed over her shoulder as she bustled away, her gray muslin skirt billowing behind her, with me close at her heel still baying for blood. Then, just we turned the corner into the locker area where Claude and Fleur were chatting, Cressida let out this weird theatrical moan followed by pitiful blubbering.

"Claude! Fleur!" Cressida whined, wrapping her sweater sleeves over her hands and dancing from foot to foot like a

smacked toddler. "Waaaaahhhh! Ronnie is being so negative and aggressive with me over this silly misunderstanding!"

Thick streams of tears were trickling down Cressida's cherubic little face. "I'm so sorry if I've accidentally caused bad karma. So vewwwwwy sorry!"

I knew, in a flash, that no one would believe me about Cressida's evil little outburst. In fact, within seconds both Fleur and Claude were hugging the little minx, trying to calm her down.

By the end of lunch break, it was agreed that to solve further problems, we should all have our astrological charts cross-referenced.

hell

Silly old Panama Goodyear! Apparently she'd got it "all mixed up" about Jimi and Suzette Laws. They hadn't been getting together twice weekly since January for clandestine groping and snogging sessions.

No, of course not!

Jimi assured me, amid all the crying and screaming, that he and Suzette were "just really good friends" who'd "grown closer" during the stressful run-up to the A-level exams. This led to them "hanging out" in each other's bedrooms late into the night, "studying" and "chatting."

Something I wasn't allowed to do.

Weirdly enough, however, the very moment I went crazy and dumped Jimi over this . . . *he and Suzette announced they were going out together!*

But remember, Jimi hadn't cheated on me and broken my heart. No, he'd waited until we'd "officially had closure" before getting freaky with another girl.

Oh, purrrrrr-leeeeeease! Which Christmas tree did they both think I'd fallen off?

After all the sobbing and hurling subsided, I just felt angry and stupid. I began staring into the mirror for hours at a time, imagining parts of me I'd alter if only Magda and Loz would buy me a birthday gift voucher for the Transform Clinic.

New nose? Yes, please.

Perkier bum? Absolutely.

Bigger boobs? Yes, big humongous boobs, definitely. Not tiny little feeble swellings that sit there adding nothing to my shape.

I hated Jimi Steele for making me feel so ugly and charmless.

(Okay, I didn't hate Jimi Steele. I felt like I'd love him forever. Mum, on the other hand, truly hated Jimi Steele and had to be physically restrained from giving him a backhander across the face in Safeway.)

The only good thing about splitting with Jimi was that Cressida Sleeth got out of my face for a couple of weeks and let Fleur and Claude get on with making me feel better.

If I'd not had the LBD during that fortnight, I don't know what would have happened. I never wanted another boyfriend as long as I lived.

The GCSE exams began five weeks ago in May. It was around then that Cressida phased out Fleur.

Fleur had served her purpose. Nowadays, Cressida knew all the hottest people to know at Blackwell. She played tennis with Panama, had several hot boys sniffing round her, and got personal invites to all the best parties. She just didn't need Fleur anymore. She was perfectly civil, but the texts, the calls, the Reiki sessions, the past-life therapy, all that just stopped.

At first I was chuffed. Now Fleur would see Cressida for the freak she really was—but it didn't work out like that. Instead, Fleur got angry with Claude for not dropping Cressida in protest. Things got weirder, more complex, more subtly nasty.

A distinct crack began to form right down the center of the group. Fleur was bitching about Claude and Cressida "leaving us both out of things" while Claude and Cressida spent their days in the library cramming for the GCSEs like weird book-ogling Siamese twins.

I don't blame Claude for being flattered by Cressida's undivided attention. Let's face it, we've both played second fiddle to Fleur right through Blackwell. And Claude truly believed that Cressida liked her the best.

I buried my head in quadratic equations and infinite verbs and tried to ignore the whole mess.

Eventually Cressida bought Claude a heart-shaped necklace to thank her for being "such an amazing friend during Year 11," which Claude wore to her geography exam. This riled Fleur so deeply that she stopped texting Claude daft good-night messages at bedtime, something the LBD have done every night since Year 9.

So, Claude refused to lend Fleur her green Morgan dress

for the Blackwell Golden Centenary Barbecue, telling her to "buy her own clothes," seeing as the Swan family "had more money than sense anyhow."

And by this point, I was finding it hard to like Claude. Or Fleur for that matter.

And that pretty much brings us up to now.

dizzy

"Hmmm . . . well, you know what the moral of that tale is?" Nan asks, crashing open the oven door and producing a tray of sweet-smelling scones.

"Er, no?" I say, my eyes red-rimmed.

"Never trust a vegetarian," she says. "Hitler was one, you know."

"Really?" I say.

"Absolutely," she tuts. "A couple of plates of corned beef hash down his neck, he'd never have invaded Poland. What's life without the odd lovely Scotch egg? Cuh! No wonder that Cressida Slime article is so bitter and twisted."

I gaze forlornly at Nan, who has flour on the end of her nose and a random sultana in her hairline. She winks at me before hobbling to the pantry and producing a tin of Lyon's black treacle, a bottle of Glenmorangie whiskey and two small glasses.

"Can I tempt you with a wee nip? Just for your nerves?" Nan asks, pouring herself a healthy-sized dram.

"Nah," I sigh. "I'll pass."

"Very noble," Nan smiles, tapping her floury nose, then taking a dainty glug of the pungent fluid. "So, anyway, what's the lay of the land now? When did you last see Claudette and Fleur?"

"Wednesday," I tell her. "It was the last GCSE exam. English."

"And?" Nan prompts.

"Well, the paper was fairly easy," I sigh. "So I was really hoping we all might go to Ruby's afterward for cakes to celebrate. But the second the bell went, Fleur chucked her pencil case in her bag and stormed out with her nose aloft."

"And Claudette?" asks Nan, picking up her whiskey and taking another dainty glug.

"She just watched her go!" I cry, tears spilling down my face. "Like she didn't care. And then the most awful thing of all happened!"

"What?" says Nan, reaching up her sleeve, pulling out a fresh cotton handkerchief and passing it to me.

"Then Cressida pranced over to Claude's desk with an evil little smirk on her face. I couldn't hear exactly what she said, but it sounded like she was firing one of her servants or something! She thanked Claude 'for all of her hard work,' then breezed out without even saying good-bye!"

"The little harridan," tuts Nan, knocking more of her whiskey back. "She dropped Claudette too, once the exams were over?"

"Yeah," I say. "When I left the exam hall, I saw Cressida jumping into the back of Panama Goodyear's Range Rover. Panama was driving and Abigail and Derren, two of the most vile snobs at Blackwell School, were there too! Claude was scurrying off up the street alone."

"Oh," says Nan.

"She won't answer her phone," I say.

The cuckoo clock in Nan's hallway chimes six times. I place my face in my hands and sigh deeply.

"What do you think I should do?" I ask, not holding much hope that a half-tipsy octogenarian can save the LBD's summer.

"Hmmm . . . well," says Nan, smothering a scone in clotted cream and pushing it in front of me, "that's as plain as the nose on your face, Veronica. *You have to save the LBD!*"

"Save the LBD?" I repeat.

"Yes!" she nods. "And quickly, before this whole affair gets any sillier."

"It's too late," I sigh.

"It's never too late to patch things up," smiles Nan. "Sure, it'll take a bit of talking and pride swallowing. But you girls can do that."

"Hmpgh," I bristle. "Maybe I don't want to be friends with them again. Maybe I've seen a side of Claude and Fleur I don't like!"

"Veronica," says Nan seriously, "no one's perfect. If you allowed only people into your life that you liked all the time, well, you'd be a very lonely person. Friends make mistakes. That's a fact of life. Bearing grudges gets you nowhere. Let an old fool tell you that for nothing."

Nan picks up her enormous white handbag, which always lives beside her ankle. She fishes around in it for a while, pulling out an envelope containing a pile of well-thumbed black-and-white photographs.

"Edith Warburton," Nan announces, handing me a photograph of a pretty dark-haired girl aged about twenty-five in a 1940s dress. "Dizzy, that was her nickname. Ahhh . . . the boys loved Dizzy! I never got a look in with those American airmen when she was around. Mad as a hatter, she was!"

"Was she your friend?" I say, examining the photo.

"For fifty years," Nan says, nodding. "I was there when she gave birth to George, her first boy. Ha! What a night that was. You've never heard language like it!" Nan looks at the photo again, biting her lip a little.

"Did you ever argue?" I ask.

"Oh, now and then," Nan says a little sadly. "But we always made up again . . . well, until 1987, when we stopped speaking altogether."

"What happened?" I gasp.

"Well," Nan says, sighing. "Young George, he got engaged to a girl called Marie. Nice girl she was, worked as a teacher . . . lovely teeth . . . Anyhow, George and Marie, they decided to get married at the local registry office. Y'know, what with them both being, er, athleticists . . ."

"Atheists?" I suggest. "They didn't believe in God?"

"That's it!" says Nan. "So anyhow, I says to Dizzy, I'll not bother wearing a hat to the wedding, seeing as it's not a religious do. Well, Dizzy took great offense at that! She said, 'Leticia, if you don't want to take George's big day seriously, then don't come at all!'"

Nan gives her best derisive snort. "Ha! As if I was going to buy a brand new hat to stand in a drafty council office," she tuts. "But Dizzy, she said I was just jealous because none of my kids had managed to get wed. The cheek of her! So I didn't go."

Nan looks at the photo again, then puts it away. "We never spoke to each other ever again," she says sadly.

"You fell out over a hat?" I splutter.

"A hat," repeats Nan. "I wouldn't phone Dizzy, Dizzy wouldn't phone me. Then George and Marie moved to Devon and she went with them."

Nan's eyes become a little glassy. "Anyway, she's gone *up there* now," she says, pouring herself another very small Glenmorangie.

By "up there," I'm surmising Dizzy's gone somewhere a little farther than Devon. "That's a shame, Nan," I say.

"I know it is," she agrees. "Life's too short for silly arguments. That's why you've got to get your girls together again. Now! Plan yourselves an adventure! A holiday? You're sixteen years old! Oooh, if I was sixteen again, I'd—"

"I can't!" I protest. "Mum's making me get a waitressing job at the Wacky Warehouse."

"Eh?" splutters Nan. "Whatever for?"

"She says I can't freeload off her all summer," I say. "She says I need to know the value of money."

At this moment, Nan begins to howl with laughter. In fact, she laughs so much she has to hold on to the oak table. Her face has dissolved into a million wrinkles.

"Hoo hoo! My Magda actually said that?" guffaws Nan. "Oooh, I've heard the lot now! Did she care to tell you what she was doing at sixteen?"

"Mmm . . . ," I ponder. "Something about being up with the lark doing housework?"

Nan nearly explodes with mirth. "Ha ha ha!" she howls.

"She was never up before midday! She never saw the sun! It was like living with a bat."

"Are you sure?" I say, feeling slightly disoriented.

"Yes, I'm sure!" says Nan. "She drove me absolutely doolally! Her and Susan Fitzpatrick—out at nightclubs until all hours! The stupid clothes! The endless procession of long-haired lout boyfriends! Then, Magda meets your dad one night at one of them ravey parties, drops out of catering college and takes off to Tenerife to work in a nightclub with him. That girl turned my hair white!"

"Pardon?" I say incredulously. "My mother dropped out of college? Mum told me she finished college before she went to Tenerife."

"Veronica," chuckles Nan. "Your mother has a very selective memory."

I will never listen to anything Magda Ripperton says, ever again.

It's 8 P.M. I already promised Mum I'd come home tonight for babysitting duties tomorrow morning, so I have to get going.

"Well, that works out nicely," Nan says as we walk down the hallway. "My program begins at 9 P.M. *Autopsy Squad*—do you watch it? It's the best thing on the box."

"I saw the episode with the kidney snatcher," I wince.

"Wasn't that great?" beams Nan, passing me my coat. She's also shoved something into my hand. An envelope.

"What's this?" I say, raising an eyebrow.

"Money," she winks. "For the summer."

"Nan . . . you don't have to . . . ," I begin.

"Oh, shush," she smiles. "Go and have a good time. Buy something daft with it!"

Nan opens the door. It's a balmy June night. Daddy longlegs are crawling around the lamp outside. I give her a big hug, trying not to crush her.

"I'll call you soon," I say. "I'll give you an update on events."

"Good girl!" smiles Nan. "You tell your mum I love her. I'll call her tomorrow after Miriam's put my curlers in."

"Sure thing," I say, walking down the garden path. As I reach the small gate, I turn around for another wave.

"Cheerio, sweetheart!" Nan shouts, her walking stick supporting her tiny frame. "Oh, and you remember what I said, eh? Save the LBD! Have courage—it's not too late!"

"I hear you!" I chuckle, walking away up Dewers Drive in the twilight clutching my warm tinfoil parcel of scones. "Love you, Nan. See you soon."

"Ronnie," Dad says. "Ronnie. Sweetheart? Are you awake?"

"Gnnngnn . . . Dad," I moan, opening one eye.

Dad's sitting in the armchair in my bedroom. It's 11 A.M. Visiting Nan must have bought me some major brownie points—they never let me sleep this late.

"I promise I'm getting up now," I say. "Will you tell Mum I'll do Seth's lunch feed?"

There's a long silence. I open my eyes and sit up. Dad's sitting very quietly, peering at me. He stands up and opens the curtains.

"Er, Ronnie babe?" he says. "Sit up. I need to talk to you."

Oh God, he's going to start doing my head in about summer jobs again. "Can it not wait?" I say huffily.

"Not really, darling," he says.

Something about Dad's tone makes me slightly uneasy.

"What's up?" I say, propping myself upright.

Dad looks at me. He looks lost for words. "Erm, Ronnie, it's . . . your nan," he finally says.

"Oh, Dad!" I say, beginning to laugh. "I should have said last night. She's not gone mad at all. You'll never believe this . . . she's only got herself one of those police scanners from dodgy Tony down the road! What a woman!"

Dad looks at me blankly. He sits down on the side of my bed. "Ronnie, darling, your nan died last night."

I feel like somebody has punched me in the mouth.

"But . . . but . . . no," I splutter. "She . . . she was . . . I was there . . . there last night!"

"I know you were, petal," says Dad calmly.

"And she was fine!" I say. "She was . . . she was totally fine. She baked scones!"

My head's spinning. I think I might be sick.

"And I . . . I was telling her about Claude and Fleur!" I say. "She . . . she was telling me what to do!"

"That sounds like Leticia," says Dad sadly. He reaches out, placing his big rough hands over mine. Thick tears are streaming down my cheeks.

"Dad . . . Dad, this makes no sense!" I sob. "Are you sure? Maybe there's been a mistake."

Dad reaches forward and cuddles me into his chest. "No,

Ron," he says. "Miriam found her this morning. She was lying in bed. Miriam says she just looked like she was asleep. Your mum's gone there now to meet the undertakers."

"But . . . she was okay last night, Dad," I sob uselessly. "She was fine."

"She was old, Ronnie," says Dad, smoothing my hair with his hand, blotting my tears into his shirt. "She was just really, really old."

Chapter 3

a good turnout

My dad and Tony, Miriam's son, and some other Little Chipping men help carry Nan's coffin. It's tiny. Not exactly £900 worth of stained golden oak, which is the price Sneddon and Sons Funeral Directors charged.

Nan would have been livid at that price.

"Wrap me in newspaper and put me in the rubbish!" That's what she used to tell us. "I don't want any fuss!"

In the end, Nan's funeral is a bit "fussy," but I think she would have approved. Nan loved a good funeral. She liked the singing and the flowers and the after-party where everyone gossips and eats pork pies. Mum once accused Nan of scouring the *Local Daily Mercury*'s obituary section for fresh deaths, because she had more fun at wakes than at bridge club.

Mum and Nan were always taking the mickey out of each other.

I don't cry at all during the service, although I nearly do when we sing "Amazing Grace," Nan's favorite hymn. It just doesn't seem right to blubber when Mum's face is so stiff and dignified. I'm determined to cope just for her.

However, when we arrive at the Little Chipping Hotel for Nan's wake, I begin to feel totally hideous. All of Nan's gang from her Tuesday Club are gathered: Tilly, Philly, Kitty and Sissy, all with their fluffy candy-floss hair, chunky handbags and walking aids. In the function room, a long, grand oak table is laden with sandwiches and sausage rolls. Old-fashioned china cake-stands heave with scones, macaroons and cream éclairs, and two huge steaming teapots are perched ceremoniously in the center of the table, waiting for service.

In the corner, Aunty Susan and Miriam sit on either side of Mum on a sofa, holding her hands, while she gazes into the middle of nowhere. Meanwhile, Dad wanders about, dispensing extra chairs to the elderly and announcing, "Crikey, what a turnout!" to random passersby.

The whole thing is beyond surreal.

I stand for at least half an hour in the center of the room, making small talk with the cotton-wool heads about my exams, waiting patiently for something to happen.

Something. Anything. I'm not sure what. It just feels like something isn't right. Then, eventually, as the guests tuck into the sandwiches and begin complimenting the scones, it finally hits me:

I'm waiting for Nan to show up.

At some weird level, I've been expecting her to hobble through the door and begin piling a plate with jam tarts and potted-meat sandwiches—which is totally ridiculous, as I'm never going to see her again.

I have to get out of that room.

In a flurry of limbs, I rush out a side door, narrowly missing a woman carrying a huge teapot, stumbling into the rather majestic hallway where at least the air is cooler. To my right is a grand sweeping staircase where, halfway up, I see a young man with his head in his hands. It's Tony, Miriam's son.

"Tony?" I say, climbing the stairs to where he sits. "Are you okay?"

Tony looks up at me. His hands are marked with bad tattoos. His dark brown eyes are full of tears.

"Oh . . . don't mind me, Ronnie . . . I'm just being soft," Tony smiles, wiping his wet hands over his shaved head. "It's just your nan . . . she was just . . . y'know, a really nice woman. She never had a go at me about stuff."

"Yeah, Tony," I say, sitting down on the step beside him. "I know."

And then I start to cry too.

Eventually, Dad finds me and decides to drive me home.

~~~~~~

chess

"Oh dear, Ron," smiles Dad as we turn into the Fantastic Voyage's parking lot. "We may have intruders. Shall we call the police?"

"Eh?" I grunt. I've not uttered a syllable during the entire drive home.

Dad points across at our beer garden where two girls are playing on the man-sized chess game: one blonde, another with dark bunches and spectacles.

I can't believe my eyes.

Claude and Fleur!

"Oh my God," I gasp, jumping out of the car. Dad smiles and says nothing.

As I approach, Fleur is waving Claude's white bishop above her head with victorious glee while Claude glares back at her.

"I thought you said you played chess, you numpty!" Fleur shouts smugly. "Were you getting it mixed up with Hungry Hippos?"

"I can play chess!" retorts Claude. "You just take so flipping long to make your moves I lose the will to live. It's like playing with a sloth!"

"Oh, *whatever*," tuts Fleur, adding the bishop to her vast pile of vanquished pieces. "A sloth who's whooping your ass!"

The girls spot me and stop bickering.

"Ronnie!" Fleur shouts, rushing over to me with her arms open. "How's it going, babe?"

"Hey," says Claude, running over and joining the hug. "We heard about your nan. Your dad called our mothers. We can't believe it. We're so sorry, Ronnie."

"Thanks," I say quietly, feeling all juddery again. I'm so relieved to see them both.

"Today has been just totally horrible," I sniff, taking a hankie out and blowing my nose. "Just totally surreal."

Claude releases me from her hug, wrapping her arm around my waist. "Look, Ronnie," she says, "I just want to say how sorry I am that I've not been there for you over the last few days. I feel terrible."

"Me too," sighs Fleur, biting her lip. "I'd have come round on Saturday if you'd called. You didn't even text, though. You must have thought I wouldn't care after, well, y'know, everything that's happened. I feel awful."

I dab my eyes and shrug. "I didn't think that . . . I just . . . ," I begin, but my voice trails off.

This has all got so stupid and complicated.

"Ronnie, we do care," says Claude firmly, taking charge of the awkward silence. "Things have just got messy between me and Fleur, that's all. No one's angry at you."

"Totally," nods Fleur.

I look at my two friends, standing there with tearful expressions.

"Look, if there's anything we can do to make you and your mum feel better," says Claude, "just give us a shout, we'll be there."

"Yeah! Anything at all," nods Fleur. "Like babysitting, or making cups of tea or running errands or, well, anything. I know what it's like when grans die. Everybody has to pull together."

"Thanks, girls," I whisper. "To be honest, I feel a whole lot better just seeing you both and, well, knowing we're all fine again."

Claude and Fleur look at each other, then look away.

There's another awkward silence.

"What?" I say.

"Well," says Fleur sheepishly, "depends what you mean by 'fine.'"

Claude crosses her arms and throws Fleur a withering look. "Leave it, Fleur," she mutters.

"No, c'mon," I say plaintively. "Surely you two must be okay now. You both came down here together, after all."

Claude fixes me with her best fake politician smile. "We're fine," she begins, nudging Fleur to shut up. "We've just got a few niggles that need ironing out—"

"But we didn't come together," Fleur announces, talking over her. "I came down here to wait for you by myself. Then brainiac here showed up. I wouldn't leave and neither would she!"

Claude tries to let that wash over her, but she can't. "And why should I have left, candy-floss brain?"

"So we decided to play chess," Fleur says, ignoring her. "Then we wouldn't have to talk to each other."

"Oh, I see . . . ," I say dryly. "Great." I sit down at one of the garden tables, shaking my head in disbelief.

"Fleur!" hisses Claude. "I can't believe you'd be so insensitive as to start this in front of Ronnie, on today of all days!"

"I'm not starting anything!" Fleur huffs under her breath. "I was just telling the truth."

"Oh, we're all telling the truth today, are we?" Claude growls under her breath. "Well, let's leave that for another day, perhaps? I've certainly got plenty of home truths to tell you!"

The pair swing around and look at me apologetically. I'm not angry at them, though. In fact, after the day I've had, they both seem rather comical.

"Anyway, Claude," Fleur says, wandering over to where I'm sitting, trying to sound breezy. "Good of Cressida to give you a day off today to come down here. Very compassionate of her."

Claude shuffles awkwardly. "Mmm," she mumbles. "I don't, er, think I'll be seeing Cressida Sleeth again."

"Pgh," snorts Fleur, folding her arms. "Oh dear. Dropped you, has she?"

Claude scowls at Fleur and doesn't answer.

"She's dropped you, hasn't she?" repeats Fleur, cocking her head to the side in a satisfied manner.

"She dropped you first," Claude retorts.

Fleur's face crumbles. "Pah . . . plgh," she splutters, struggling to get the upper hand again. "Yeah, and as if I was bothered."

Her rattled expression seems to suggest otherwise.

"It was a relief to get rid of her. And to get shot of you too! It's not like I've missed you," Fleur tells Claude, wagging her finger. "I mean, look at you! You're just so . . ." Fleur makes her fingers and thumbs into circles, placing them around her eyes to mimic spectacles. *Oooh, look at me, I'm Claude Cassiera! I study for nine hundred hours a week! I iron a sensible crease into my thongs! I get my thrills highlighting textbooks with neon pens!*

Claude's face stays poker straight.

"Cuh!" continues Fleur. "And at least I don't spend my nights on the Internet chatting to geeks about books!"

Claude simply gazes at Fleur. "Well, you'd have a job doing that, Fleur," she replies, deadpan. "You've not read any books."

Fleur's nostrils flare crossly. "I have so!" she says.

"Really?" says Claude, sitting down at the table opposite me. "What was the last thing you read?"

"That's easy. It was *To Kill a Mockingbir—*" begins Fleur.

"That you weren't forced to read by Mr. Swainson for GCSE English?" Claude interrupts cruelly.

Fleur looks totally stumped now. Her cheeks begin to flush pink. "Hmmm . . . ," she huffs eventually. "Okay, it was the July *Vogue* swimwear special."

Fleur looks sheepishly at Claude, emitting a small embarrassed groan. I let out a small involuntary chuckle. Claude's trying her best to stay serene, but her mouth is creasing upward at the corners.

Fleur prances across, sitting her very small posterior down at the table opposite her enemy, folding her arms.

We sit in silence for what seems like an eternity. I feel absolutely stumped at where to begin sorting this all out.

"Okay. Look, both of you," Claude says eventually, taking a deep breath. "I just want to get something off my chest. I want to apologize."

"Eh?" says Fleur, staring at Claude, rather gobsmacked.

"What for?" I ask.

"For getting so . . . so sucked in by Cressida Sleeth," Claude sighs.

"Well . . . we all did, at first," I mumble.

"You didn't, Ronnie," corrects Claude. "You knew she was a vile stirrer. You said rather expressly she was trying to split us up."

"I did too, Claude!" pipes in Fleur. "I've been telling you for the last month."

"Okay, okay, I know," admits Claude. "But, Fleur, you've been a total nightmare recently. I didn't care what you thought."

"When have I been a nightmare?" gasps Fleur.

"Whoa! Hold on," I say, frowning at Fleur to shut up. "Let's not start fighting again."

We all glare at the table in silence. A small group of Fantastic Voyage customers filters into the beer garden, giving our angst-ridden table a wide berth.

"Listen," says Claude softly, turning to Fleur, who's clearly fuming but trying to keep a lid on things for my sake. "I shouldn't have been so tight about lending you that green dress. I'm sorry, right?"

"Doesn't matter," whispers Fleur, her bottom lip jutting petulantly.

"But it's just that . . . ," Claude continues, "you've got tons of amazing clothes. And I . . . well, I just haven't. So I get a bit precious about lending stuff. Especially when you're being totally frosty and horrible with me anyway."

"But I . . . I've not got that much stuff," Fleur protests rather feebly.

This is nonsense. Fleur's bedroom is ram-jammed full of girly fabulousness of the extreme ka-ching variety. She's never short of a £20 note for a new T-shirt or a designer lip gloss.

"And of course, Cressida spotted this," continues Claude. "And she started harping on about the whole money thing, saying that you're way too materialistic. And that you don't respect our monetary differences . . . and I started thinking, yeah! She's right! Fleur is really spoiled."

Fleur looks horrified at Claude. Her huge blue eyes well up with tears. I mean, all of this is true, but Fleur doesn't need to hear it, does she?

"Suffice to say, I feel like a right spanner now," Claude sighs. "Why did I listen to Cressida?"

Fleur shakes her head slowly. I pass her a tissue and she wipes her eyes.

"Hmmm," Fleur sighs. "*You* feel like a spanner, Claude? At least you didn't let Cressida practice acupuncture on you with nonsterilized sewing needles."

Claude and I gasp in horror.

"Fleur?" I say. "You didn't? Cressida's not a trained acupuncturist!"

"Thank you, Ronnie," says Fleur, blushing slightly. "I know that *now*."

Claude catches my eye and we both can't help giggling.

"Oh, girls, don't be cruel!" sniffs Fleur, rolling her eyes. "Some of those needles really hurt! Cressida assured me it would prevent the stagnation of my chi and make my butt tiny like hers."

Fleur buries her face in her hands again, groaning with shame.

I know this is meant to be a serious discussion, but I can't help cracking up laughing. It just feels so good, having my girls here with me. I'd rather we were bickering in the beer garden than in our bedrooms alone.

"Look, girls, can we sort something out here?" says Claude, taking control of the situation. "I really don't want us to argue anymore."

"Me neither," I say emphatically.

"And I know things have got really dodgy lately," Claude says to Fleur. "But Ronnie needs us both right now. The bambinos need to present a unified front. It's not too late to make this a good summer."

"We should make a plan!" I say, remembering what Nan advised me to do on the last night I saw her. "We could still have an adventure!"

Fleur seems to be thinking about it.

"C'mon, Fleur!" pleads Claude, grabbing Fleur's hand. "Let's call a truce."

"Erm . . . I don't think so," Fleur says.

"Oh, why not?" I sigh. "Claude's apologized! Do you want her to beg?"

"No! It's not that," Fleur protests. "Of course I want us all to be friends. But it's just that . . . I'm going away for the summer."

"What?" says Claude. "Where to?"

"Destiny Bay," Fleur says. "I've applied for a summer job in a hotel. It's looking pretty certain that I start next week."

"Destiny Bay?" I squeak. "Where MTV holds the Big Beach Booty Quake? The total party resort with all the clubs and beach bars?"

"Uh-huh," groans Fleur.

"Destiny Bay!" repeats Claude. "That surfers' resort where they broadcast all those surf and bikini competitions from?"

"Er, yeah, that's the one," says Fleur apologetically. "There's this really exclusive hotel about a mile from the main resort called Harbinger Hall."

"Harbinger Hall!" I cry. "MTV hired nearly the whole hotel for a weekend last year when they were staging the Big Beach Booty Quake!"

"That's it," says Fleur, her lip wobbling. "Oh my God! I'm so sorry! I just e-mailed my resume to Miss Scrumble, the personnel lady, on the off chance. I didn't expect her to call me!"

Claude and I stare at Fleur, utterly aghast.

"When do you go?" I ask, feeling my life beginning to trickle down the drain.

"Next Tuesday," Fleur says. "Until late August."

"Nooooooo!" I moan.

We all sit in silence again. This has to be the worst day of my life.

"Well," sighs Claude eventually. "I know this sounds like a peculiar thing to say after all that's happened but . . . I'll really miss you, Fleur. I can't believe you're going."

"Oh, don't, Claude!" says Fleur. "I thought the LBD was finished. I'd never have applied otherwise! And Paddy was on my back 24/7 about getting a job. He's never stopped nagging!"

"I know how that feels," whispers Claude sadly. "Mum's giving me a hard time too. She just can't get a job in this town that pays like her old one. I need to find work extra quick. Things are getting a bit desperate."

Claude stares into the distance. She looks really worried.

"What happens if things don't get better?" asks Fleur.

Claude looks at us both, then bites her lip. "Well, let's not think about that now," she says. "I just have to start earning soon."

We all sit rather dumbfounded for about ten minutes. A candy wrapper tumbles mournfully around the beer garden as I unravel a thread on the hem of my funeral skirt. This is officially the end of the world.

"Right," announces Fleur, after an eternity of woe. "I've got it. And don't either of you dare say no!"

We've known Fleur far too long to ever agree to that.

"Come with me to Destiny Bay," Fleur tells us firmly. "Both of you. Come with me? Please, just say yes?"

"Oh, Fleur, I can't," I begin, thinking of Mum and the whole Nan business and of Seth and all my Post-it note chores. I can't just leave.

Claude just looks stunned.

"Come to Destiny Bay!" repeats Fleur, grabbing our hands. "Let's call Miss Scrumble at Harbinger Hall and ask if there are other jobs!"

"I can't see how I can—" Claude begins.

"Aha! Don't even say it!" Fleur shrieks, putting her hand to Claude's mouth. "Not a word, unless it's yes! Say that the LBD will spend the summer together at Destiny Bay! Just say it!"

Claude and I stare back at Fleur with eyes as wide as saucers.

We couldn't do that, could we?

Or could we?

Four days later

"Daaaaaaa-aaaaad!" yells Fleur so loudly her next-door neighbors' back teeth rattle. "How do we make a conference call?"

"What?" shouts Paddy Swan from his bedroom next door. "What now?"

"Connnnnnnnnnnn-ference call!" yells Fleur again. "What do we do? Come and show us!"

Paddy Swan sticks his head around the door to his office, raising one sardonic eyebrow at the LBD sitting perched around his computer, making full use of his "mission control" facilities.

"Well, just press the 'conference' button, then dial, you

blithering imbeciles!" scoffs Paddy. "Where have you three been going every morning for the last five years? Blackwell School or Burger King?"

"Gnnnngnn, Fleur!" groans Claude. "I told you it was that button!"

"Hmmph, you say that now," tuts Fleur as Paddy appears wearing a sharp, navy blue bespoke suit, clutching a handful of neckties.

"Ladies," he announces seriously. "Which tie? The blue or the gray? C'mon, hurry! I'm lunching with Mr. Jefferson Smythe in half an hour. He's a very important new client. This meeting could end up paying for Fleur's mother's next crucial jaunt to a Himalayan health farm. If it goes well, we can get rid of her for two whole weeks!"

"Excellent," says Fleur without even looking up.

"The blue one," says Claude confidently. "It goes with the pin stripe."

"Really, Claudette?" asks Paddy, holding the tie beside his face. "It's not too . . . old fogey?"

Paddy Swan has been acting very oddly since he turned forty-four last month. Not only has he taken up the martial art tae kwon do and started high kicking up and down the lawn each dusk, but last week he threatened to purchase a mint-green Lambretta scooter and a Maharishi parka. Well, until Fleur threatened to run away with the circus in shame.

"Nooooooo! It's not old fogey, Mr. Swan!" assures Claude, ever the smooth talker. "It's more . . . *Secret Service*."

"Ahhh! Secret Service!" beams Paddy. "I like that, Claudette. You can come here again."

As if he has any choice, I think. We've practically lived here since Year 7.

At this point Paddy breaks into his very worst Sean-Connery-as-James-Bond impression. "The name's Schwan . . . Paddy Schwan," Paddy rasps, looking into the mirror while fastening his tie. "On Her Majesty's shecret shervice. Lish-ensh to kill . . ."

Fleur visibly shrinks with embarrassment. "Dad, will you get out?" she moans. "We're calling Harbinger Hall!"

"Very well," sniggers Paddy, clearly elated at humiliating his youngest child. "You girls can leave the money for that call on my desk."

"Put it on my bill," tuts Fleur, dialing the number. "Oooh! Shh, everyone . . . It's ringing! It's ringing!"

The fact that I'm here, waiting to speak to Miss Scrumble, Harbinger Hall's head of personnel, is the freakiest of deakiest turn of events. Ever since our Monday meeting, Fleur has talked and pleaded until she was blue in the face about the LBD going to Destiny Bay. She yaddered incessantly about MTV's August Big Beach Booty Quake. (Psycho Killa, God Created Man and the Scandal Children are all rumored in the tabloids to be playing there, plus there's a surf competition and a massive beach party.) Fleur never shut up about the hot surf dudes, cliff-top parties, sunbathing, snogging and skinny-dipping in store for us if we'd just agree to go.

Fleur's smooth talking certainly paid off. By Wednesday evening Claude was wavering toward "yes" and had even convinced Gloria that Harbinger Hall was a great place for Claude to make some cash.

It was all down to me then. But it just didn't seem right.

71

I couldn't disappear for a nine-week party when Nan had just died, could I? Not even if a summer in Destiny Bay sounded like the most exciting, fabulous LBD adventure in the entire cosmiverse.

I mean, even if I do agree to go, when is the time to hit Mum with it? Tuesday? When she and I collect Nan's ashes from the crematorium and drive to the town hall to sign some death certificates? Or Wednesday, when we go to Nan's house to close off the gas and electricity (the day Mum spends five hours staring at Nan's very small fluffy slippers and walking stick while crying)? Okay, then, what about Thursday, the day Mum doesn't get out of bed at all and I spend my afternoon talking Seth out of pushing chocolate chip cookies into the VCR?

The fact is, I can't bring the subject up, and that is that.

But on Thursday night, I am sitting in the bar after closing time, keeping Dad company while he closes up, when the subject of summer presents itself of its own accord.

"What is your gang up to then," Dad asks, "now that you've stopped arguing? Any plans for summer?"

That's when I tell him, in my very best, noncomplaining voice, that Fleur and Claude are planning to go to Destiny Bay.

"Destiny Bay?" Dad says, replenishing the bottled lagers in the main bar's refrigerator. "Isn't that where they hold that Crash Bang Wallop Wobble Your Bottom Party in the summer?"

"The Big Beach Booty Quake," I say. "Yeah, that's it."

"Saw something 'bout that today in *The Sun,*" Dad mutters. "That Psychic Billy bloke is coming, isn't he?"

"Psycho Killa," I correct him. "He's a rapper."

"That's him!" Dad says. "And that bunch of twerps who always sit on tall stools wearing jackets with no shirts?"

"God Created Man," I sigh, thinking of the lead singer Sebastian Porlock's oiled chest. "They're a boy band."

Dad works away in silence for a while, but I can see his brain clanking. "What about you, then? Don't you fancy gallivanting on MTV with your booty quacking then?" he says dryly.

"Pah! Me in a thong bikini?" I tut. "I'm far too short and squat for that."

Dad gazes into the middle distance, as if he is mulling over something. I feel selfish now for even mentioning Destiny Bay. "You're not short, Ronnie . . . you're perfect," Dad says sagely, wandering off to collect some ashtrays. *"You're just the right height to rest a beer on."*

The following afternoon, I'm in my bedroom clunking away on my bass guitar when Mum summons me to the den. She is sitting on the sofa, wearing a chunky dressing gown over a tracksuit with her hair scraped into a wonky bun, watching *30-Minute Home Revamp Madness!* with a zombielike enthusiasm typically reserved for the long-term unemployed or the recently bereaved.

She looks terrible.

I don't think she's slept properly for days. Dad said she'd been up all Thursday night because she kept having a recurring dream that Nan was calling to say good-bye but she couldn't find the cordless phone.

"Hey, Ron. How's tricks?" Mum asks. Beside her on the sofa, Seth lies flat on his back in a scarlet rompersuit, his soft little snores punctuating the living room's sad silence.

"I'm okay," I say. "How are you?"

"I'm . . . strange," Mum says, shaking her head slowly.

"Do you want a cup of tea?" I ask. All we've done for the last week is make and drink tea. It feels constructive.

"Nah . . . I've had about eighteen cups today," says Mum, nodding at the mugs strewn all over the lounge table. "My back teeth are floating."

We sit in silence staring at the TV, watching someone in wacky dungarees going buck wild with a potato printer. Finally Mum speaks. "Oooh, God yeah, that was it," she says distractedly. "I need to talk to you about the summer. About that hotel job."

"Oh, Mum . . . forget it," I blush, feeling petty and self-centered. "It's nothing. I'm cool about staying here."

"Really?" asks Mum, looking straight at me, furrowing her brow.

"Yeah, really," I lie.

"Oh . . . well, that's ironic," Mum says. "Because I was about to tell you to go for it."

I nearly fall face-first out of the armchair in surprise. "Pardon?" I splutter. "Mother, don't be daft."

"I'm not being daft," she says. "You're not hanging around here for a summer being miserable, watching me being miserable. I've been thinking . . . about everything. About the whole point of being here. About this whole stupid life business."

"What about it?" I say.

"Well . . . It's just over so . . . so quickly! Puff! Gone!" Mum tuts. "So you may as well enjoy yourself."

"But what about Wacky Warehouse?" I splutter. "What about looking after Seth?"

"Stuff Wacky Warehouse!" Mum says vehemently. "Oh, and as for babysitting, I've decided I'm finding a good part-time nanny for Lord Fauntleroy here."

"Splghgh?" I gasp. "Really?"

"Yes," she says, sounding scarily driven. "And I'm going to revamp that menu downstairs in the Fantastic Voyage, start cooking more pan-European and Thai dishes from now on. Experimenting! That's what used to make me happy. *I want to be happy.*"

Mum looks at me and bites her lip. I think she might start crying again.

"Well, Toothless Bert won't like any of this," I tell her, naming a regular barfly who lives on Mum's burgers and scampi.

"Toothless Bert can go and walk in the River Lees till his bobble hat floats for all I care!" announces Mum defiantly.

I stare at her in disbelief.

"Look, Mum," I say, grabbing her hand. "Are you totally sure about this? Because if you're not, I'll stay. I'm worried about you, Mum." My voice begins to crackle too, although after the week we've both had, I feel like I have no more tears left to cry.

"Ronnie, I'm 110 percent absolutely completely sure," Mum says, grabbing my hand back. "It's what Nan would have wanted. She hated people moping about feeling sorry for themselves."

At that point, a tear falls down my face. I reach forward and give Mum a big hug. She feels cold and fragile. She gives me a huge cuddle back, just like she used to when I was a little girl. I can't believe it is possible to hate someone and then love them and worry about them so much in the space of a few days.

"Go and have an adventure," Mum whispers. "Just do it. I packed a suitcase and went to Playa Las Americas in Tenerife when I wasn't much older than you. It was the best summer of my entire life."

I sit back on the sofa and look at Mum curiously.

Tenerife?

Now, that reminds me of something. I know this isn't the correct moment to bring it up, but I absolutely can't help myself.

"Mum?" I begin.

"What?" she says, playing with one of Seth's tiny feet. He stretches and gurgles a little.

"Y'know when you were at catering college?"

"Yeah. What about it?"

"I was just wondering . . . Did you actually *finish* your diploma before you ran off to Tenerife with Dad?"

Mum looks at me, flabbergasted. She shuffles nervously in her seat. "Why?" she asks, her eyes narrowing. "Who's been talking?"

"Erm, well," I say, trying to suppress a smile, "it was just something, er, Nan said the last time I saw her."

Mum's cheeks flush pink, but then a smile spreads across her face, the first that I've seen for a week.

"I can't believe it!" Mum chuckles, a tiny tear falling down her face. "I can't believe that little old lady grassed me up."

"Thank you for calling Harbinger Hall, Precious speaking. How can I direct your call, please?" says the operator.

"Shh!" hushes Fleur. "Personnel Department, please. Miss Scrumble's office."

"Connecting you now, madam," says the operator.

Fleur, Claude and I gaze anxiously at the telephone's speaker. "Miss Scrumble," announces a rather dull, nasal voice.

"Er, good morning, Miss Scrumble," says Fleur, with a very sweaty top lip. "This is Fleur Swan speaking. Do you remember me? We spoke the other day about a summer vacancy beginning next Wednesday?"

"Ah, yes, Miss Swan," Scrumble says drably. "Thank you for calling. I'll just locate that application form. . . . You're our new waitress, aren't you?"

"That's right!" beams Fleur.

"With the impressive resume?" Scrumble says, sounding like she's never been impressed by anything in her life. "Three years' waitressing experience with silver service skills, wasn't it?"

"That's me!" smiles Fleur.

"What!?" mouths Claude in disbelief.

"Shut up!" mouths Fleur back.

"Fluent in French, German and with some conversational Japanese too?" Scrumble says in her monotone.

"Oui! Bien sur! Zut alors!" Fleur says. "Oh, I'm like a sponge when it comes to languages."

"Unbelievable," I mutter under my breath. Five years of French lessons and Fleur can still hardly find her way to a Parisian bathroom and back.

"But, you see, the thing is, Miss Scrumble," Fleur begins, "since I spoke to you, two of my equally dynamic friends, Claudette Cassiera and Veronica Ripperton, have also expressed an interest in working at Harbinger Hall. Are there are any other vacancies coming up?"

After a very long silence, Scrumble speaks. "Hmmm, well," she grumbles. "There's irony in your questioning. I sacked three waiters this morning. They're being marched off the premises as we speak."

Miss Scrumble sounds like she really enjoys that side of her job. Her voice turns a little giddy at "marched off the premises."

"Oh, that's terrible," Fleur says, giving us the thumbs-up. "I'm so sorry to hear that . . ."

"I've no time for laziness, Miss Swan!" blurts out Miss Scrumble, sounding a little unhinged. "And these three vile articles, Saul, Clemence and Stephen, hmmpgh, well, they tested the absolute limit of my patience! They may have sounded applaudable on their resumes. However, one week at Harbinger Hall and it turns out they're in Destiny Bay only to surf and party. No work ethic whatsoever."

"Disgusting," Fleur says, cutting straight to the chase. "So you've not replaced them yet?"

"Er . . . no," says Miss Scrumble, sounding a little breathless from her outburst.

"Fantastic!" Fleur says.

Claude and I have to stop ourselves from squealing!

"If your friends are interested," Scrumble drones, sucking the joy out of the air with her voice, "tell them that the jobs are live-in positions. I would be housing you and whoever the other two successful applicants are in the West Turret."

"The West Turret?" repeats Fleur, trying to muffle her excitement. "Is that like a separate apartment?"

"It's a fully contained three-person apartment with beds, bathroom, TV, kitchen and a sea view," Scrumble sighs. "It's basic but clean."

"That sounds . . . great!" says Fleur, going almost purple with glee.

Claude and I can hardly breathe. The LBD sharing our first apartment?

"I'll speak to my friends right now, Miss Scrumble!" Fleur garbles. "And I'll . . . I'll ask them to e-mail resumes to you! And then I'll call you to check you've got them! And I'll do it right away!"

"Not so fast, Miss Swan," Scrumble interrupts crossly. "Now I've remembered what I needed to say to you. I've made a note here on the last page of your application. There's a problem with your character reference."

"Er, really?" says Fleur. "But I included one! Mr. Patrick Swan. He knows all about how hardworking and trustworthy I am!"

"I'm sure he does, Miss Swan," Scrumble says dryly. "He's your father."

"Hmmm," says Fleur flatly. "That is also true."

"Family members do not make suitable references, Miss Swan," Miss Scrumble whines. "And I was going to request that you simply find another willing body, but after today's unfortunate sackings, the rules are being tightened."

"Oh?" gulps Fleur.

"From now on," says Scrumble. "All prospective Harbinger employees under the age of eighteen must provide an exemplary reference from their headmaster. Now, will that be a problem?"

"Er, pah, pgghhhgh . . . mmm, well, I'm not sure . . . ," splutters Fleur.

"Because you appear to be the model pupil, Miss Swan. Let's see . . . spelling bee champion two years in a row? Chairwoman of the Blackwell Debating Society too?"

"Erm," winces Fleur. "Doesn't that excuse me from getting the reference?"

"No. Rules are rules," grumps Scrumble.

"But we're already on vacation!" Fleur pleads. "How will we find our headmaster? Maybe he's gone away on a cruise. What if—"

"You and your chums have till six o'clock today," interrupts Scrumble, almost as if she's enjoying being a right royal pain up the bum.

"Six o'clock?" Fleur gasps.

"Six o'clock," Scrumble repeats. "Don't be late. Good afternoon to you."

"But, Miss Scrumble!"

The line goes dead.

"We're doomed," I groan, placing my forehead on Paddy's cold desk and beginning to bang the surface slowly.

I'd have given up then, but Claude refuses to be beaten. "Right, let's not panic!" she announces as the LBD paces nervously around Fleur's bedroom. "All we need to do is find McGraw . . ."

"Chloroform him," I mutter. "Give him a frontal lobotomy, then get him to give us references."

"He'll give me a reference anyhow," Claude announces rather capriciously.

"Well, whoopie-do you!" Fleur retorts. "Is that, perhaps, because you've spent five years with your nose wedged up his bum crack?"

Claude doesn't even flinch at this abuse. "Look, Miss Conversational Japanese, do you want us to live in the West Turret or what? Do you want a summer adventure?"

"Of course I do," groans Fleur. "More than anything in the entire world!"

"Good!" says Claude. "And while you're thinking about that, can I also add that I bumped into our ex-guru Miss Cressida Sleeth in the mall this morning, with her new best friend Panama Flipping Goodyear. They were shouting remarks about that *Moulin Rouge* video Cressida saw of us dancing in our underpants! I wanted to crawl under a bus."

"Oh my God," groans Fleur, flushing crimson. "I forgot about that!"

"Well, Cressida hasn't!" Claude says. "Look, let's go and find old grumblechops McGraw, shall we? Let's get away from this town. Away from Cressida Slime and Panama Bogwash!"

"But be realistic, Claude," I say. "The last time Fleur saw McGraw was when he caught her photocopying her bum cheeks in the IT lab!"

"Uggghhh! That's right," sighs Fleur. "You were supposed to be watching the door, Ronnie!"

"Yes, Fleur, silly me," I say dryly. "That was my fault, wasn't it?"

"Okay, no arguing!" implores Claude. "Girls! Let's be logical here. McGraw's a very busy man. Surely he has better things to do than remember every petty little prank his pupils have committed. He'll have forgotten all about the photocopier by now, surely."

"I suppose so," Fleur says. "There are nine hundred and fifty pupils at Blackwell. He's got plenty of other pupils to worry about."

"Hmmm, okay, that's a good point," I say, brightening a little. "But where do we start? It's 2 P.M. now."

"Easy!" says Claude. "We know where McGraw lives, don't we? Pomfrey Manor! It's near Gelt Woods, about nine miles away. It's down a little private road. Let's get the bus over there and visit him."

"Okay," agrees Fleur nervously. "Let's do it."

Frankly I'd rather remove my own wisdom teeth with pliers, but there is no other way.

~~~~~~~

their Pluffy little faces

"This just makes no sense," sighs Claude, gazing up at Pomfrey Manor's intimidating green cast-iron gates. "How can someone not own a doorbell?"

"Hmph! Well, he hates the human race, doesn't he?" Fleur tuts, slumping defeatedly against the manor's impenetrable ten-foot-high brick wall. "He likes being uncontactable."

"Well, I think it's sad," Claude says. "Apparently his phone number is a closely guarded secret too, nowadays, because of the number of prank calls he gets. Who'd be pathetic enough to do that?"

Fleur shoots me a "please shut up" look.

"Beats me, Claude," I shrug, scowling back at Fleur. "Some people just have no respect."

I stand on tiptoes, pushing my face up to the gold letter box. Inside, a long dusty driveway leads to a detached, rather disheveled mansion surrounded by junglelike lawns. The luscious grass is ankle deep. Trees and bushes grow wild, and numerous flowers and shrubs grow every which way they please. It's hardly the prim, neatly kept garden I was expecting.

"He's obviously not short of a few quid, is he?" mutters Claude. "This place seems huge."

"Well, my nan reckoned that his parents were loaded," I say. "I think he inherited the house. He's lived here all his life."

"Wow," says Claude. "So your nan knew him when he was a little boy?"

"Yeah," I say, smiling a little. "Nan knew everyone."

"What was he like?" Claude asks.

"A right little misery, apparently," I laugh, picturing Nan saying it. "She said he used to walk down the street when he was seven, eating his licorice pennies with a face like he was off to his own execution."

Claude and Fleur chortle merrily at the idea.

"Do you think he's home?" Claude asks.

"Difficult to say," I sigh. "There's no car there. But the upstairs windows are open. There are a few lights left on too."

"Mr. McGraaaaaaaaaw!" yells Fleur, her voice echoing redundantly through the surrounding meadows. "Hellllllllloooooooooo!"

This is hopeless. He could be on holiday. Or have killed

himself. Or be away visiting equally suicidal relatives. But—and it's a major but—there's also a small chance he might be home. There's an even more minuscule possibility that we can persuade McGraw to sing our praises to Scrumble.

Claude looks at her watch again anxiously. "Oh no! It's nearly 4:30 P.M.!" she groans. "We've got an hour and a half! We're totally scuppered now."

"Nonsense," says Fleur, with a tiny mischievous smile. "I think we've got to get a little proactive."

"How?" says Claude, rattling McGraw's letter box again uselessly.

"Watch me," says Fleur, looking determinedly at the wall before walking over and taking the black drainpipe in both hands.

"Fleur! What are you doing?" I ask.

She doesn't reply. She simply grips the pipe firmly, thrusts one sneaker into a gap in the bricks and pulls herself a few feet up the pipe.

"Fleur! No!" gasps Claude. "Stop it!"

"Stop worrying!" yells Fleur, scaling farther up the pipe, displaying a rather shameless amount of pink thong under her black miniskirt. "Look, if he's too stubborn to own a doorbell, how else can he expect visitors?"

"Burglars, more like!" shouts Claude. "Get down! What if somebody sees?"

"Got a better plan?" Fleur yells down at us. "Look, stop panicking! If McGraw's in, we'll just tell him that he left his front gate open. Ha! I'm a genius."

"Fleur!" I shout. "You'll kill yourself!"

"Oooh, flipping heck, this is quite high, isn't it?" Fleur giggles, ignoring me completely. As the blonde bombshell reaches the top of Pomfrey Manor's wall, she clambers up, perching her bum on the top.

"Oh, hurray!" she shouts. "There are some tall trees here on the other side! We can climb down them into the garden."

"I'm not climbing anywhere!" shouts Claude. "You'll get us arrested, you stupid nork!"

"Look, I'm going in!" smiles Fleur, jumping down out of sight. To our horror, Fleur vanishes over the wall into Pomfrey Manor!

"C'mon!" Fleur's muffled voice shouts. "It's easy! Stop being scaredy-cats. Do you want to go to Destiny Bay or what?"

"Ignore her," Claude says, crossing her arms. "She just wants attention. Let's not give it to her."

"Girls, have you started climbing yet?" Fleur yells again. "Come on! It's not that scary once you get used to be being . . . ugh . . . oh dear . . . hang on . . . owww . . . some of these branches are a bit . . . slippery!"

"Fleur!" we yell. "What's up?"

"Damn! I've caught my skirt," shouts Fleur. "Oh, hell! Oooooooooh noooo, I think I'm going to . . . aaaaaaaaaaaaaaaaagh-hhhhhh!"

There's a loud rip, followed by a tremendous crashing of branches . . . then a deathly silence.

"Fllllllllllllleur!" we yell. "Fleur! Are you okay?"

But there's no reply.

"Oh my God! Fleur, I'm coming!" shouts Claude, running over and starting to climb up the drainpipe. "Ronnie! Come on! Fleur could have broken her neck."

"Oh Jesus," I sigh, watching Claude's denim-clad bum shimmying up the wall.

"Fllllleeeeeeeur!" Claude shouts, making grand headway. She's almost at the top in moments. "Speak to me, Fleur!"

"Oh, poo," comes a little voice from behind the wall. "I've crushed all his begonias."

"Ha! You're alive," Claude shrieks, perching on top of the wall and looking down into the garden. "You're alive . . . you're . . . oooh, my God! Fleur, where's your skirt!? I can see your butt cheeks!"

"Mmm . . . yeah," groans Fleur. "It's on one of those branches. That's our next problem."

As Claude disappears, I sit down on the curb and ponder why I ever missed the LBD. I could be eating chocolate chip muffins in my bedroom with the curtains closed now.

"Come on, Ronnie!" yell Fleur and Claude. "Your turn!"

I stand up, take a big deep breath, walk over to the wall and begin to climb. The pipe's quite slippery now with all the sweaty hands that have pawed it. Why did I wear flip-flops? If I look behind me, I'll probably vomit. I climb frantically, spurred on by sheer terror.

"Hurray!" shouts Claude as my auburn plaits and petrified face loom over the top of the wall. "C'mon, Ronnie! Not far to go now!"

"Uggghhh, Fleur!" I groan, climbing onto the top of the wall, spotting Fleur's miniskirt, which is hanging in three torn shreds off various branches. "You're almost naked!"

"Concentrate, Ronnie!" shouts Claude. "Some of those branches are quite dangerous."

"Gnnnnngnnn!" I groan, clinging on for dear life.

Ten minutes later, after much careful maneuvering, I'm back on solid ground, being hugged ecstatically by Fleur and Claude.

"Good work, everyone!" shouts Fleur, pure euphoria sweeping over our little huddle.

"Ha!" laughs Claude. "It takes more than a ten-foot wall to beat us!"

"Precisely . . . we're invincible!" I giggle proudly, looking around. "So, er, what shall we do next?"

"Well, we should . . . er," Claude begins, but then she pauses and looks quite anxious. It's just then that we realize that we've broken into our headmaster's property, and that Fleur is standing in only a thong and a T-shirt with her bottom hanging out.

Some people might say we are potentially in a lot of trouble, but then something else very terrible indeed takes our minds off it.

The sound of dogs barking. Yapping, growling and drawing closer by the second!

"Oh hell!" says Claude. "Oh please, God, no!"

"Is that what I think it is?" I shudder.

"Guard dogs!" squeals Fleur, as the terrifying noise gets louder.

"Runnnnnnnnn!" shouts Claude, as three massive, slobbering, hairy dogs appear on the horizon around the left-hand side of Pomfrey Manor. "Run as fast as you can!"

"Aaaaaaaaaaggghhhhh!" we squeal, tearing in the opposite direction. I don't dare look behind me! All I hear is dogs panting, drooling and yapping, beside themselves with excitement, clearly sizing the LBD up as a tasty, protein-rich, between-meals snack.

Suddenly a black dog manages to charge past me, turning itself around to go in for the attack. Aaaaaaaaagh! Behind me, I hear Claude screaming, stumbling, beginning to sob. Fleur's screeching loudest of all. I think she's being bitten on the bum. It's like a horror movie! All I can do is fall to my knees, cover my face and wait for the savage mauling to begin.

"Get off me!" screams Claude. "Get off! Owwwwwww!"

"Aaaagggghhhh! Mr. McGraw! Save us!" I yell pitifully as a slobbery, rough tongue licks across my face.

"Get off! Get off!" Claude howls. "Agh! My face!"

But then bizarrely, I hear Claude giggle.

A rough canine tongue licks across my ear again, accompanied by a blast of breath that isn't exactly minty fresh.

I dare to open one eye.

Standing before me, peering straight at me, is an enormous black pedigree poodle, with a preposterous fluffy Afro, impish coal-black eyes, a shiny black button nose and daft, strategically shaved fluffy "leg warmers." The dog gazes at me playfully, tilting its head to the side, before holding out one dainty paw to shake hands.

"I don't believe it," I say, gasping for breath.

As I turn around, Claude is tickling the belly of an equally ridiculous pure white poodle that is lying on his back, waving his paws gleefully in the air. The third poodle, a gingery pink canine freak, prances about merrily, yelping and wagging its absurdly cotton-woolly tail, clearly elated to have new friends to play with.

"They're as daft as brushes!" smiles Claude, rubbing the white poodle's ears.

"I thought we were going to die there," I pant. My jeans and T-shirt are covered in grass stains.

"Well, Fleur sounded like she was being killed," Claude says. We both freeze. Where's Fleur? She's vanished.

"Fllleeeuuuur!" we yell, starting the poodles off barking again. "Fleeeeeuuuuur!"

"I'm up here!" Fleur snaps crossly, somewhere above us.

"Where?" shouts Claude.

"In this tree!" squeaks Fleur, sitting on the branch of a nearby oak. "I'm not coming down. Not until those horrid things have gone! Those horrid . . . evil . . . demons!"

"They're only poodles, Fleur," I laugh. "Come down!"

"Shan't!" she trills tearfully as the three poodles yelp and strain at the tree. "I won't. Make them go away!"

"Fleur, you're not usually scared of dogs," I say.

"Make them go!" howls Fleur, sounding near hysterical. "I hate them! Hate them!"

"Fleur?" says Claude, sniggering slightly. "Have you got an irrational fear of poodles?"

"Gnnnnngnnnn! Yes!" Fleur yells. "My aunt Irene used to breed them. I . . . I hate them! With their horrid little fluffy faces and their evil eyes, which are always full of black, yucky, smelly sleep dust! And their . . . ggnnngnnn . . . stinky dog-food breath! And their yellow-brown teeth! Yuk! Look at them! I feel sick. Look at their eerily flamboyant haircuts! And their . . . their . . . poo-encrusted bums! Uggghhh!"

"They haven't got poo-encrusted bums," I laugh, picking up

the black poodle's ridiculous tail to examine, then wrinkling my nose. "Oh . . . hang on, you may have a point there."

"Fleur, you must come down," Claude pleads, trying not to laugh. "We're in real trouble here. We have to work out what to do."

But just then a long dark shadow moves across the LBD's path, accompanied by a dismally familiar voice. "Well, you can start," a man's voice booms, "by telling me why you're trespassing on my property!"

Aggghhh! It's Mr. McGraw!

He's not looking at all happy. All the veins are protruding out on his spindly neck, and his eyes look on the brink of explosion. Despite the summer sunshine, McGraw's wearing his trademark heavy-tweed, three-piece suit with thick brown brogues and a primly knotted brown tie, his face dripping with sweat.

"Zanzibar! Zeus!" he shouts, beckoning his poodles over with his skeletal hand. "Zsa Zsa! Come to Papa!"

"Mr. McGraw," begins Claude, pasting on a big nonthreatening smile. "This isn't how it looks!"

"Claudette Cassiera?" McGraw gasps, suddenly recognizing one of his burglars. McGraw only ever sees Claudette when he's awarding her school prizes for wonderfulness. "What is the meaning of this?"

"We needed to speak to you," stutters Claude.

Just then a rustling in the trees above sets the poodles off yelping again.

"And who's up there?" yells McGraw, becoming quite incandescent with rage now. "Get down now! I'm calling the police. Do you hear me? I'll have you all locked up!"

After a few seconds, Fleur's bare bottom emerges from the tree like a pink full moon. Mr. McGraw's typically gray face is now a deep shade of scarlet.

"Fleur Swan!" he fumes, finally meeting the face that matches the ass.

"Good afternoon, Mr. McGraw," smiles Fleur, trying to sound breezy.

"Fleur . . . Swan," repeats McGraw, with a tone of insurmountable woe, shaking his head slowly.

"Yes, Mr. McGraw?" Fleur winces.

Our headmaster lets out one of his trademark dismally long sighs. He pinches the nodule of skin between his eyes, then points in the direction of a nearby garden shed. "There is a pair of gardening trousers in that shed, Miss Swan," he snaps. "Put them on immediately! Then all three of you get into my study and wait for the police. For once, I am quite literally at a loss for words."

an arduous task

In McGraw's study, the grandfather clock reads a quarter to six.

The LBD have been sitting on stiff-backed dining chairs, with our Harbinger Hall dreams well and truly dashed, for more than half an hour. Outside the office, McGraw crashes around Pomfrey Manor, slamming doors and berating the world. I don't think I've ever heard him so angry. Eventually, he appears, takes a seat behind his desk, and snatches up the receiver of his antique telephone, pausing momentarily to scowl at our row of faces.

"Fleur Swan . . . Claudette Cassiera . . . and . . . who are you?" he says, pointing at me.

"I'm Veronica Ripperton!" I huff.

"Are you from Lymewell Academy?" he asks sniffily.

"No! I go to your school," I say rather incredulously. "For the last five years!"

"Hmmm . . . whatever you say," McGraw sighs. "The police can run a full ID search on you. In fact, a summer in a young offender's institute might just do you some good. I'm a great advocator of the short, sharp shock method . . ."

McGraw's spindly finger dials a 9.

"Mr. McGraw," squeaks Claude, "please don't call the police! Please let me explain why we wanted to see you."

McGraw sighs even more deeply. He places the handset down. "Make this outstanding," he growls.

"Mr. McGraw, er, sir," Claude begins, "well, the thing is . . . er, we really desperately want summer jobs at a hotel. Harbinger Hall in Destiny Bay, to be exact. But we need exemplary character references from our headmaster. So—"

Mr. McGraw cuts her off in midflow. "So breaking into my house, trampling my begonias, nude streaking across my lawn, scaring the bejesus out of me and my prizewinning poodles, whom, may I add, have very sensitive dispositions, was the way to charm me, was it?"

"Hmmm . . . well, when you put it like that," Claude mumbles, her lip wobbling.

McGraw peers at Claude, a tiny microscopic flicker of sympathy passing over his face. "Claudette," he says gently. "I find it very difficult to believe you're involved in something like this. Very difficult indeed. You're a model pupil! The sterling job you did helping Cressida Sleeth settle into Blackwell was remarkable. All that wonderful coaching! That girl is predicted ten A-stars at GCSE, you know."

Claude blanches at the mention of Cressida Slime.

"And that's why I feel these fledgling hooligan instincts should be nipped in the bud," McGraw says.

"But I'm not a hooligan," whispers Claude.

"Whereas you!" McGraw snorts, pointing at Fleur. "You . . . satanic creature!"

"Mr. McGraw!" says Fleur, petulantly folding her arms. "Now that's just unfair."

"Oh? Unfair is it?" McGraw jibes, leaping up and marching over to a tall silver filing cabinet, the clatter of his chair setting Zanzibar, Zeus and Zsa Zsa yapping hysterically in the hallway all over again.

As McGraw roots through reams of files, the poodles howl and scratch the door, pushing their moist black snouts underneath it. Fleur grimaces and wipes her hands nervously down her ridiculous oversized tweed gardening pants. After some searching, McGraw produces a bright red document wallet, with a Polaroid picture taped to the front of it. The photograph is of a very familiar blonde girl, sticking her tongue out.

McGraw flings the file down on his desk, opens it dramatically, and clears his throat to speak. "Fleur Iris Swan," he announces. "Blackwell School behavioral record."

"Oh, poo," mutters Fleur.

Oh my God! McGraw actually keeps duplicates of all his school files at home. We're doomed!

"Year Seven," begins McGraw, reading from a list. "During morning assembly chaired by the Gideon Bible Association, shouted the phrases 'You suck!' and 'Bite me!' making the Gideon representative cry."

Fleur examines her pink sparkly nail varnish sheepishly.

"Year Seven!" McGraw continues. "Smeared Marmite along the backs of door handles throughout Blackwell School, leading to numerous dry-cleaning bills and a one-mile area stinking of beef extract."

"There was no proof that was me!" whines Fleur as Claude winces in shame. That Marmite stunt was totally Claude's idea. McGraw simply refused to believe her confession.

"Silence, Swan! I'm speaking!" shouts McGraw, pointing at his file. "Year Seven: brought a car jack to school and stole the rear left wheel of Miss Blythe's Renault Clio."

"Mmm . . . okay, that was me," mutters Fleur.

"The list goes on and on! Let's skip to the final entry, shall we? Year Eleven: cracked the IT room's photocopier screen with bottom cheeks."

"Gnnnnngnnn," groans Fleur.

"Yes, gnnngggnnnnnn!" repeats McGraw, his saggy gray face reverberating in annoyance as he snaps Fleur's file shut. "Why, oh why should I honor your character? Tell me one good reason."

"Because . . . because she wants to change!" blurts Claude.

"Eh?" McGraw, Fleur and I chorus.

"She wants to change!" repeats Claude. "She was just saying while we were waiting here for you . . . she's riddled with guilt and wants to turn over a new leaf!"

"That's right!" says Fleur, clasping her hands together. "Mr. McGraw, I'm giving you my solemn bond. Give me one last chance—I won't let you down! I'll be the hardest-working waitress Destiny Bay has ever seen. Okay, I've done some childish things in the past, but this is my chance to grow up. To enter the world of work. Plllleeeeeeease!"

McGraw stares directly at Fleur for one long, slow minute. It's now six minutes to 6 P.M.

"No," he says, picking up the phone again and dialing.

"Mr. McGraw!" gasps Claude, leaping up and crashing her hand down on the phone, cutting off McGraw's phone call. "Please listen to me for a second. I need to tell you the truth."

McGraw looks taken aback. What can Claude possibly say?

"I really, really need this job, Mr. McGraw," Claude says, her eyes filling with tears. McGraw looks stunned. "The Cassieras really need the money. And this job is a live-in position, where the tips will be excellent if I work hard. I'll be able to save money to send back home to my mum."

McGraw looks at Claude in shock.

"Mum's lost her job, you see," Claude continues, "and things are getting kind of desperate with bills and the mortgage. She spent all her life savings when Dad was dying, you see. And my big sister lives in London now and she's penniless too, so she can't help out. We're totally . . . broke. Mum's been talking about selling the flat and moving to Cornwall to live with Aunty Sissy. She lives more than three hundred miles away!"

Claude's voice cracks up now. Fleur reaches across and grabs her hand. We didn't know things were so bad! Gloria is even considering moving away? Taking Claude with her? The LBD are truly cursed.

Will McGraw hammer the final nail in the coffin?

The grandfather clock reads four minutes to six.

McGraw looks rather shaken up by Claude's speech. He doodles a picture on his phone pad awkwardly, refusing to meet Claude's gaze. "When would you be finished?" he asks after an excruciating silence.

"Pardon?" says Claude.

"Finished," repeats McGraw crossly. "When would this term of summer employment cease?"

"Late August," Fleur pipes up. "Just in time for us to begin sixth form."

We look at McGraw expectantly. His face gives nothing away.

"Why?" says Claude.

"Because I have some autumnal employment that would keep you out of trouble," says McGraw. "We'd call it remunerations for the stress you've caused me this afternoon."

"Does . . . does that mean you'll give us references?" splutters Fleur.

"Not strictly," huffs McGraw. "You've not heard my offer yet."

"We'll do anything!" Fleur says. "Gardening? Painting? Car washing? We can start September first. We're your girls, Mr. McGraw!"

"Dog grooming?" announces McGraw, arching one eyebrow. Fleur's face freezes.

"Having met my three magnificent prizewinning beauties," McGraw boasts, "you'll have noticed the plethora of loving attention they need lavished upon them. They're magnificent animals. But without their weekly shampoo, blow-dry and tooth-brushing session they can get quite, er, unhygienic. It's a very arduous task keeping poodles."

Fleur puts her hand over her mouth. Her face seems to flush green.

"Their little eyes get quite caked in sleep," continues McGraw, "and their, er, other parts can get quite matted and unsavory."

"Oh God," mutters Fleur, swaying on her seat.

"We'll shampoo your poodles, Mr. McGraw!" smiles Claude. "Every week!"

"For a year?" threatens McGraw.

"Oooh! Er, okay! For a whole year!" grins Claude, scrambling around in her pocket for the Harbinger Hall telephone number. "As many times as they need it! We just love poodles. Mmm! Those fluffy little faces! So cute. Fleur can't wait. Can you, Fleur?"

"I can't wait," says Fleur in a robotic voice.

"Have we got a deal?" gasps Claude, pushing the piece of paper under his beaky nose. "It's getting late now—will you call Miss Scrumble?"

McGraw looks at the telephone number, then at all three of us before slowly shaking his head. Then he begins to dial.

"A whole year, mind!" McGraw warns. "That's one hundred and fifty-six shampoos! Ah . . . yes, good afternoon to you. Could you direct my call to Miss Scrumble's office, please? Samuel McGraw here, headmaster of Blackwell School."

Chapter 4

thumbs-up

"Apparently Esperance Beach is the best beach to hang out on," announces Fleur authoritatively as the train chugs slowly south-bound toward Destiny Bay. "That's the hippest beach with the best breaks! Much less mainstream than Misty Beach. Esperance is where all the hottest surfers go."

"What do you mean, breaks?" asks Claude, offering around a box of egg-salad sandwiches that smell vaguely of farts. Claude's been so much more chill ever since we got jobs. We'd never realized how stressed she'd been about her mum and their money problems.

"Breaks are waves," Fleur says. "I've been brushing up on my surf jargon. I'm in the mood for a bit of summer lovin' with a surf dude. I need to speak the lingo."

"Awww," I groan. "I feel a bit sorry for Baz Kauffman. He liked you, y'know?"

Poor oily-headed Baz was chucked the very instant McGraw put that phone down and confirmed our places at Harbinger Hall. According to Fleur, things were "fizzling out" anyway. Apparently Baz's hair product overload was starting to annoy her. Fleur reckoned they couldn't snog without their foreheads becoming glued together. Plus his ears were full of old flaky gel. Double-spew!

"Look, I'm doing this for you!" says Fleur, filing her nails absentmindedly into Claude's egg sandwiches. "How can I help you find a new boyfriend if I'm not allowed to flirt with his friends?"

"Pgghh," I splutter, not believing Fleur's benevolence for a second. "I don't want a boyfriend. I can't be bothered. Cuh! Boys are just a total waste of time."

"Have you gone insane?" tuts Fleur. "What's the point of coming to Destiny Bay if you're not up for snogging a surf dude?"

Claude laughs, scatter-gunning me with egg salad. Fleur puts down her nail file and wrinkles her nose at me.

"Ugh . . . I get it now," she moans. "You're still hung up over that Jimi baboon-breath Steele, aren't you? Gnnnngnnn! Oh, how I hate him! I wish you'd let Magda beat him up when she wanted to."

"I never even think about him," I blush.

"Really?" asks Claude tactfully. "So you've stopped hacking into his Hotmail account now? 'Cos y'know, Ronnie, that was a bit freaky. Even for you."

"He changed his password," I say, remembering far darker days just after Jimi ran off with Snuff Monster when I used to sit on his garden wall because "being near him was better than nothing." Jimi's mum, Doris, used to bring me out mugs of tea.

Let's never speak of that ever again.

"I'm over Jimi Steele," I say firmly.

"Good," says Claude. " 'Cos would you really want him back anyhow after he's spent six months being groped by Frankenstein Beak?"

"No," I say quietly. It'd be nice to think he wanted me back, though.

"Anyway," says Fleur. "Don't worry, there'll be no shortage of hot boys at Destiny Bay. It's going to be one long snog-athon!"

I look at Fleur witheringly.

"What's up now?" laughs Fleur.

"Well . . . it's okay for you, Fleur, isn't it?" I tut. "You can speak to boys! You're an excellent flirt. You've got all the best lines. Me? I start acting like a day-release patient the second anyone vaguely hot comes near me."

Fleur and Claude start giggling. They're not arguing with me.

"Take last month at that Blackwell Centenary Barbecue shambles," I moan. "When Miles Boon walked over to me for a chat."

"Mmm, Miles Boon. He looks so hot right now!" swoons Fleur. "He's been training for a charity half marathon. He's totally buff."

"I *know*!" I howl. "So he walks over, and I think, oooh, flipping heck, better start flirting. So I said hello . . . and I gave him two thumbs-up!"

"You did what?" splutters Fleur. "Two thumbs-up? What, like this?" Fleur holds both her thumbs aloft in an "I'm wacky!" manner.

"Uh-huh," I affirm. "That's it."

100

"Why?" she says in disbelief.

"I don't know!" I wail. "And then . . . Claudette, what did I start talking about?"

"Slugs," Claude winces.

"Slugs," I repeat, placing my head in my hands. "My brain just flipped out and I started jabbering on about garden pest control."

"I thought it was quite interesting," says Claude kindly.

"Then, worst of all, when Miles started making excuses to leave, I said, 'Hey, call me sometime.' *And I made a phone sign with my hand!*" I illustrate, pulling my thumb and little finger into the internationally accepted gesture of the phone, before clamping it to my face.

"Noooo!" howls Fleur, biting her fist. Claude's trying not to laugh.

"I can only surmise," I conclude solemnly, "that if I ever want another boyfriend, I may need to cut my own hands off."

Fleur and Claude start laughing so loudly now that other people in the train carriage are tutting and rustling newspapers. I can't blame them for being cross at us really. The LBD have giggled, gossiped and goofed about for well over four hours now. It's not as if Fleur Swan has any volume control on her head either—at one point she coerced the entire carriage into a Mexican wave.

However, at least when we're chattering, it stops me worrying about stuff. I mean, I'm really excited about Harbinger Hall. I'm doing what my nan (RIP) specifically told me to do: I'm off to have a proper adventure. But this hasn't stopped me worrying that I'm making the biggest mistake of my life.

I mean, come on. I'm hardly the world's most competent waitress, am I?

Last Christmas, when I worked at the Fantastic Voyage, so many customers got drenched with soup and gravy that Mum considered serving a complimentary rain bonnet with each dish. The dishwashers used to high-five me whenever a customer got the correct order. I once dropped a chicken drumstick right into a woman's Louis Vuitton handbag. She didn't realize until two weeks later when her wardrobe was full of bluebottles.

Needless to say, I mentioned none of this on my Harbinger Hall application form.

Another thing freaking me out is that I've never been away this long from Mum and Dad before. What if I get, like, really homesick? What if I end up having a complete schizoid fit in the first week and can't exist without my mother, like the wet fart girls that had to get picked up early from Brownie camp?

(Okay, this is a long shot. My mother was being extra-specially annoying this morning. Not only did she follow me around the house for two hours checking I had fresh underwear on and giving me unsolicited advice about my bowels, but she then embarked upon a really embarrassing "facts of life" speech. Well, she tried to. At the first smattering of the word "penis" passing her motherly lips, I locked myself in the bathroom, placed a finger in each ear and hummed "Rule Britannia" until she retreated.)

Despite this, I still felt pretty choked, standing on Platform 4 waving good-bye, knowing I'd not see them for eight weeks.

"Go on, bail out on me," Dad groaned. "Leave me with the ayatollah! You just have a good time, forget my plight!"

"See ya, Dad," I said, getting a big lump in my throat. "May the force be with you."

Then Mum gave me a big hug and pushed me onto the train. "Gone for the whole summer. My little girl!" she smiled, her lip wobbling furiously. "It's the end of an era!"

That set me off crying. I'm such a sap.

Fleur, on the other hand, virtually high-kicked her way onto the train, ignoring Paddy's sarcastic comment that he'd "see her next week when she got fired." And as for Claude? Well, she just kissed Gloria and hopped aboard. She just seems really focused on earning some cold hard cash.

"So, anyway, Esperance Beach," says Fleur. "That's where the in-crowd surfers hang out. Y'know, the locals? The pro surfers? All the coolest folk? That's where we'll be doing most of our sunbathing."

"How do you know all this?" says Claude.

"Hmmm, well, big sisters have to be good for something, I suppose," smiles Fleur. "I e-mailed Daphne in Guatemala, and she put me in touch with her friend Suki, who did the last summer season at Destiny Bay."

"At Harbinger Hall?" says Claude.

"Er, no," says Fleur. "Suki was a tequila girl at the nightclub Utopia. Basically, she stood around in very small, tight shorts with bottles of tequila in a holster belt, blowing a whistle, charging two pounds a shot for tequila. But apparently all the clubbers used to give her at least a pound tip per shot! She made enough in eight weeks for a ticket to Sydney. How amazing is that?"

"Her mother must be *very* proud," mutters Claude.

Fleur twitters on, oblivious. "So anyway, Suki was giving me the Destiny Bay lowdown. Apparently all the Aussie and Kiwi surfers crash at the Banana Hostel or Sam's Surf Shack. Or the beach bar called A Land Down Under. Plus there's an amazing café called Cactus Jack that's excellent for watching sunsets! Oh, and there's the Destiny's Edge Beach Club, which has a roof terrace where they have seventies theme parties. Oh, and there are lots of secret cliff-top parties too!"

Fleur's eyes are alive with excitement. "I can't wait," she giggles. "We're free! Free to do what we please!"

"Fleur, the breakfast shift begins at six o'clock in the morning," Claude reminds her. "We're not *that* free."

"Oh, Claude," tuts Fleur. "We're only clearing a few plates. How hard can it be?"

"The place holds two hundred guests," says Claude. "That's a lot of plates to clear away."

Fleur's face goes a little white.

"Incidentally, Fleur," Claude prods, "have you ever cleared a table before?"

"Of course I have!" insists Fleur. "Sometimes when Mrs. Duke, our housekeeper, has the day off, I . . . y'know, put my own breakfast bowl in the dishwasher."

"Well done, you!" cheers Claude.

"Oh, shut it, Claude," laughs Fleur. "You won't rain on my parade. This is going to be the best summer ever! We're freeeeeee!"

"Girls, I think we're here," I say as the train begins to pull into a very small old-fashioned station. "Get your bags together, we're getting off."

"Wonderful!" smiles Fleur, taking out her compact and applying hot-pink lip gloss. "Ahhh . . . no Paddy, no Mr. McGraw, no exams, no Cressida Sleeth, no Panama Goodyear, no hassles!"

We grab our bags, suitcases and rucksacks and tumble off the train, scanning the platform apprehensively. Destiny Bay Railway Station is absolute bedlam, jam-packed with tourists, commuters and gangs of surf boys lugging surfboards. It's nearly 6 P.M., but the sun is still blazing down, drenching us all with sweat.

Suddenly I'm feeling nervous again.

I don't see Scrumble anywhere. What if she's forgotten us? What if we're stranded literally hundreds of miles from home? We know nobody!

But just at that very second I spy a figure in the crowd that absolutely, 110 percent has to be our new boss, Miss Helga Scrumble. She is standing underneath Destiny Bay's station clock, wearing an expression that could freeze fog.

squarepants

Miss Scrumble is the most peculiar-looking individual.

She isn't fat. There isn't a spare ounce of flab on her. But she's still a chunky box of a woman. Small, smaller than me, even, with wide shoulders, wide hips, a distinct dearth of waist and a flat, almost rectangular-shaped head. Scrumble's dark brown hair is chopped into a severe asymmetric bob. Thick black spectacles are perched upon the end of her snoutish nose. Jutting from her square body are stumpy arms and little hoof-feet.

Despite the sweltering July sun, she is clad in a gray pinafore, black shirt, black opaque tights and black leather shoes. She could be any age between 18 and 72, but I'm opting for about 45.

"Miss Scrumble?" smiles Claude politely.

Scrumble's beady eyes meet ours. She scans the LBD sniffily, fixing upon Fleur's butt-cheek-scraping hot pants.

"Harbinger Hall?" Scrumble says, sounding like a less chipper version of my old Speak 'n' Spell machine.

"Yes!" we all chorus.

"Walk this way," says Scrumble, scurrying away. From behind she looks like SpongeBob Squarepants's frumpy grandmother.

"Phew, it's hot," smiles Fleur, trying to break the awkward silence as we load our luggage into the trunk of Scrumble's clapped-out Volvo Estate car.

Scrumble pauses to glare at Fleur as if she were an imbecile. "It's July," she replies, with the cold dead eyes of a death row inmate. "It's Destiny Bay. Obviously it's hot."

"Mmm, yes," says Fleur, doing her best "silly me" face.

"And besides," sighs Scrumble, eyeing Fleur's long brown legs and bare, toned arms with badly concealed bitterness, "I'd have thought, in that outfit, you'd be positively *chilly*."

Fleur's eyes narrow. She opens her mouth to say something . . . but then she shuts it again firmly. *Thank God.*

Seconds later, we're out on the road, whizzing through the resort toward Harbinger Hall. Destiny Bay, or what we can see of it, seems like a lot of fun. Well, I think so anyhow. We pass through the town at about 120 mph! Scrumble drives like an absolute lunatic, pedal to the metal, cutting cars off at intersections, terrifying pedestrians and cranking the gearbox noisily as the Volvo's engine roars in disgruntlement. Scrumble clearly has issues about this whole being square shaped thing—this is payback time for the planet.

"Oooh, look! There's A Land Down Under!" Fleur yells as Destiny Bay's landmarks whiz past us. "And the Banana Hostel! And Utopia! And woweeee, look! Misty Beach! That's where they have the Big Beach Booty Quake!"

Misty Beach looks like paradise! Its pure white sands are packed with girls in thong bikinis and buff boys with straggly blond locks carrying surfboards. Several games of volleyball and Frisbee are in progress, while ice creams are slurped and cocktails drunk. It looks like absolute heaven—although our faces are reverberating with too much G-force to see the finer details.

Quickly, we're through the main resort, climbing upward on a coastal road, clear blue ocean to our right, lush green forests on our left, the LBD gripping on to our seats in terror as Scrumble overtakes cars on hairpin bends, beeping her horn furiously and splatting kamikaze rabbits that dare to cross her path. Thankfully, after a mile or so of wacky racing, Scrumble chucks on a right-turn signal and cuts over the oncoming traffic.

"Well, you could see me coming, couldn't you?" she yells incredulously as a red-faced surfer-hippie in a VW camper makes an exceedingly rude gesture at her.

"Harbinger Hall Hotel!" gasps Claude as we hurtle up the long gravel driveway through exquisitely tended gardens, narrowly missing two old duffers in a golf cart.

"Indeed," says Scrumble, screeching to a halt.

Before us lies the most breathtaking, sprawling redbrick Gothic ex-stately home. Two beautiful yet rather intimidating turrets mark the east and west wings, and dozens of stained-glass windows twinkle in the early evening sun. In front of Harbinger's main entrance, which is a silver portcullis at the top of beautiful marble stairs, stands a doorman in a dark green top hat and tails. Several snooty-looking guests are climbing from Jaguars and Mercedes and heading up the steps. None of the clientele looks anything like Big Doggy, the Scandal Children or "Duke of Pop" Spike Saunders. This bunch looks more like Queen Elizabeth II's posher, even more in-bred relatives.

"You will never use that main entrance," Scrumble announces, nodding toward the grand portcullis. "That's for guests only. Staff use the rear entrance. It's back there beside the refuse area."

Fleur wrinkles her nose, then stays remarkably silent.

"It's like a palace!" Claude says, seeming a little shocked.

"The hall was erected in 1732 by Edmund, Duke of Harbinger," drones Scrumble, switching into History Channel mode. "It's been the scene of many regal gatherings, war committees and bloody executions. In 1886, Harbinger became a hospice for fever sufferers, then eventually in 1901 a mental institution. In 1978, the Hall was bought and renovated by local hoteliers, the Vanderloos."

"It's really, er, posh," mutters Fleur.

"Harbinger Hall is the area's most exclusive hotel," announces Scrumble officiously. "We attract a mature, affluent clientele who visit for the breathtaking coastal views, the golf and our top-of-the-range spa facilities."

"But what about pop stars?" blurts out Fleur. "Didn't MTV hire most of this place last year? For the Big Beach Boo . . . , erm, party?"

Scrumble wrinkles her nose in discomfort. "Hmmmpgh! Don't remind me! They've just rebooked for August too. The Scandal whatnots are playing, and some Bicycle Killer character is flying in from Los Angeles."

"Psycho Killa the rapper!" gasps Fleur, her eyes becoming glassy. "And the Scandal Children!"

"Not that you'll be fraternizing with any of them," growls Scrumble, "aside from serving them their breakfasts. Now, are we clear on that?"

"Mmm . . . yes, we're clear," we all groan.

"Good," says Scrumble, waddling off.

Suddenly, Misty Beach, with its chilled-out sunny surf vibe, seems rather a long way away indeed. And as for Mum, Dad, Seth and the Fantastic Voyage? Well, they seem like another cosmiverse entirely.

you've gotta smile (no really, you've got to)

"Rules," announces Scrumble, waddling around her office dispensing waitressing uniforms. Fleur has already been given a long frumpy bry-nylon pinafore that I can see her mentally customizing with scissors and glitter. The pinafore I've been handed is so shapeless I can only imagine that my predecessor was a pregnant Shetland pony.

"I'm a great advocator of rules," Scrumble drones.

"Yet obviously not the Highway Code, you complete freak," Claude mutters under her breath.

"I beg your pardon?" says Scrumble.

"I said, it's good to have a moral code," Claude smiles. "It gets one through the week."

"Precisely, Claudette," says Scrumble, opening a file and thrusting three sheets under our noses. "So, read these and learn them by heart."

We begin to read. Fleur is the first to let out a whimper.

HARBINGER HALL EMPLOYEE BEHAVIORAL CODE

1. Punctuality is paramount.

2. A waitress's personal appearance must be immaculate. No jewelry. Neutral makeup only.

3. *The customer is always right.*

4. Waitresses behaving in a sarcastic, rude or surly manner to guests or management will be punished.

5. While visiting the resort of Destiny Bay, Harbinger Hall waitresses are *ambassadors* of the hotel. Bringing the hotel into disrepute is unacceptable.

6. Dismissal from Harbinger Hall will result in loss of hotel accommodation *with immediate effect.*

---

7. Waitresses will NOT canoodle with the guests.

8. Waitresses will NOT entertain members of the opposite sex in their accommodation. Spot checks will be made.

9. Waitresses must provide their own meals and NOT eat from the kitchen.

10. A happy disposition is compulsory! All waitresses must look cheerful and jubilant while in view of the guests. For appropriate width of smile see affixed Diagram A.

"These seem . . . er, reasonable," says Claude.

"Neutral makeup!" shudders Fleur. "How old am I, thirty?"

"I'm sure I'll be *just fine* with this no-sarcasm rule," I say dryly.

"Accommodation," says Scrumble, ignoring us all. "Now, collect your belongings, girls, and follow me to the West Turret. And remember, we're heading out into Harbinger Hall now, so everybody *smile*."

In a flash, Scrumble is through her office door, pulling a weird "happy-happy-joy-joy" face so unnatural she just looks like she is wrestling a trapped fart. We march through Harbinger Hall's rather ostentatious gold-and-marble reception, chaotic with check-ins and check-outs plus dozens of bellboys carrying luggage, turning right down a sumptuous pastel-colored main thoroughfare, which is bedecked with chandeliers, past Lady Tattershall's Ballroom, then past Captain Morgan's Dining

Room, where dinner is in full swing and a small orchestra is playing.

As news spreads of Scrumble approaching, you can literally see the expressions of Harbinger Hall's staff strain into weird variations of the requisite cheerful face. People are pulling weird forced smiley faces everywhere!

"Good evening, Miss Scrumble!" says one waiter as we pass by, pulling what is quite frankly a Count Dracula face. "What a lovely evening we're having."

"Good evening, Jeremy," Scrumble bristles as she turns to us. "See, girls? Everybody has a smile at Harbinger Hall."

"Make them stop," mutters Fleur. "They're frightening me."

"This way for the West Turret!" points Scrumble, taking a swift right. "Come on, girls, don't dilly-dally."

Suddenly a rather cute bellboy appears walking toward us, with blond hair and a smart green jacket.

"Well, look here," smirks the lad. "More West Turret inmates?"

"That will be all, Joseph," grumps Scrumble, shooting him a filthy look.

"Good luck up there!" he quips.

"Eh?" I shout after him. "What do you mean?" But Joseph just wanders away, chuckling to himself.

"Ignore him," commands Scrumble, ushering us onto a dark, rather eerie spiral staircase labeled STAFF ONLY.

"How many steps is it to the West Turret?" asks Claude, gazing upward.

"One hundred and eighty-eight," announces Scrumble, ushering us up the dark stairwell. "They'll keep you fit."

After much huffing and panting, we finally reach a large white door. Scrumble turns a large black key in the lock, and with a creak and a crash our entire world suddenly seems brighter.

The LBD has a new headquarters! And it's really rather fabulous!

Our new apartment consists of a plain white living room with a threadbare sofa, a creaky armchair and an antique TV. In the kitchen in the corner, there's a tiny oven, a fridge and an eighties-style microwave. The adjoining bedroom has three single beds with an en suite bathroom, which is little more than a cupboard with a toilet and a shower. Okay, it's not much to write home about—it's even a tiny bit depressing—but it's clean, it's all ours and now it's home!

"Here's a set of keys," says Scrumble. "The other set is missing, so you'll have to share them. Now, is this all to your liking?"

"It's amazing," whispers Claude, staring around the apartment, getting a little glassy eyed. "Thank you."

"It's just . . . wow!" says Fleur, running into the bedroom and throwing her suitcase on the comfiest-looking bed near the window.

"We can see the sea!" I shout, throwing open the large living room window, letting in a blast of salty air. Our apartment overlooks a garden that reaches right to the cliff's edge. To the left, we can see the lights of Destiny Bay twinkling a mile away along the coast. Ahead lies the ocean, stretching as far as the eye can see. Far in the distance, a lighthouse shines out, warning ships away from the rocks.

I stand there for a second, gazing out to sea at the regular, revolving beam, remembering a daft song that I used to sing for Nan when I was a little girl called "You Can't Keep a Horse in a Lighthouse." I learned it at school in Year 3, and whenever I went to Nan's, she used to make me stand on a dining chair and sing it for her and Granddad.

A small lump forms in my throat. I'd never have done any of this without Nan. Made friends again with Fleur and Claude. Gone to Destiny Bay.

I can't stop replaying the last time I ever saw her. Standing there in her doorway at 11 Dewers Drive, waving me good-bye. I wish I'd run back and given her one last hug. And told her thank you.

I was an idiot. I really thought she'd be around forever.

"Hey, Miss Scrumble, can you get down to the beach from here?" asks Fleur, pointing at the cliff path.

"Pardon?" barks Scrumble. "Beach? Oh, well, there is a cove down that path, but it's just, erm, spiky rocks, algae and, er, dead seagulls. Your nearest sandy beach is in Destiny Bay . . . Now, anyway," Scrumble looks at her clipboard, "your first breakfast shifts are tomorrow morning. You're scheduled for the lunch shifts too. Assemble at 5:45 A.M. in the dining room and introduce yourselves to Siegmund, the general manager. Good evening to you."

"Five forty-five . . . ," gasps Fleur.

But Scrumble has already vanished.

"Come here, girls," mutters Claude, dragging me and Fleur into an impromptu tearful LBD group hug. "We're here! We've finally made it!"

bigger than God

"Who in Mary's name are you three?" sighs Siegmund Brewster as we amble into the vast dining room promptly at 5:45 A.M. Siegmund, with his neatly coiffed dark hair, fabulously expensive black suit and beguilingly shiny shoes, is peering at us oddly. I'd swear his eyebrows have been pruned into perfect arches. They're just too perfect.

The LBD, needless to say, don't look so glossy. Having sat up till after 1 A.M. last night gossiping about Baz Kauffman's halitosis, my eyes are sliding down my face.

"Hello, Siegmund. I'm Claude, that's Fleur and that's Ronnie," Claude announces. "We're your, er, new waitresses."

"My new . . . what? Where's Saul, Clem and that other boy gone to? Did they quit?" gasps Siegmund, putting his hand to his mouth in amazement. "Ha! Oh well, never mind. Three more lambs to the slaughter! Where does Scrumble find you people?"

"You . . . you didn't know we were coming?" stutters Claude.

"Hmmm . . . ," says Siegmund, scanning his memory theatrically. "Now, I do remember a ghastly memo of some description crossing my peripheral vision."

"Great," sighs Claude, relieved.

"But I didn't read it," frowns Siegmund. "Scrumble should know by now, *I don't do memos.*"

"Oh," we groan. This is a highly auspicious beginning.

"*Mais, ça ne fait rien*, you're here now," smiles Siegmund, clapping his hands. "Huzzah for that! Willing waitresses are always welcome around here . . . Now, I'm taking it that you girls all know how to wait tables?"

"That's right," says Claude. Fleur examines her shoes.

"*Wunderbar!*" Siegmund nods. "All right, so follow me. I suppose I should introduce you to the rest of the cast."

As the LBD stand, mouths open, catching flies, Siegmund turns on his heel and flounces off to the end of the dining hall, crashing through the white double doors into the kitchen.

"Oh and incidentally," yells Siegmund, turning again. "My official title is general manager. But I'm like God around here. Honestly. The 'powers that be' just won't let me put it on my name badge."

By the small derisive snort he gives before chivvying us into the kitchen, I'm guessing he means Miss Scrumble.

"Actually," he adds, "I'm bigger than God."

Inside Harbinger Hall's kitchen, a bulky man wearing chef's whites with a ruddy face and eyes like pieces of coal is whisking a bowl of yellow gunk furiously, while beside him two younger lads are chopping herbs and kneading dough.

"Rosco," Siegmund shouts to the older man, "attention, *s'il vous plait.* Let me introduce, er, Fanny, Claire and Maud, our new waitresses."

I was about to correct him, but then I figured we may well be fired before anyone learned our real names. Best not complicate matters.

"Ladies, this is Rosco Flanders, your head chef. Oh, and those are Gene and Leon, his two assistants."

While Rosco gives us a quirky military-style salute, his two deputy chefs wave hello. Leon is rather small and ferrety, age about twenty, with a silly mustache, and Gene is the same age, rugged with sandy hair and big friendly blue eyes.

"Hey! Are you living here?" Gene pipes up rather mischievously, directing his question to Fleur.

"Yes, we're in the West Turret," Fleur says.

Leon and Gene look at each other in mock horror, then begin laughing. Quickly Leon is prancing about in a spooky zombie manner, while Gene cracks up.

"What?" the LBD howl.

"Rather you than us!" chuckles Leon.

"Boys! Boys! Less of the nonsense," barks Siegmund, rolling his eyes. "Girls, ignore them, they're just excited to see beautiful women. I've had them locked in here making eggs Benedict since February."

The LBD decide to ignore them.

"Now," continues Siegmund, "before you begin, I need to warn you about Rosco. You may find he shouts a lot."

Rosco nods in agreement.

"He's allowed to do that," says Siegmund. "We think he had an unhappy childhood. But if he *throws* anything at you, like, say, a shoe or an espresso machine, just tell me and we'll review the situation. Right?"

"Throws anything?" Claude and Fleur gasp. I just chuckle. It'll take more than a shouting chef to scare me—I've lived with one for sixteen years.

"Any customers out there yet, Sieg?" asks Rosco.

"Not yet," replies Siegmund, checking his Rolex. "Give them five minutes, though, and they'll start to flock."

The chefs smirk as Siegmund cranes his neck to peer through the serving hatch. "They're on holiday, for crying out loud!" Siegmund continues. "Can't they just have a lie-in?"

"Weirdos," grumbles Rosco, opening the fridge and producing a ginormous tray of duck eggs. "I'd ban them. Ban the lot of them."

"You'd ban all of the customers?" says Claude, looking rather shocked.

"Hmmpgh, yes . . . make my job a lot easier," grumps Rosco before wandering off muttering something profound about Cumberland sausage.

"Oooh! Spoke too soon," tuts Siegmund. "Here's one now! It's Colonel Three-Minute Egg! Right, you, Fanny? You take him. Grab a menu and go give it to the old man with the navy blazer and the military tie. Take his order . . . believe me, it'll be a three-minute soft-boiled egg with wholemeal toast. Well, it has been at 5:57 A.M. for the last four weeks."

"Who, me?" I shudder.

"Well, you've got to start somewhere," laughs Siegmund, throwing a large red leather menu at me.

"Er, oooh, okay," I stutter, my stomach doing double somersaults. I thought I'd at least get a training session.

"Oh, and a word of advice," yells Siegmund. "*Don't* let him start talking about the Second World War. I've sat through the Siege of Monte Cassino with him twice this week already."

"Okay," I nod, biting my lip.

"Oh, and Fanny . . . one other thing," adds Siegmund, as I waltz into the dining hall. "Smile!"

at your service

The LBD's inaugural breakfast shift passes by in a blur.

It's a cacophony of kippers, eggs, bacon, croissants, extra spoons, missing forks and Highland marmalade, as legions of hungry, impatient and exceedingly snooty guests pour into the dining room, requiring greeting, seating and their orders taken. As soon as their bums are perched upon the scarlet velour seats, their moans commence for racks of toast, jugs of milk, organic butter and oceans of coffee. Chucked in at the deep end, the LBD, accompanied by a rather spiky Russian waitress called Svetlana, have no choice but to get to work, scampering all over the room, carrying plates, scribbling orders and attempting to keep the guests happy.

I don't think I've ever seen Fleur Swan being so quietly focused and polite in my entire life! She doesn't even throw a hissy fit when Gene and Leon put a comedy dog poo on a piece of toast and send her off to Table 5. It turns out our deputy chefs are big customers at Destiny Bay's joke shop, Joe's Jokes, and love nothing more than winding newbie waitresses up with severed fingers, plastic flies and fake blood. Horrid boys!

"Ignore them. You're doing just wonderfully," winks Siegmund as I spin past carrying three plates of eggs Florentine, before pirouetting back toward the kitchen to shout some new breakfast orders to Rosco.

"Cheers, Siegmund!" I grin.

Of course, Claude, who's only ever waitressed once before at a local wedding, takes to the job like an absolute pro, finding the time to smile and make small talk with every one of her customers. Claude's guests appear to be leaving the breakfast hall with a spring in their step and joy in their heart, ready to embrace the day, commenting on Claude's wonderful service. How does she do it?

"That's bizarre," muses Siegmund as I pass his podium around 10 A.M., wincing as my toe pokes through my tights inside my shoe. "Room 205 has just left your colleague Miss Cassiera a fat twenty-five-pound tip."

"Wow!" I say. "That's, like, good, right?"

"For the breakfast shift, dear heart, it's a miracle," announces Siegmund, observing Claude as she helps a customer put on her mink stole. "It seems we may have a star in the making."

"What a surprise," I laugh, rolling my eyes. But then I notice Svetlana, with her sleek black bob and horn-rimmed specs, shooting Claude the filthiest of looks. I put my head down and get back to work.

Officially breakfast is served until half past ten, which means that at exactly twenty-nine minutes past ten, virtually half of Harbinger Hall deluges the dining room, sheepishly begging for eggs. And by the time the breakfast guests have cleared out, it's time for the lunch crowd, and they're more demanding than ever.

Just after 1 P.M., I have my first meeting with a Harbinger Hall resident whom Siegmund affectionately terms Carbzilla, a.k.a. Mrs. Blaire Fontague, a huge woman-mountain with a dyed-black beehive and an ass as big as a TV set. I can see Fleur visibly blanching as Carbzilla crashes into the room. Very wobbly people give Fleur the heebies. I'm concerned she's going to trot over and start making Carbzilla do squat thrusts and ab blasts right then!

Not that it is poor Mrs. Fontague's fault she's so fat. Oh no. Apparently, as Carbzilla explains to me in intricate detail, it's evil carbohydrates that make her so flabulous. That's right, carbohydrates, *not* the two large mojito cocktails she sloshes back while perusing the lunch menu, questioning me on every single lurking gram of carb in every dish.

After twenty dizzying minutes Carbzilla opts for the baked chicken parmesan with a side of steamed asparagus . . . accompanied by a full bottle of merlot and a sticky toffee pudding with extra double fudge sauce and crème fraîche. Gnnngnnn!

"Marvelous to see you again, Mrs. Fontague!" shouts Siegmund as Carbzilla waddles out. "Same time tomorrow!"

"Can't hang about!" yells Carbzilla back. "I've got an appointment at the beauty spa. Having one of those body-contouring seaweed wraps!"

"Good for you!" replies Siegmund, taking his voice much quieter. *"Get them to wrap one round your gob."*

But the prize for the day's most very, very unbelievable guests? That has to be Mr. and Mrs. Segatti from Room 109, a bone-thin middle-aged Italian couple with mean eyes and thin lips who bitch at Fleur about every little piddly thing from the second they sit their scrawny bottoms down.

Eventually, after a huge hissy fit over a forgotten bread basket, things just get too much for our most sensitive bambino. Fleur snaps and storms out of the hall, chucking her apron behind her. Claude and I discover her outside, kicking the dustbins and sobbing.

"That's it!" squeals Fleur. "I'm going home. Scrumble can stick this job. I can be on the next train and in my own bed on Disraeli Road by tonight. This was the stupidest idea ever! I'm a rubbish waitress!"

"Fleur, calm down," I plead. "Please don't go home."

"I'm going home!" repeats Fleur. "I've just had Leon frightening the life out of me too. Did you know the West Turret is haunted? By an executed earl who roams the apartment with his head in his hands!"

"What?" I gasp.

"Oh, Fleur," tuts Claude. "Just ignore him. He tried that with me too. It's a load of old tosh. He's winding us up."

"A headless earl," I shudder.

Claude frowns at me to shut up.

"Fleur," says Claude, wrapping her arms round her, "you're just tired. And that Italian couple would test anyone's patience. No wonder you've lost your temper."

"But they just called me a blonde bimbo and threw a fork at me!" sobs Fleur. "They've not even had their main courses yet! I'm sorry, girls, but I'm quitting."

"Okay, lady," says Gene, who'd been sitting on the step

smoking a cigarette. He pulls a clean white napkin from his pocket and passes it to Fleur in a gentlemanly fashion. "Nobody needs to quit."

Fleur blows her nose noisily.

"Now listen to me," Gene says, batting his long black eyelashes. "Maybe it's time you girls learned a few Harbinger special emergency moves. For dealing with nasty customers."

The LBD look at him curiously. We move closer.

"Okay," says Gene, with a small mischievous twinkle. "Now, when you take the Segattis' starter plates away, make sure you take all of their other cutlery too."

"All of the cutlery?" we repeat.

"Yes, I mean the cutlery for the main courses too. Get me? You can take these knives and forks back when you serve their main dishes."

"But why?" sniffs Fleur, dabbing her eyes. "That makes no sense."

"Watch and see," chuckles Gene, ruffling Fleur's hair at the front before sauntering back into the kitchen. "Hey, and no quitting. Quitting is not allowed!"

Mr. and Mrs. Segatti's behavior doesn't improve one tiny iota during the remainder of their lunch session. They bawl at Fleur, bicker loudly with each other and even accuse Siegmund of overcharging them. Yet, despite the torrent of abuse, Fleur starts feeling a little rosier. She even serves the Segattis' desserts with a tiny joyous spring in her step. Because, yes, she might be a "brainless bimbo" in their opinion, but at least she hasn't just eaten lunch using knives and forks gently warmed inside Gene's three-day-old underpants.

By the time Siegmund officially lets us go at 4 P.M., the LBD look like walking corpses. We can barely climb the 188 steps to the West Turret. All our fabulous intentions to quick-change into bikinis and hit Misty Beach to catch the late-afternoon rays are dashed in favor of crashing on our beds, facedown in star shapes, groaning in unison.

"I ache," mumbles Fleur into her pillow. "I ache worse than after a sixty-minute butt-blast class."

"Mngggh," moans Claude, wrapping herself in a duvet. In seconds she's doing her usual impression of a chain saw. Ugh. When I agreed to share a room with her for an entire summer, I'd forgotten about Claude's atrocious snoring problem.

Just then I notice a slip of paper lying behind our front door. It's a note from our friend Miss Scrumble, with a timetable attached. Somebody has clearly been having a lot of fun on their PC, because to my utter horror it appears that the LBD are scheduled to work double shifts *every single day for the next fourteen days!*

Aaaaaggggggh!

"Fleur!" I say, poking my blonde buddy, who had quickly slipped into a comatose sleep. "Listen to this!"

"Mnnnn? Wah?" mutters Fleur, curling up into a fetal position and cuddling her pillow. "Wassamatter?"

I gaze at her. She looks so peaceful.

"Erm, nothing," I grump, chucking the schedule on the bedside table quietly. "Just get some sleep."

I lie on my rather lumpy single bed, simmering quietly with

rage. *Right, Scrumble, you square-assed slave driver,* I think. *You can stick the Big Beach Booty Quake. Stick Misty Beach. Stick the West Turret! Stick your flipping job up your . . . jumper. I've had enough!*

Just then I hear a creepy dragging noise and, if I'm not wrong, a small groan, upstairs in the attic.

That's it, I think adamantly. *I'm going home.*

MTV PRESENTS

IN ASSOCIATION WITH
IT'S A GIRL'S WORLD AND DEMONBOARD SURFING

Saturday, August 14
LIVE FROM MISTY BEACH, DESTINY BAY

THE BIG BEACH BOOTY QUAKE

hosted by CHLOE KISSIMY AND LONNY LARSON
BROADCAST LIVE ON MTV!
Show begins at 11 A.M.

FEATURING LIVE PERFORMANCES BY
PSYCHO KILLA and the MORTUARY TEAM
THE SCANDAL CHILDREN
GOD CREATED MAN
PLUS A LIVE DJ SET FROM WARREN ACAPULCO

ALSO FEATURING:
THE INTERNATIONAL DEMONBOARD SURF CHAMPIONSHIPS
(FIRST PRIZE 60K!)

AND . . . THE SEARCH FOR MISS ULTIMATE DEMONBOARD BABE!
(FIRST PRIZE 20K)

THE BIG BEACH BOOTY QUAKE "HEAVEN AND HELL" AFTER-PARTY
AT THE UTOPIA NIGHTCLUB, SPONSORED BY DEMONBOARD SURFING.

FOR VIP GUEST LIST CALL 08983-799000.

Chapter 5

cometh the mailman

I tear open the small white envelope, which has my mother's familiar swirly hieroglyphics across the front, and pull out her letter. A crisp £20 note falls upon my lap. Ha! Good old Mum. I begin to read . . .

> *19 July, The Fantastic Voyage*
> *Hellooo . . . anyone there?*
> *Earth calling Ronnie.*
> *It's your mother here. Remember me?*
> *Well, lambkins, that's two weeks you've been gone now. Things must be looking up, eh, kiddo? Not a peep out of you for days?*
> *I take it you're not coming home. Jeez, Ronnie, it was hard hearing you crying like that on the first night without jumping in the car and racing to get you. . . .*

Pah! Pardon? What fantastic nonsense my mum gibbers! Me, Ronnie Ripperton? Fearless Amazonian warrior? Sobbing on the phone to Mummy like a homesick child? The woman's clearly delirious. I mean, okay, I was a bit sniffly . . . but, well . . . cough, moving on . . .

Believe me, Ron, newbies always get lumped with the crappy shifts. That's waitressing for you. Make sure you stand your ground and get some time off to have fun. Be assertive! Remember, you learned from the best!

Hmmm. Don't worry, Mother, the LBD have been making time for fun. I mean, sure, the hours here at Harbinger are long, and Scrumble may well be a heinous right-angle-ridden old boot, but Siegmund, Rosco and all the other kitchen misfits always cheer me up.

Plus they announced the lineup for the Big Beach Booty Quake the next day . . . and it rrrrrocks! The whole MTV gang are staying here! And Destiny Bay is just so cool. I feel alive!

There's always something fab happening. Like last Saturday night, Gene and Leon gave the LBD a lift in their van up onto the cliffs at midnight for a campfire party with a huge gang of their surfer buddies. And Jose, this hottie from Pamplona in Spain, said I had a bum like "two little apples," and he gave me his e-mail address if I ever want to visit for the bull-running weekend. Fleur and Claude and I stayed out till 5 A.M. having crazy limbo dancing competitions with some New Zealand dudes. And Claude learned to walk through hot coals! We got a lift home on the back of the Harbinger Hall milk truck! And the next morning, when Fleur was doing breakfast shift, she vomited in the waste disposal, then fell fast asleep against the dishwasher with her face in a plate of porridge! Ha ha ha!

And . . . erm . . . actually, Mum, you're never going to find out any of this. No way. Because you'd hit the roof.

But suffice to say . . . am I coming home? Of course I'm flipping not . . .

. . . Oh, yeah, Ronnie, ignore those "headless earl" stories too. Allegedly there was a "dead weeping waitress" haunting the first place I chefed at. Never saw her either, funnily enough. It's just another classic newbie wind-up . . .

I read that last bit again, then pause to look around our apartment, which I notice is totally covered in Fleur's clothes, makeup, plates and cups. Fleur seems to move through the apartment like a tornado of mess, shedding her belongings and making things unimaginably untidy. Sometimes I feel like her mother, walking about picking up her lipstick and stained tissues and hanging up her dresses.

I'm glad we're living here together, though. I wouldn't want to be here alone. The West Turret definitely has a creepy feel to it. It's steeped in a fairly gruesome history, after all. Plus, and I might be going mad here, things keep disappearing. Biscuits, cheese, bread . . . it's like we've got a bulimic poltergeist. If it is Fleur and Claude gobbling it all up, they're flipping good actresses when questioned. And what's that weird dragging sound in the attic? Claude says I've got an overactive imagination and next year I should take an A-level in "getting a grip." Hmmph! She won't be so smug when we're being chased to our doom by an ax-wielding ghoul carrying a severed head spewing out cookies and stolen sausages.

There's more . . .

Anyway, Ron, me and Dad are cool. Seth sends regards. He continues to rule the house, as ever . . . the poo never endeth. We're all still getting back to normal after everything. I have dodgy days, but today I'm feeling pretty chipper. Every day without Nan things seem to get a little bit more back to normal, but then that makes me sad too, as I feel further away from her. It's a no-win situation. Every little thing reminds me of her right now. I spend my days ranging from hysterical giggles to sobbing while serving pints of beer. The customers must think I'm bonkers.

Hmmm . . . more than a large twinge of homesickness there. Must fight it.

Anyway, in other news, Susan and I went shopping in Westland Mall yesterday. Susan's doing great at Slimming World (ahem, again) and needed all new nonbaggy knickers and a new "over-the-shoulder boulder holder." (Yes, she's still not sick of that joke.) Guess who we bumped into in House of Frazer? That Cressida girl you were lumbered with last term!

Euuuugh! I'd almost forgotten about her.

She was with that snooty little madam with the dark hair from Larkrise Manor. Panama, is it? Anyway, they were in the fitting rooms trying on thong bikinis the size of microchips. Skinny whippets they both were too. Annoying. Saying that, they were chatty enough, asking what you were up to, etc. Don't worry, Ron, I put them straight. I told them that you, Claude and Fleur were all at Harbinger Hall in Destiny Bay having the time of your lives! You should've seen their faces. Priceless!

Right, must run and catch last mail. Ring me soon! Love you loads. You may be all grown-up and living away from home now, but you're still my little girl.

Mum xxxx

Ha ha ha! Excellent! Stick that in your caldron, Sleeth! Thought you could split the LBD up, didn't you? Instead, we're tighter than ever before and having triple the fun.

Friends forever!

Nothing can muck things up now.

P.S. Nearly forgot! Saw that sniveling little excuse for manhood Jimi Steele yesterday morning . . . waiting for the staff minibus for the Wacky Warehouse! Ha! Ha! Ha!

Oh my God! Ha ha ha! Today just gets better and better. Love you too, Mum!

That very second, Fleur Swan appears from the bedroom clad in a green Chinese silk kimono, kitten-heel slippers and a fluffy pink eye mask pulled up over her forehead. She walks over to the fridge, opens the door and pulls out a carton of orange juice with a yellow Post-it note attached to the spout.

"Claude's orange juice. Keep off!" reads Fleur, taking the note off temporarily to take a long refreshing gulp. "Sheeeesh, Claude's on fire with those Post-it notes, isn't she?"

I roll my eyes and try not to laugh.

"Oooh, another one," laughs Fleur, rooting about in the fridge and producing some butter. "It's like a treasure hunt! What does this say? *This is not communal butter.* Ha ha!"

"Oh, and apparently we're rationed to three sheets of toilet paper per bathroom visitation," I announce. "There's a Post-it note above the loo. Apparently we're using too much."

"I'm going to use four sheets!" laughs Fleur. "I laugh in the face of authority."

"You're a braver girl than me," I mutter.

"Hey, is that the mail?" she smiles. "Is there anything for me?"

"There was one for all for us," I say, nodding at the postcard and letter on the coffee table.

Fleur grabs her card and begins reading . . .

Miss Fleur Iris Swan
The West Turret
Harbinger Hall Hotel
Destiny Bay
DBX1 423

FAO: Fleur Swan
Where in God's name is my Olympus XJ-216 digital camera? Can I have nothing in this house without my children relieving me of it? You, girl, really are the absolute limit. Consider it deducted from next year's allowance.

Yours, incandescent with rage,
P. Swan (Father)

P.S. Come home soon, darling. House is utterly tedious without you.
x

"Poor Paddy," says Fleur, shaking her head slowly. "He's a heart attack waiting to happen. He should take up Ashtanga."

Fleur picks up the aforementioned "borrowed" digital camera from the breakfast bar. She snaps a shot of me lying on the sofa, then begins examining some snaps we took at the cliff-top party.

"Aaaggggggghh! Delete! Delete!" squawks Fleur, staring aghast at the camera's screen. "Bingo wing alert! Noooo! I've got flabby corned beef arms in all of these. Yuk!"

I just smile at her. I'm not playing her "oooh, I'm so ugly" game today.

"Who's that from?" Fleur says, nodding at my letter. "Jimi Steele?"

"Noooo!" I grimace. "Mother."

"Gossip?" says Fleur.

"Hmmm, well," I smile, "Mum ran into Cressida and Panama, trying on bikinis in House of Frazer!"

"Did she?" says Fleur, her eyes glowing. "Did she see what size bikini Panama was? Has she put on any weight? Did she have cellulite? Oh, Ronnie, go on, tell me she had big shoals of cellulite swimming up each wibbly thigh!"

"Er . . . well," I say.

"And a third nipple?" suggests Fleur. "Glowing in the center of her chest like an all-seeing eye?"

"Mmm . . . no," I sigh.

"Damn it, Ronnie! What is the use in you?" chuckles Fleur. "Well, was Cressida hairy then? With rufty-tufty locks sprouting from her navel to her knees . . . like a pair of furry knicker-bockers?"

"Nope," I say.

Deep down, we both know Panama Goodyear and Cressida Sleeth are pretty much perfect. Panama's the only girl at Blackwell who looks hot in satin hipster hot pants. (When I tried on a pair at It's a Girl's World, Fleur laughed so much she had to cling on to the cubicle door to steady herself.)

"Pggh . . . bet Cressida's been invited along to Panama's daddy's villa in Ibiza, eh?" groans Fleur. "Panama, Abigail, Derren, the whole shower. They go every summer, don't they?"

"Hope so," I say. "Cressida's allergic to sunlight, isn't she? I hope she dissolves into a puddle of bile."

"Me too," agrees Fleur, double-checking the waitressing schedule pinned to our fridge. "Not that we care about them anyway. We're having a super-fabulous time here! Plus, today's our first full day off together."

Fleur throws open the West Turret's living room curtains, letting sunshine pour into the room. "Wow! Scorchio!" she hoots. "Right, Ronnie, I'm taking a long soak, then applying my sun cream. Then, we're off to Destiny Bay to cause a rumpus."

"Sounds like a plan," I smile.

"And you're in charge of waking up Claude," says Fleur.

"Oh, thanks," I groan. "She was working till 1 A.M.! She said not to wake . . ."

Fleur swings open the bedroom door where Claude is snuggled in her duvet, gob open, emitting noises like a broken lawn mower.

"Morning, Claudette!" screams Fleur as Claude sits up in bed with glued-shut eyes and Halloween hair. "Are you awake?"

"Shplgh gnnnn," she growls. "Go away!"

"But you've got mail," Fleur says, chucking Claude's letter onto the end of her bed.

"Hmmm . . . It's a mum-o-gram," Claude mumbles, picking up her reading specs and ripping it open.

"Now then, both of you!" warns Fleur. "Find your itsy-bitsiest bikinis! All armpits and lower legs need to be defuzzed! We're on a mission. The Argies are coming. I'm so excited I could spew!"

"The who?" I say, wrapping my sensible dressing gown a little tighter.

"The Argentinians! Santiago Marre and all his Argentinian surf buddies. They're arriving at Destiny Bay today. Ha ha ha! Game on!" cackles Fleur, vanishing into the bathroom with a copy of *Harpers and Queen* and a large white bath towel under her arm, leaving me lying on the sofa with a bemused expression.

Just then, I notice something extremely unsettling. Claude appears to be slumped forward in bed with her face cupped in her hands.

She appears to be crying.

Gloria Cassiera's letter lies discarded on the carpet beside her bed.

♪pill

It's noon later that day, and the LBD are chilling on Misty Beach. Destiny Bay's famous sandy cove is extra-specially jam-packed today with buff boys, near-naked babes, Frisbee chuckers, lush surf junkies, surf groupies and of course, several miserable-faced grown-ups with kids attempting to enjoy a fuddy-duddy day trip despite all the heaving cleavages and canoodling couples.

As the July sun beats down, a chilled-out DJ set drifts over from Cactus Jack's roof terrace accompanied by wafts of jerk chicken sizzling on the Cactus Jack barbecue. To my left, Fleur Swan, almost dressed in her lemon thong bikini with gold ties, is noisily slurping a double-flaked 99 cone with neon sprinkles and strawberry sauce. On my right, a highly subdued Claudette Cassiera is applying SPF 6 to her voluptuous brown curves. Claude's barely spoken since she got up three hours ago. And we're not buying her migraine story one little bit.

Fleur catches my eye and raises an eyebrow as if to say, "What do we do?"

I take a deep breath and ask Claude for the tenth time if she's okay.

"I'm totally fine," says Claude, doing a fake smile. "Stop fretting! Hey, Fleur, tell us about what Siegmund knows about Booty Quake. He had gossip, didn't he?"

"Ooh, erm, okay," says Fleur, vanilla ice cream dribbling down her hand. "Well, word is that Psycho Killa's people have preordered three cases of Cristal champagne. Ten thousand quid, that costs!"

"Flipping heck," says Claude.

"I know," nods Fleur. "And Dita Murray, lead singer with the Scandal Children, has demanded that the entire Barclay Suite get repainted ivory and lighted with white Diptique candles or else she won't perform."

"But that's ridiculous!" I say. "Isn't the Barclay Suite ivory anyway?"

"It's eggshell," says Fleur. "And Dita doesn't do eggshell. Only ivory. It's going to cost two thousand pounds to redecorate."

"What a total waste of money," tuts Claude, adjusting the straps on her hot-pink bikini top. "Imagine what some people could do with that . . ."

She starts to say more, but then she shuts up, folding her arms in front of her, her brow in a perfectly centered furrow.

It should be mentioned here that Claude Cassiera, despite her grouchy mood, looks unbelievably fabulous in swimwear. For a mere lumpen-bodied mortal like myself, it's simply heartbreaking. Little wonder stripping off for summer fills me with dread. Claude's ebony skin has a litheness, a firmness, a depth of color and shine that isn't available in bottles. Her bottom is a perfect rounded feminine peach, her tummy cutely curved and her belly button neatly inward. Annoying. Worst of all, she has a great whopping set of boobs, which enter rooms before her, bounce perkily when she walks, and if necessary, can win arguments on her behalf.

She's got no reason to look so glum.

"Claude, this is driving me mad," I say. "What's up with you?"

"Oh . . . nothing," she says. "I just really need to chill today."

"Cuh," tuts Fleur. "Chill out? It's like hanging out with my depressed aunt Enid. What's up with you? We won't give up, y'know. You'll have to tell us."

"It's nothing," persists Claude, folding her arms.

"Oh, c'mon, Claude, stop lying," I say plainly. "It's about that letter. What's going on?"

Claude's lip wobbles. She pulls down her oversized Top Shop sunglasses.

"What was in the letter?" probes Fleur.

Claude's lips just become tighter.

"Are you feeling homesick?" I venture. "Are you missing Gloria?"

"Oh my God!" gasps Fleur, sitting bolt upright. "You're homesick, so you've decided to go home, haven't you?"

Claude doesn't argue. My stomach lurches horribly.

But then Claude's face crumples and she gives a little snort. "Of course I haven't, you pair of total numpties!" she splutters. "I love it here! I'm having the time of my life. Just having our own apartment. No mother, no curfews, earning my own money! It's like a dream."

"Oh, hurray," sighs Fleur. "You had me worried then! You can't leave us, Claude. Can she, Ronnie? That would suck, big style."

Claude's lip wobbles a little. We've not got to the bottom of this.

"Ha!" chuckles Fleur, her candy-floss brain leaping ahead. "I've just had the most fantabulous idea. I'm asking Paddy if he'll extend my bedroom at Disraeli Road out over the garage. Then we could have our own self-contained apartment! Let's live together during Year Twelve too."

As Fleur beams at her own ingenuity, Claude goes to speak, but something stops her. As a long involuntary sigh slips between her lips, a tiny tear trickles down her cheek.

I reach forward, grabbing her hand. Fleur stops grinning instantly.

"Right, Claude," I say firmly. "Spill it."

"Don't, Ronnie," Claude whispers. "It'll just wreck the summer."

"Oh, don't be a spanner, Claude," tuts Fleur. "Nothing can wreck summer."

Claude stares into nowhere for a good twenty seconds. But then, she pulls the decidedly crumpled, tear-stained letter from her beach bag and hands it to me. I take a deep breath and begin to read.

19 July, Lister House
Dear Claude,
Hello, darling. Wonderful to hear you on the phone yesterday. Thank you so much also for the money you transferred into my account today. £250! Claude, you're an angel. Dad would have been so proud of you . . .

"You sent two hundred and fifty pounds home?" gasps Fleur. "Flipping heck, Claude!? You've been working your butt off!"

"Tell me about it," nods Claude.

Now, Claude, I've been thinking long and hard about our money problems. Please don't be too angry at me, but I've some bad news. I just feel it's illogical for us to stay at Lister House. I could cope with the mortgage and bills no problem when I worked for Mr. Rayner, but it seems all I can hope to earn around here now is half of that. Things are getting serious, darling. Today I totted all the debts up and we owe £16,869 . . .

I stop abruptly, trying to appear unhorrified.

You're working so hard, darling, and for that I'll always be grateful, but we're fighting a losing battle. The only solution is to put 27 Lister House up for sale and move in with Aunty Sissy. I'm going to call the real-estate agents today. I hope you're not too angry. Mossington is only 375 miles away, not the end of the world. This is really hard for me too. I don't want to leave Lister House either, it's got so many memories. (You and Mika as babies, Dad when he was well and happy. The list goes on . . .) But in times like this I just think of the sacrifice our Lord Jesus Christ made for us. God's love and spirit pushes me through the pain.

Have a really good summer, darling. Try to make the most of your time with your friends.

God bless, Mum xxxx

I put down the letter. My hands are actually shaking.

"Hmmm," says Claude, lying back on her sun lounger wearing a face of nigh-calm acceptance. "I particularly liked the God's spirit pushing me through the pain bit." She sighs. "Sometimes she sounds like she's plugging an isotonic energy drink."

Fleur is floundering around for words. "That . . . that whole letter was a joke, right?" she stutters.

"Erm . . . no," I say, scanning the paragraphs through again for a hidden "P.S.: APRIL FOOL!"

"Mossington? Where the hell's Mossington?" splutters Fleur. "Did you just say three hundred and seventy-five miles away? Is that the place you went on holiday to once that takes like sixteen squillion hours by train?"

Fleur's voice is becoming rather shrill now. "But Claude," she pleads. "What about your A-levels? This totally sucks! Your mum's not thinking straight. You can't just—"

"Apparently Mossington High School has a sixth form where the physics and chemistry departments are, sort of, well, okay," Claude says calmly.

"Sort of *okay*?" I repeat. Claude was intending to be prime minister one day.

"And I can begin in September, if need be," Claude explains. "They've saved me a provisional place."

"Oh my God," I mumble. "You knew you were going, didn't you?" It's all beginning to seem real now, now that the shock is wearing off.

"No, it was never certain," sighs Claude. "Mum thought she'd find a new job that paid well. But if she didn't, then we agreed—"

"But . . . but you can't just leave!" butts in Fleur. "What about the LBD? What about Blackwell? What about 'friends forever' and all that drivel we've been spouting? What about . . ."

Claude sinks farther into her lounger. "We'll stay in touch," she says, aware of how super-lame that sounds. "I'll be online loads . . . and we can text one another."

"Great," tuts Fleur, her eyes narrowing. "Yeah, 'cos that's the same, isn't it? Y'know something, Claude? We should have just let Cressida finish us off. And after everything I've done to keep us all together!"

"Oh, pipe down, Fleur," I tut. Sometimes I just want to slap her. How's this about her "pain" all of a sudden?

"Stop freaking out at me, Fleur!" says Claude, her lip wobbling slightly.

"Pah!" tuts Fleur. "I feel like freaking out! Why are you both so calm? Why don't either of you care?"

As Fleur leaps to her feet in a fury, shoving aside her sun lounger, something seems to snap within Claude. She leaps up too, grabbing Fleur's wrists and shaking them crossly.

"Of course I care! You silly moo!" she snaps, her voice cracking. "This is the end of the world! Do you think I want to be Billy-No-Mates, living in outer Bumgrape-on-the-Nowhere, receiving LBD updates by text? Well, do you?"

As Claude's voice is becoming louder, the entire beach appears to have paused to spectate our dispute.

"Well, let's do something then!" pleads Fleur. "We'll make a plan! Have Ronnie and I let you down before?"

Claude shakes her head slowly. "There's no point, Fleur. I've been fighting this for months," she says, sounding defeated. "It's over."

The back of my throat feels sour.

"Don't say that!" tuts Fleur, pulling her hands from Claude's, grabbing her sarong and storming across Misty Beach in the direction of Cactus Jack's.

"I'm only saying it because it's true, Fleur!" Claude shouts after her.

Then she sits back down on her sun lounger and begins to cry.

a lifeline

"Are you angry at me, Ronnie?" says Claude gingerly.

Since Fleur's departure, half an hour ago, we've been sitting silently on our sun loungers watching a group of surf girls having a ball in the midday sun.

They look so carefree. I feel quite jealous.

For the first time since Year 7, Claude and I are fresh out of chitchat. If Claude leaves town in September, it'll be the end of an era. To say I'd miss her is an understatement. It'd be like having an arm removed.

I bet we look hilarious to passersby, sitting in the middle of this growing beach party, looking like case study diagrams from the textbook *Recognizing Suicide*.

" 'Course I'm not angry, babe," I say. "Neither's Fleur. She's just upset. This is huge."

"Hmmm, well," groans Claude, pointing across the beach toward the boardwalk. "If she's not angry at me, Ronnie, she's certainly angry about something."

As I turn to look, around twenty meters away, Fleur Swan is stomping through the sand toward us, wearing a highly indignant expression, churlishly demolishing sand castles in her path.

"Oh, boo-hoo!" Fleur barks at two freckly brats who've just witnessed their sand Arc de Triomphe being trampled under her flip-flop. "It's only sand. Get over it!"

A long shadow falls over our sun loungers.

"Hello, Fleur," I say, gritting my teeth, noticing that she's holding a flyer for MTV's Big Beach Booty Quake. "You've come back then?"

"Well, yes," says Fleur sheepishly. "Sorry about that last eruption. I just went schizoid for a moment. But, I've had time to think about stuff now, and I have in my hand the solution. Claude, you are *not* going to Mossington in September. I've saved the summer!"

"Erm . . . really?" says Claude.

143

"Really. Now, the MTV Big Beach Booty Quake . . . that's three weeks away," says Fleur, scanning through the flyer. "Broadcasting live on MTV . . . show begins at 11 A.M. . . . live performances by the Scandal Children, Velvet Cobweb, Psycho Killa . . . da da da . . . ah, here it is! Also featuring the Demonboard Surf Championships . . . and the search for Miss Ultimate Demonboard Babe!"

Fleur looks up triumphantly, displaying two rows of white teeth.

"What?" shrugs Claude. "I don't understand."

"Oh no. Nooooooo," I groan, understanding immediately.

"Miss Ultimate Demonboard Babe!" repeats Fleur. "Big cash prizes are to be won!"

"But we can't surf!" protests Claude.

"Claudette, it's a beauty contest," I grimace, slapping my forehead.

"It's . . . it's a what?" splutters Claude. *"A beauty contest?* Fleur! How will that help me? Are you tripping or something? Have you been at your mother's diet pills again?"

"Nooooooo! I'm deadly serious," snortles Fleur. "One of us could win this."

Fleur is dancing excitedly from foot to foot now like an African tribeswoman with a bladder problem.

"Pghh! Well, it certainly won't be me," harrumphs Claude. "Because I . . . in fact . . . *we* the LBD are morally opposed to any sort of beauty pageant."

"Are we?" says Fleur.

"Yes, we are, Fleur!" splutters Claude. "Especially ones with swimwear sections where women are paraded around like cattle on auction day!"

"Oh, shut up! No one's forced at gunpoint to enter," giggles Fleur, clearly about to force us both at gunpoint to enter. "Beauty contests are fun! And besides, I'm not one of those feministical thingies. What's the problem?"

"Gnnnnnn," groans Claude. "The problem, Fleur, my butterfly-brained amigo, is the sexist concept of girls being rewarded not for their intellect, but for looking pretty in a bikini."

Fleur looks confused. "What, you'd have a problem with winning twenty thousand pounds?" she says.

"Pgghh!" tuts Claude. "As if money makes the whole concept any less oppressive toward women—"

Claude stops her rant abruptly. She arches one eyebrow and grabs the flyer from Fleur's hands. "How much is first prize?" she says.

"Twenty thousand pounds," repeats Fleur matter-of-factly. "I'm going to give it a shot. Obviously, you and Mrs. C. can have the cash if I win. Or should I say, *when* I win."

Claude's mouth drops wide open. "You'd . . . do that for me?" she whispers. "But . . . I couldn't take . . . I mean, wow!"

Claude is utterly gobsmacked.

"Yes, you could," says Fleur firmly. "I'm not letting you go, Claude. I've got to do something! You can't go to that crappy Mossington place. And besides, you're in charge of sleep snot and poo bums when we wash McGraw's yucky poodles. You can't abandon me!"

Claude's face is an absolute picture.

It's moments like this when I remember why Fleur Swan is a life necessity. Okay, she's crazy as hell, totally conceited, and a liability at times, but there's something about her that makes me and Claude feel bulletproof.

"But let's all enter!" Fleur urges. "Let's triple our chances!"

"Mmm . . . erm," I say, sucking in my tummy.

"Twenty thousand pounds," mutters Claude to herself, her eyes as wide as saucers. "That would be incredible. It would solve everything."

"Would it really, Claude?" I ask.

"Totally," she replies.

"Well, that's that, then," says Fleur, whipping her phone from her beach bag. "Let's call the hotline now and register. Ha! And it's broadcast live on MTV too! Everyone at Blackwell will see it."

"Oh God," I groan.

"And we'll have to start working out a training schedule," says Fleur. "Y'know, fresh fruit, exercise, exfoliation, two liters of water a day. We'll have to detox. I'm going to buy some of those detox socks that purge the toxins out of the soles of your feet."

As Fleur gibbers on and on and on, Claude is absolutely silent, staring ahead with a small grin spreading across her face. It seems the mere possibility of clearing her mum's debt is making her more relaxed than I've seen her for a long time.

And that's why I find myself agreeing to this whole ludicrous Miss Demonboard Babe idea. Because I'll do anything to keep Claude at Lister House and the LBD together. Anything. No matter how daft, far-fetched or likely the scheme is to humiliate me on a nearly naked international televisual level.

Because, okay, it's a long shot, but at least now we have a lifeline.

♂pooked

So here I am in the West Turret, alone.

It's about 5 P.M. and I'm standing before a full-length mirror, wearing only my fave pink halter-neck bikini and Claude's silver high heels. I'm having a sneaky go with them while she's working.

Twenty-four hours have passed since I agreed to this totally shameful Miss Demonboard idea and I'm already regretting it big time.

I mean, first, my mother will flip out if she sees it. Sure, she doesn't watch much MTV. She likes VH1 Classic, where she can watch ye olde hits from the medieval ages, but that doesn't guarantee Seth won't sit (or poo) on the control, filling the screen with his teenage sister jiggling her bits to a Psycho Killa track, wearing little more than pipe cleaners and diamante nipple tassles. (Fleur's already spoken to Siegmund, who says he can locate us some sequins and fabric if we want to make bikinis. Aaaaaaagh!)

And what if Jimi and Snuff see me? Or Cressida and Panama? Panama Bogwash will laugh till she pukes. Last September, when the LBD did Triplet Day, she informed me that I "take pear shaped to a new eerie dimension of dumpy."

She's such a spiteful moonfaced hag.

I pinch a whole centimeter of flesh on the side of each thigh and wibble it about, pivoting around for the umpteenth time to examine my butt cheeks.

Right, that's it. I have to get out of this competition! How easy is it to break your own arm?

Okay, I'm probably over-thinking things, as ever. I'm exhausted and a little grouchy. After the beach drama yesterday, the LBD headed over to A Land Down Under for a party thrown by a gang of gorgeous Argentinian surfers who'd just hit town. The party was fabulous! Plenty of tanned Argie muscle to ogle and an excellent grime DJ from London playing a loud, raw set that had everyone spilling out onto the beach, shakin' their booties like mad.

A mere ten minutes after arriving, we'd lost Fleur Swan in a melee of bronzed pecs, testosterone, beer cans and processed beats . . . only for the scurrilous minx to reappear in the West Turret at 5:45 A.M., crawling into bed beside me, stinking of cider and surfboard wax, begging me to cover her breakfast shift. Apparently Fleur Swan was "unwell."

By 6:10, I was being chased around the dining hall by Colonel Three-Minute Egg, false teeth rattling in his skeletal hand as he attempted to demonstrate he had "a delicate palate and a misformed esophagus that can't cope with hard yolk."

Uggghhh! Fleur Swan must die.

Back in the bedroom, in the West Turret, I adjust the straps on my bikini and let out another gut-wrenching sigh. This will not do at all.

Nan used to call me a classic beauty, but what does that

mean exactly? Why didn't I ever ask her? That's another secret she took away that I'll never know.

I spin around and judder my butt fat again. No one deserves to be exposed to this horror. Especially the Demonboard Babe judges. If I chucked myself down 188 stairs, surely I'd crack a rib at least?

Just then, something creaks loudly upstairs in the loft.

I stop in my tracks and glare upward.

Gnnnn, old buildings creak, Ronnie. Get over yourself, I tell myself, wandering into the kitchen and grabbing a Diet Coke from the fridge. That's weird—my leftover Chinese food is gone from the bottom drawer. Both Fleur and Claude are on strict detox plans. They totally refused even a mouthful of noodles the other night.

Who's been in here?

Okay, I'm officially beginning to get spooked out again. This happens every time I'm in this apartment alone. I'm such a sap.

I take a deep breath and try to focus my mind elsewhere.

Grabbing one of Claude's Mistress Minny novels, I balance it on my head and decide to try out some posture exercises, like Fleur's been bullying me to.

"Well, hellloooo, Destiny Bay!" I announce as I sashay across the floor, practicing my "personality interview." "My name is Ronnie Ripperton, contestant number one. My long-term goals include unifying the children of Israel and Palestine via the funky power of disco dancing . . . and, er, finding a vaccine for hemorrhoids!"

"Achooooooooooooo!" erupts a very definite sneeze somewhere above me.

Oh my God! That was totally real. I didn't imagine it.

Clump, clump, clump thump some rather heavy footsteps.

I'm literally rooted to the spot in terror. My heart is thudding loudly against my chest.

I try to scream but only a futile squeak comes out.

The ghostly footsteps gravitate over to the loft's trapdoor entrance just above the sofa.

I can hear heavy breathing.

Oh my God! This is it. It's just like in the slasher movies. They'll find me bludgeoned to death in a puddle of my own entrails. Aaaaaaaaaagh!

Just then, the loft door falls open. I can't breathe.

Out of the dark hole in the trapdoor, a ghostly face emerges.

It's the headless earl!

"Aaaaaaaaaaaaaaaaaaaaaaaaaaaaagh!" I screech, finding my voice and falling over backward into the sofa.

"Aaaaaaaaaaaaaiaaaaaaaaiaaaaaaaaai! Get out! Get out!" I yell. If this is a nightmare, let me wake up!

But as my screaming goes on and on, I begin to realize half the racket is coming from the ghost itself.

"Shut up!" the earl is shouting, looking as shocked to see me. "Stop screaming! You're freaking me out!"

What? I'm freaking him out?

"I . . . I . . . eh? Aiiiiiiiiiii!" I screech again at the dismembered head. "Get out of my flat, you hideous ghoul! This is my home!"

"Hmmmph," tuts the earl slightly huffily. "It was my home first."

"That's . . . erm," I splutter, becoming more flummoxed by

the second. "That's irrelevant! Look, you're clearly trapped in some sort of ghostly time stasis. Move on to the next world!"

"Are you on magic mushrooms?" asks the spectral vision rather sarcastically. His voice sounds distinctly northern.

I glare at him rather crossly. The earl appears to be about seventeen, with huge brown eyes, longish auburn curly hair and a smattering of freckles. His head, I now see, appears to be attached to a muscular pair of shoulders.

"Nice bikini, by the way," the earl adds cheekily.

"Look, who are you?" I yell, feeling thoroughly foolish as well as rather naked. "What are you doing up there?"

"Erm, well, that's a long story," he says. "Look, would it be out of the question if I came down? I can explain everything."

I fold my arms across my boobs.

"Okay," I huff.

Quickly a pair of feet in black flip-flops dangle through the loft door, followed by a pair of toned calves, some navy knee-length surf shorts, then a toned, tanned torso with a buff chest, and finally a rather handsome yet cheeky face. His hair is matted into little occasional dreads and encrusted with bits of sand. I grab my mobile phone from the coffee table, dial 999 and place my finger on "call."

"Hey, chill! Please!" pleads the lad. "Hey, I'm not a mad ax man or anything. Honest! I just needed somewhere to crash. I had no choice after Scrumble sacked me."

"What?" I bark. "I don't believe this! How long have you been up there?"

"Erm . . . ," winces the lad. "About three weeks."

"But that's when we arrived!" I snap. "Hang on—were you

one of the waiters Scrumble sacked for being lazy, useless good-for-nothing surf freaks?"

"That's us," smiles the boy proudly. "But Clem and Stevie went back to Lancashire. I decided to stay. And when Scrumble forgot to take my keys . . ."

"But . . . but how? Why? Where do you sleep?" I scream, my mind racing with questions.

"I've got a sleeping bag. Oh, there's plenty of room up there," he beams. "It's pretty freaky, really! There's all sorts of interesting heirlooms and knickknacks. In fact—"

"So you thought you'd just squat illegally in the loft?" I yell, interrupting him. "You thought you'd just sneak about, steal our noodles, watch our TV, and spy on us . . . like a freaky perv!"

The lad's face goes white.

"Hey!" he shouts. "I've not been spying! I'm not a perv. I'm totally, er, unpervy! The anti-perv, in fact."

"But, but, how did you manage to miss us?" I shout at him. Then my eyes rest on the LBD's waitressing schedule, containing our names, phone numbers and daily routine, stuck to the fridge door. "Hmmm . . . clever," I tut.

"Well, not exactly foolproof," says the lad sheepishly. "So which one are you then: Veronica, Claude or Fleur?"

"Veronica," I say sternly.

"I'm Saul Parker," he says with a small grin.

Saul holds out his hand to shake. I stare at it crossly, then back at him. Eventually, he lets his arm fall back to his side. I'm not in the habit of fraternizing with burglars.

"Look, Veronica," Saul says, batting his long brown eye-lashes, doing his best "sorry" face, "can I just express my utmost regret and complete shame about spooking you out? I totally and utterly apologize."

Okay. He's cute. But he's not winning me over that easily.

"Apology *unaccepted*, Mr. Parker!" I say firmly. "Pack up and ship out!"

"But . . . but I've nowhere else to go," he says pathetically. "It's just for another three weeks. Until the Booty Quake. I'm entering the surf contest!"

"That's not my problem," I say, cold as ice.

"Aw, have a heart, Veronica!" pleads Saul. "Look, I know I'm in the wrong here. I should never have been crashing up there . . . but . . . you have to understand! Surfing is my life, Veronica. It's an obsession. An illness even! And competing at Demonboards, well, that's a life ambition and—"

"Can I just butt in?" I say sharply. "I've got three words for you, Saul: Sam's Surf Shack. Make a reservation!"

Saul looks stunned at my bluntness. But then a broad grin sweeps over his face.

Why is it that the ruder you are to boys, the more they like you?

"Well, I suppose I could sleep on the beach," he says pathetically. "I'm broke, y'see. Blew all my savings last summer surfing in Fuerteventura. That's where I won my wildcard entry to the Demonboard finals. Wish I was back there now . . . least the locals were friendly."

I narrow my eyes at him, and he stops talking.

"I'll go and get my sleeping bag then," he says, shuffling his feet like a little boy. The teensiest pang of guilt flickers across my face.

Then Saul turns quickly, grabbing my arm gently.

"Let me stay! Please!" he pleads. "I'll be totally quiet! And I'll replace all the cookies and noodles and stuff!"

"Noooo!" I shout. "Scrumble will throw all of us out. Claude will go berserk!"

"That won't happen!" cries Saul. "Hey, and here's a plan: what if, as a payback, I teach you to surf too?"

"What?" I gasp. Now he's got me. I'd love to learn to surf. "Could you really teach me?" I ask.

Saul smiles broadly. His teeth are lovely and white. "Sure! I've still got Clem's board," he says. "And his suit! It'd fit you okay. He's quite a small bloke."

My mind is racing now.

Learning to surf is 100 percent more appetizing than being a Demonboard Babe. And if I must do this totally lame-ass bikini thing to save the LBD, then why shouldn't I have a little fun of my own?

"You're thinking about it," grins Saul, flaring his cute nostrils.

"I'm . . . oooh! Gnnnnnnnnngnnn!" I groan, knowing I want this more than anything in the world.

"It's a yes, isn't it?" hoots Saul. "Oh, I'm stoked, man! This'll be so great. Me and you, Veronica, riding the green monsters!"

"Eh? Errr . . . oh," I moan, starting to giggle. "Oh, yes! Okay, yes! Teach me to surf!"

But just then we hear footsteps climbing the 188 stairs to the West Turret. It must be Claude coming back from her shift!

"Later!" yells Saul, jumping on the sofa, flipping down the loft door, then in a freaky flying-baboon-type motion, swinging his entire body up into the loft before snapping the door shut behind him.

He's gone!

In a flurry, I kick Claude's silver shoes beside her bed, grab my dressing gown and try to look normal.

"Yo!" grins Claude, sauntering in and grabbing the last can of Diet Coke from the fridge. "Ha! Fleur's downstairs getting screamed at by Scrumble for swapping shifts with you this morning. Scrumble's yelling so hard, Fleur's hair looks like it's in a wind tunnel."

"Really?" I grin. "Y'know something, Claudey? Scrumble grows on me."

Claude cracks up laughing. She lies down on the sofa, picking up the *What's On in Destiny Bay* guide to find tonight's party.

"So, any gossip?" she asks.

"Nah," I say, wearing my best poker face. "Just a normal day really."

Chapter 6

booty camp

Six entire days pass, and I don't hear another peep from Saul Parker. Or a thump, sneeze, cough or chuckle, for that matter.

When we girls aren't out waitressing, partying, chasing Argie sex gods or at the beach, and I have a moment alone, I try banging on the loft door with a broom, shouting Saul's name and even luring him down with the aroma of sizzling bacon. Nothing.

Have I imagined the entire episode? Or has he moved on? Found himself a less grumpy landlady? Or hitched back to Wigan with his surfboard under his arm?

It would probably make things a lot simpler if he has. I mean, if Scrumble does one of her "spot checks," finds him and kicks us all out just before Booty Quake, well, Claude and Fleur will blank me till 2047.

So, yeah, it's all for the best. I just wish I didn't feel so . . . so stupidly disappointed.

But learning to surf would have rrrocked.

And, if I'm being completely honest, Saul Parker, despite being a talented cat burglar and looking like the shock of a good deep hair-conditioning treatment might kill him, seems like a pretty wild kind of lad to kick about with for a few weeks.

Not that I fancy him or anything. He just seems sort of, cool, y'know? A bit of a wrong'un. Precisely the sort of lad my mother warns me to steer clear of (usually before attempting to hook me up with Aunty Susan's Scottish country-dancing godson).

"Think sexalicious! Think va-voom! Think curves!" Fleur Swan cries breathily, waving her arms, while Claude Cassiera fiddles with the wiring on a laptop computer.

"Wah?" I say, crashing back to earth, totally forgetting about Saul Parker's neat smattering of freckles and broad shoulders.

The LBD are in the conference room of Harbinger Hall's Business Suite, sitting around a magnificent oval oak table.

"I was giving you runway tips for the contest," tuts Fleur. "I don't need to remind you how important scooping this twenty thousand pounds is, do I, Ronnie?"

"No, Fleur," I say through very tight lips.

I wish *she'd* move to Mossington.

"Hey," interrupts Claude, flicking a switch on the side of the overhead projector. "That's it, it's hooked up. Can we hurry this along, please? I'm working in twenty minutes. I'm helping get the Windsmore Suite ready. We've got VIP guests arriving tomorrow!"

"No problem," says Fleur, tapping a key on the laptop. "So, let me introduce you to Miss Demonboard Babe contestant number one: Svetlana Varninka."

On the far screen, a huge image appears of a stunning, sullen, athletic brunette with a geometric bob. She's dressed in a black bustier, French knickers and green high heels. It looks like an underwear shot from an expensive catalogue, but the girl's face is weirdly familiar.

"Svetlana?" I gasp, feeling dwarfish, rotund and sausagelike. "That's Svetlana the Russian waitress. Miss Flipping Premature Menopause with whom I serve coffee each morning! She's entering Miss Demonboard Babe?"

"She certainly is," Fleur says firmly.

"Fleur Swan!" says Claude. "Where did you get this photo?"

"Hmmm, well, I'd heard a rumor Svetlana used to model part time in Russia," says Fleur matter-of-factly. "So I, er, borrowed her portfolio from the East Turret and scanned some shots."

"You stole it!" Claude gasps.

"Look, let's not get bogged down in details," tuts Fleur. "Do you want to see what we're up against or what? It took me hours of arduous flirting to get the lowdown on who the other contestants are."

"Flirting? Who with?" I say. "Who told you all this?"

"Oh, I called Demonboard's head office in London and targeted their office assistant," Fleur says. "Julian, he was called. Bit dim. Putty in my hands!"

"Fleur, that's immoral," says Claude, her eyes alive with excitement. "And normally, y'know, I'd be outraged. But in this case, I'm going to say well done! Right, let's get on with it. Show me the pictures. Bring it on!"

Fleur taps the keyboard. The next slide shows a curvy blonde girl with long shiny hair, clad in tiny red sports shorts, long funky hockey socks and a cropped gym top, sweating it out on the Harbinger Hall treadmill.

"Wow!" says Claude. "Is that Precious Elton from reception?"

"Snapped two hours ago on my camera phone," says Fleur, raising an eyebrow. "According to Carbzilla, Precious has been doing two hours of Hatha yoga each day for a fortnight and eating only fruit, vegetables, seeds and grilled meat. Oh, and she's just had her hair colored three shades blonder. She's looking pretty buff, eh?"

"Amazing!" coos Claude.

I retrieve a packet of Chocky Wocky Doo-Dahs out of my handbag and stuff one in my gob defiantly.

"What about Carbzilla?" I ask dryly. "She's not entering too, is she?"

"Goodness no!" says Fleur. "She still weighs a cubic ton. I just served her a midmorning banana daiquiri in the Jacuzzi."

"Damn it," I mutter. "She was my one hope of not coming in last."

"Ronnie," tuts Claude.

"Now, what's interesting," says Fleur, ignoring me and pointing at the screen, "is that none of these girls is an anorexic bone bag. Look!"

Fleur clicks through another ten slides of equally stunning barmaids, waitresses and surf instructors from around Destiny Bay. Small doe-eyed brunettes, tall Amazonian blondes, quirky-looking indie girls, chicks with bunches, brown-skinned babes, pale-skinned honeys, girls with faces like angels. Each girl possibly prettier than the last.

"The look is 'healthy and alive,' " continues Fleur, "so from now on we're focused on getting into shape!"

"Agreed!" grins Claude. Claude loves a project.

159

"Now," says Fleur, dishing out some papers, "both of you take one of my healthful eating tip sheets."

I gaze forlornly at the sheet, which is filled with lots of low-fat, low-fun, windy, farty things that make you poo and wee a lot.

"What's up now?" chuckles Fleur.

"Cuh," I scoff. "It'll take more than a few bags of Puy lentils to get rid of this," I moan, whipping up my T-shirt and playing the opening bars of "The Ace of Spades" by Motörhead on my belly, just to illustrate.

"Oh, shut up," sighs Fleur. "Ronnie Ripperton, as well as being extremely pretty, you have the tiniest of nonexistent stomachs, which looks perfectly womanly to me. You've just got a poor self-image! Which isn't surprising considering you wasted two years dating a lying, cheating, chromosomally challenged skateboarding baboon."

"Hmmm . . . but," I begin.

"But if you're so keen on having washboard abs, then do some crunches!" quacks Fleur. "The closest I've seen you get to aerobics this year was when you pulled a groin injury doing Riverdance at my birthday sleepover."

"Hmmmph," I say, wriggling in the grip of truth.

Just that instant my phone vibrates and squeaks in my pocket. It's a text sent from a number I don't recognize.

FROM: 079782 432871
TIME: 2:33
HEY VERONICA—IT'S YOUR LODGER. STILL WANNA RIDE THE WAVES?

Do I wanna ride the waves? Eh?

Oh my God! Saul Parker! My heart nearly leaps through my chest.

"Who's that from?" noses Claude.

"Oooh, erm." I'm blushing now. "Just Mum. She's mad I've not called her for days."

"Girls, girls! Can I have your attention?" persists Fleur. "Right, who agrees that we all swim twenty lengths of the pool each morning? And do fifty crunches a day before breakfast shift? And . . ."

But Fleur's voice is just background static now. I'm thinking about surfing with Saul. Should I text him back right away? Or make him wait? But what if I leave it and then he thinks it's a no, so he vanishes again?

Does this mean he's still kipping in the loft? Is this going to end in disaster?

Oh God, this is hopeless. I can't help myself. My hands are moving out of control with my mind by this point. I start tapping out an answer.

FROM: RONNIE
TIME: 2:36
REPLY: AH . . . YOU'RE ALIVE. ARE YOU? WHAT HAVE YOU GOT IN MIND?

I press "send."

Uggghhh! That "You're alive" bit made me sound like I was worried about him. Which I soooo wasn't, by the way.

Oh God. Why am I such a total loser with the opposite sex? It's Miles Boon all over again. Yuk.

Brrrrrrrrrrrrrrr! Another text!

FROM: 079782 432871
TIME: 2:38
REPLY: CAN YOU MEET ME AT 5AM TOMORROW BY THE GATE TO HARBINGER'S CLIFF PATH? X

Can I meet him tomorrow? What are my shifts? Oh my God, yes, I'm off tomorrow until 2 P.M.! I begin to text a reply.

"Ronnie!" nags Fleur. "Stop texting! That's soooo rude!"

"Sorry! Sorry!" I blush, with a huge grin spreading across my chops. "Okay, what were you saying again?"

"I said," repeats Fleur, "will you at least promise to add some fresh air and exercise to your daily routine?"

FROM: RONNIE
TIME: 2:42
REPLY: YES! NO PROBLEM AT ALL. SEE YOU THERE X

"Yes! No problem at all," I tell Fleur with a mischievous grin.

rendezvous

I barely sleep a wink that night. I wake up at 2, 3 and 4 A.M., checking my watch.

Eventually, at half past four I slide out of bed. Fleur and Claude are dead to the world; Fleur emitting dainty breathy snores, Claude letting out big breathy snores like an asthmatic elephant on a slide trombone. I pull on a bikini, some track pants and my big blue baggy hoodie, scribble the girls a note saying I'm off "to exercise" and creep out of the apartment.

Harbinger Hall is freakishly silent. All the guests and staff are safely tucked in beddy-bye-byes, aside from an occasional cleaner polishing a marble floor or scaling a ladder to fiddle with a chandelier shard. As I pass reception, Frank the nightwatchman is deeply asleep, the peak of his dark green hat pulled down over his eyes. I tiptoe past him, then run through the hotel, past the health club and through the pool area before unbolting one of the back doors leading out into the gardens.

At the bottom of Harbinger's gardens lies a steep cliff path leading down to a private cove. A dusty sign on the path's gate reads

PRIVATE COVE EXCLUSIVELY FOR THE USE OF HARBINGER CLIENTELE ONLY. TRESPASSERS WILL BE PROSECUTED.

I loiter by the gate for about twelve minutes, feeling increasingly foolish.

This wouldn't be the first time I'd been stood up by a boy. I waited for Jimi outside the Warner Village Multiplex one Friday night until the usherettes took pity and sent me out some chili fries.

I look at my watch. It's twelve minutes past five.

"Saaaaul!" I shout, doing that half-quiet shout you do when searching for a dog late at night. "Saaaaul!"

To my horror, the hedge begins to rustle.

"Ha ha! Morning!" yells Saul, his cheeky face and crazy brown hair appearing like the rising sun from behind the leaves. "You came! Sweet!"

"Jeez! Aaaagh!" I squeal, nearly splatting face-first into the hedge. "Look, monkey-boy, could you just stop doing that? Stop . . . hiding in places! Lurky Lurkason! What's wrong with you?"

"Ha ha!" Saul chortles. "Look, lady, one of us is a fugitive around here, remember?"

I pull a twig from my hair and straighten my track pants, trying to regain my dignity.

"C'mon then," says Saul, standing there in his black hoodie, long khaki shorts and flip-flops. He opens the gate and beckons me in. "Ready?"

"Erm, yeah," I smile, stepping inside.

As we begin to descend the steep cliff path, the view ahead is awesome. As far as the eye can see is vast, calm blue ocean, with a magical amber sun shimmering as it ascends. Wow!

Instantly Saul and I are chattering furiously about the past six days. Saul has certainly been a busy lad. A load of his old mates from Lancashire, who all have daft names like Goggy, Pickle and Doss, had been down at Destiny Bay that week, so they'd been surfing at Esperance Beach all day, then partying hard all night before crashing out in the back of their smelly camper van. Yes, all five of them in one van.

"Yuk," I groan. "I bet that place smelled good in the morning."

"Hmmm," winces Saul. "Goggy hadn't changed his socks since we were in Fuerteventura."

"Lovely," I say. "And you've not been back to Harbinger Hall at all?"

"Just the once. Thought I'd best keep a low profile," Saul said. "Y'know, in case you'd grassed me up to Scrumble."

"I wouldn't have done that," I tell him quietly.

Saul smiles as if that means a lot to him.

During the rest of the walk, I make Saul laugh about what I've been up to this week. I tell him about Claude's latest detox plan, which involves drinking pint after pint of a bizarre green slimy liquid (only £3 a bottle from the local health food store), and how Fleur spent the week waiting for an Argie surf god called Santiago Marre to call, after she pushed her phone number into his hand at that party at A Land Down Under.

"Ugh! That guy's a right nork," groans Saul. "He's ridiculous. He's always on the front of *Surf King* magazine, flexing his muscles. What a ponce."

"I know," I giggle. "But try telling Fleur that."

Then I tell him about my week at work and how Gene the sous chef and I have been dealing with a particularly rude crowd of guests.

"No! Not the spoons down the underpants trick! That's rank!" howls Saul. "Oh my God, behind the cute face, you're actually evil, aren't you?"

"I try my best," I giggle proudly.

Fifteen minutes later, slightly out of breath, we reach what to my total surprise turns out to be a perfect picture-postcard cove. Fresh, clean sand and smooth pebbles. Not a dead seagull or a spiky rock in sight!

"But, but . . . wow!" I gasp. The tide is ebbing away, leaving fresh wet sand unmarred by human feet. "But Scrumble said this was all rocks!"

"Yeah, well, Scrumble hates surfers," Saul smirks. "She just doesn't want word spreading about this little gem."

We wander out onto the wet sand, leaving two fresh sets of footsteps behind us. Waves are building up and crashing brutally against the cliffs on either side of the cove. It feels cool to be so isolated. There's no one here but me, Saul and the sea.

"You come here every day?" I ask.

"I keep a board down here," Saul says, pointing at a little ramshackle beach hut back by the cliffs. "But sometimes I go to Misty. Sometimes Esperance. I'm just crammin' in as much water time as I can. If I could even take third position at Demonboards . . . y'know, win some cash? Then I'm off to Oz."

"Australia?" I say. "To surf?"

"Yeah! The plan is to buy myself a little camper van," Saul grins. "Load up the board, head toward Noosa Cove, maybe even check out Bondi . . ."

Saul's voice trails off. "Then what's the plan?" I prompt.

"Then the plan is . . . *no plans,*" he says. "Just to have a good time."

That sounds wonderful. But totally alien too. My parents have my life mapped out till I'm twenty-two years old.

"But what about A-levels?" I ask. "Or university?"

Saul sort of winces. "Probably not," he says. "Got kicked out of my last school."

"Why?" I ask.

"I ran off to the Hebrides halfway through Year Eleven for a surf contest," he says sheepishly. "Got suspended for four weeks. How's that a punishment? It was more like a treat! I never went back."

Saul stops. He picks up a small star-shaped shell from the sand, examines it, then hands it to me. "Don't need exams for what I wanna be anyhow," he says.

I put the tiny shell in my hoodie pocket. "What do you want to be?" I say.

Saul thinks about it for a little while. "Free," he says.

My first surf session, even if it is a lesson in extreme humiliation, is as cool as hell. Most of the morning I spend on dry land, floundering on my belly on a borrowed surfboard, wearing a wet suit that makes fart noises, learning about paddling out, duck diving and wave etiquette. Eventually Saul and I wade out into the awesomely cold ocean for some "water time," although to my shame all I really manage is a lot of girlish flapping around swallowing mouthfuls of white water.

For a newbie surfer, I suck big time, but it still rocks just to be there. Especially when Saul shows me how it's really done, paddling out into the stronger breaks, jumping up onto his board, then ripping along, pulling all sorts of twists, tricks and turns like some sort of Extreme Channel surf king. Amazing.

Later on, we wander back to the sand and lie in the sunshine just laughing and chattering. Saul is dissing all the rich-kid "shubee" boys on Misty Beach who wear £5,000 worth of Rip Curl clothes but don't even own a board, while I tell Saul all sorts of LBD stories about Triplet Day and about when we broke into McGraw's property and trod on his poodles. And about last

167

summer when we went to Astlebury Festival and renewed our friendship with Spike Saunders, international Duke of Pop.

"Wow! You've met Spike Saunders?" Saul gasps.

"Two times," I say, trying to sound matter-of-fact. "But, hey, that's another story."

Saul is just dead easy to chat to. Somehow I find myself telling him about Nan and her police scanner and how she talked me out of getting that job from hell at the Wacky Warehouse and into having an adventure instead. And how she died promptly that night, before I could flake out on her and change my mind.

"Aw, she sounds cool," says Saul. "You must miss her loads."

"Well, the weird thing is," I say, "I still feel like she's here. Especially when I do mad stuff like this. I mean, me on a surfboard?"

"She'd be proud of you," Saul nods. "You were really good."

Later, I even confess to Saul how Claude and Fleur and I are all actually in training for the bikini contest and how we need to win the money to keep Claude from moving away.

"You're going to be a Miss Demonboard Babe?" says Saul. "Just to make your friend happy?"

"Er, 'fraid so," I say bashfully.

"Wow, that's true friendship," Saul says, looking seriously impressed. "This Claude chick must mean the world to you."

"Yeah," I say, feeling a bit choked.

"Jeez!" I gasp, checking my watch. "It's half past one! I'm working two to ten! Gotta go!"

"I'll walk ya," Saul says, leaping up.

We scramble up the cliff path together. My legs and arms are stiffening from my surf lesson, so I'm a little unsteady on my feet. Saul notices this and links my arm. Just as friends.

His right biceps feels good and strong pressed against me.

"Okay," he says as we reach the top of the path where the bushes are. "Gotta leave you here. I'll wait till it's quieter before I risk coming out."

We stand looking at each other for a second.

There's a tiny awkward pause.

"So, erm, thanks for the surf lesson!" I say, poking Saul's biceps.

"Awww, hey, no worries!" he smiles, ruffling the front of my hair. "Thanks for everything. Y'know, letting me crash in the loft and all that. You're a star, Ronnie."

"No worries!" I say.

"Hey, I meant to say," adds Saul. "Don't suppose you're going to that beach barbecue at A Land Down Under tomorrow night, are you?"

"Yeah," I say. "We're all going. Fleur bagged us some passes through the organizer."

"Oh . . . right, cool! Well, maybe . . . y'know, we could, like, hang out."

"Er . . . yeah," I say. "I'd, erm, like that!"

There's another weird pause. We stand peering at each other for an awkward moment.

Shall I just go now?

Just then Saul moves forward. He cups my face in his hands and kisses my lips softly. Then he lets me go.

It feels like a major electric shock has zapped right through me. Ha! I go totally and utterly gooey! More gooey than I think I've ever felt before. My cheeks frazzle hot pink!

"I'll ring you," he grins, turning to walk away.

"Yeah!" I beam, somehow preventing myself from making a dorkish phone-hand gesture.

Aggh! This summer just gets better and better!

"Oh, hey . . . Veronica?" Saul yells as I start to walk away.

I stop and turn around.

"That Demonboard bikini thing," he says. "Don't . . . y'know, stress about it. 'Cos, I mean . . . y'know . . ."

"Y'know what?" I ask.

"Well, y'know . . . *you*," he says, waving his hand around to gesture to the whole package of me. "I've seen you in a bikini. It's sort of . . . y'know . . . *wow!*"

Saul winks and disappears back down the path.

"Oh?" I say. "Er, cheers!"

Hee hee hee!

I float back through the gardens feeling most irregular indeed. The corners of my mouth appear to be hooked to the lobes of my ears with invisible love string, and my brain is sloshing and frothing merrily around inside my skull, replaying Saul's kiss again and again.

Aaaaggghhh! Total meltdown!

I'm either in love, or I'm having a sort of brain hemorrhage.

I levitate through the health spa, past the dining hall into the heart of Harbinger Hall, my mind racing with images of Saul's gorgeous face, his great hazel eyes and his impish nostrils. About how rockin' he looks when he's carrying his surfboard, with his dready hair blowing about in the breeze and that wicked naughty grin on his face.

Saul Parker kissed me!

Saul Parker thinks I'm a top Demonboard Babe!

I feel amazing.

I breeze along the main corridor, heading through the hectic reception lobby. At the reception desk Precious is checking in a crowd of young glamorous women. The scent of beeswax soap hangs in the air.

Ah! Life is marvelous! I love Harbinger Hall!

"So let me get this straight," a new guest is sniping at Precious in a weedy yet assertive voice. "You're actually telling me you don't offer a macrobiotic option on breakfast?"

"Erm," flusters Precious, "I don't think so. I mean . . ."

"Oh, for God's sake," a second rather shrill, plummy voice says. "What sort of backward little hovel is this? Let me remind you we're VIPs! That's Very Important Persons, if your special needs teacher can't help you figure it out. Do you seriously expect me to eat normal old sausages like an everyday plebby civilian?"

I stop in my tracks.

No!

Nooooooo!

It can't be. I must be having a brain seizure.

I stare closely at the reception desk, my heart thumping. A tiny, elfin blonde girl in a floaty summer smock and bangles is waving around a gold AmEx card.

Cressida Sleeth.

Five-foot-nothing of pure, unfettered evil.

And standing beside Cressida is a taller brunette, clad in a Chloe summer dress, huge dark Dior sunglasses and a red string kabbalah bracelet around her right wrist.

The ground begins to feel highly unsteady beneath my feet.

It's Panama Goodyear.

"And can you make a note that I need kabbalah water on my breakfast tray each sunrise," Panama quacks, thumping the reception desk with her Marni wallet. "You do know what kabbalah water is, don't you? It's blessed by kabbalah priests."

Oh God.

Please.

Nooooooo.

~~~~~~~~~~~~~~~~~~~~~~

scrumbled

"Clauuuude, Fleeeeur! Oh my God! Listen," I cry, racing into the apartment, sweat running down my face. "It's terrible! The worst thing ever!"

Weirdly, Claude and Fleur are standing in the lounge wearing freaky fixed smiles.

"They've followed us," I say. "It's awful! Cress—"

But we're not alone. Because lurking in the kitchen with a clipboard under one arm is Miss Scrumble.

"Oh, hello, Miss Scrumble," I gasp. "What's happening?"

"Two crucial points of business," sighs Scrumble, peering suspiciously around the apartment, "the former being very grave indeed."

Scrumble directs the last part of the sentence to Fleur. "Hang on. What have I done now?" gasps Fleur.

Scrumble sighs and puckers her mouth into a perfect cat's anus. "Boys," she tuts.

"Boys?" repeats Fleur.

"My sources report," drones Scrumble, "that a boy has been spotted creeping out of this apartment on various occasions over the last month."

This day had taken a serious nosedive.

"Canoodlement is occurring in these staff quarters," Scrumble says, "which contravenes Section 8 of the Harbinger Hall Employee Behavioral Code."

"But that's totally impossible, Miss Scrumble!" I cry, sounding like a bad daytime soap actress.

"I don't know anything about that!" says Fleur, looking very confused.

"What a load of rubbish!" Claude says. "Somebody is lying to you."

"Svetlana wouldn't—" Scrumble begins, before coughing and starting again. "My source isn't known for telling lies."

"That Russian is going to pay for this," mutters Fleur as Scrumble begins to waddle around our apartment, snooping into the bedroom, looking under beds and behind wardrobes, sticking her snout into every nook.

"This is a very fine line that you're walking, Fleur Swan," Scrumble squawks, standing just beneath the door to the loft. "What Siegmund Brewster sees in you beats me. I'd have had you thrown out weeks ago! But, oh no, he knows best, apparently."

"But," protests Fleur, "I've not—"

"Enough!" grunts Scrumble, raising a stumpy hand. "Let this

be a warning to you. One more strike and your feet won't touch the ground!"

Fleur folds her arms and stands there visibly simmering.

I feel really guilty. But not guilty enough to grass myself up.

"Now, moving on to topic two," says Scrumble, checking her clipboard. "The new VIP guests have just checked into the Windsmore Suite."

"Are they pop stars?" asks Fleur, brightening slightly.

"No, Fleur, they certainly are not," I groan, shaking my head.

"In actual fact," says Scrumble, "they're a group of extremely wealthy young ladies here for a summer break. One of their fathers has kindly given over his gold AmEx so the girls can have unlimited spending while they're here. That makes them VIPs by our standards."

"How nice," says Claude bitterly.

"So," continues Scrumble, ignoring her, "it's of paramount importance that they feel pampered during their stay."

"Fine," shrug Fleur and Claude.

"Oh God, please kill me now," I mutter. A bead of sweat trickles down my back.

"Tomorrow," Scrumble continues, "the guests have requested a traditional English afternoon tea party to be served in their suite. Cucumber sandwiches, scones, cakes, tea, that sort of thing."

"Consider it done," says Claude, opening the door to chivvy Scrumble out.

"Thank you, Claudette," says Scrumble, waddling past. "Oh, and just one other thing: all purchases for the Windsmore Suite guests are being charged to the AmEx card of a Mr. Alan Sleeth."

174

Claude's mouth drops wide open. "Mr. Sleeth?" repeats Claude.

Fleur's eyes widen. Then I swear her face turns puce.

"Yes, Sleeth," repeats Scrumble, referring to her clipboard. "But the bill for the accommodation itself is being picked up by a Mr. Goodyear."

Chapter 7

more tea, cressida?

"Right, everyone stay chilled," Fleur warns us as we trek miserably to the Windsmore Suite pushing trolleys laden with tea-party treats. Scones, cream cakes, dainty little sandwiches, petits fours, gallons of Darjeeling and Lapsang souchong tea and of course we haven't forgotten Panama's kabbalah water. The Windsmore Suite witches have ordered the lot.

"Let's not give them a reaction," hisses Fleur. "Then they'll check out and buzz off."

"Hmmm . . . hope so," I mutter, trudging behind, pushing a trolley bearing a large pomegranate and white chocolate cream gateau under a silver serving platter.

Claude just walks behind like a little mouse. Cressida and Panama's arrival seems to have really floored her. She's coped with so much of late, but this seems different somehow.

"C'mon, Claude," I say, wrapping my arm around her shoulder. In one of the grand mirrors lining the main corridor, I catch sight of our little gang, traipsing along in our skanky bry-nylon green pinafores. Even Fleur, with her long legs and platinum blonde hair, struggles to look glam in these frumpy outfits.

"Okay, remember. Cool as ice," says Fleur, knocking on the suite's door and clearing her throat. "Hello? Room service!"

Inside the Windsmore Suite, a chorus of sniggers rings out.

"Ennnnnter!" shouts Panama Goodyear in her unmistakably nauseating tones.

"I can't go in," whispers Claude. Her hands are shaking.

"We have to," I say.

With heavy hearts, we wheel the trolleys into the suite's living area. It's worse than I even imagined. Around the suite's antique dining table sit Panama Goodyear and Cressida Sleeth looking glossy, well groomed and as smug as humanly possible. Euugh!

Whereas Panama's look is a little more "bo-ho chic" than usual, Cressida's hippie image seems a tad more dressy and blinged up. They're both wearing red cord wristbands around their right wrists. It's like the gruesome pair have melded into one.

Worse still, they're accompanied by Leeza Palmer, Panama's terrifying über-bimbo buddy. Bizarrely, they're all far bustier than I ever remembered them. Proper D-cup whoppers. Especially Leeza, who had droopy spaniel's ears last time I saw her, but now has DD monsters. Freaky.

"Oh, thank you, God!" grins Panama, clapping her hands together. "It's true. They are working as servants here. Hilarious!"

Fleur takes a deep breath, announcing calmly, "Afternoon tea is served."

I try to say a businesslike hello, but I'm too bitter to breathe. Just then, from an adjoining bedroom appears Abigail

Munro, probably Panama's loyalest of bum kissers, also with new all-improved cleavage. She can barely contain her glee.

"Oh, girls, loving the uniforms," she winks, sitting herself down.

As we begin to unload the plates, cups and food, the humiliation is asphyxiating me. Cressida Sleeth, clad in a pale blue floaty vintage Marc Jacobs summer smock, is peeping coyly at us from behind her blunt-cut fringe. Her face is a dictionary definition of conceited. Just like it was on the day of the last GCSE exam.

Play it cool, Ronnie, I repeat to myself. *Remember what Fleur said.*

"Gosh, they're all very quiet," Panama announces as we begin unloading the plates of cream scones and jugs of milk. "Taken a vow of silence?"

The first flicker of annoyance passes Fleur's face.

"Maybe they're tired?" suggests Cressida. "All this skivvying and slaving must be exhausting." She pauses, gazing directly at Claude. "We're so very blessed our parents aren't dependent on us for money."

Claude cringes with embarrassment.

"Oh, Cressy," sighs Panama. "Don't be mean! You know Claude's mum is broke as a joke."

"She's . . . she's not," says Claude unconvincingly.

"Yes, she is!" chuckles Cressida. "She had an interview with my daddy at Farquar, Lime and Young last month. She was begging for work! Claiming she was a highly qualified legal secretary. Ha!"

"What?" gasps Claude.

"Sadly, all Daddy needed at that time was a toilet attendant," Cressida smirks.

"But, we're . . . she's . . . ," splutters Claude. A small tear appears in her eye.

I can't stand this any longer. "Oh, why don't you just leave her alone?!" I growl, as the Sisters Grim collapse into satisfied titters.

"It's just a little joke," smirks Abigail. "Can't she take a joke?"

"Ha ha ha! Ronnie Ripperton speaks!" guffaws Panama, pointing at me. "Her period of mourning is over. Hurray for us!"

"Wah wah, Jimi Steele!" torments Leeza. "Let me sit on your wall, Jimi Steele! Let me hack into your Hotmail account, Jimi Steele!"

Ugh! Cressida really has told them every little LBD secret. All I can see are four faces smirking and pointing at me. I'm trying to be cool, but a red angry mist has descended.

"Okay! Enough!" Fleur yells, turning to Panama. "Listen, Panama, why are you here? Surely you've not driven three hundred miles just to laugh at us in our bry-nylon uniforms? Why aren't you in Ibiza?"

Panama rolls her eyes. "Tsk. Fleur, *no one* goes to Ibiza anymore," she sneers. "It's full of fat thirty-year-old has-beens at 'back to the nineties' retro-house nights."

The girls look to one another and smirk. "Anyone who's anyone is coming down here for Booty Quake," says Leeza patronizingly.

"Plus we all decided to enter Miss Demonboard Babe," simpers Abigail. "Just for the hell of it."

As Claude lets out a little whimper, I drop a teacup in horror.

"And when we found out you three little trolls were working here," continues Panama, "well, I said to my daddy, book me a suite ASAP!"

Somehow Fleur's face is a vision of Zen calm. I've never seen her so composed. "Okay, girls," she says serenely. "You've had your slave/master degradation kick now, haven't you? What more do you actually want?"

Panama ponders for a moment.

"Oooh, let me see . . . ," she wonders aloud. Then her eyes widen. "Oooh, I know! How about a pole-dance? Do your *Moulin Rouge* again! In your underpants and bra! Cressida tells us that home video was hilarious!"

"What?" groans Fleur, flushing scarlet. "Oooh . . . gnnnnnngnn!"

"I've got an idea too," squawks Cressida. "Maybe Fleur could tell us about the time she convinced herself she was pregnant . . . just because she'd let Baz Kauffman touch the outside of her tights!"

"Hee hee! The immaculate conception!" guffaws Panama. "I wish my mummy would buy me a *Your Body, Yourself* sex education textbook."

Fleur's mouth drops open. She's totally lost for words.

The entire gang is in hysterics now, laughing, singing *Moulin Rouge* songs and waving their arms. "More tea, waitress!" shouts Cressida, waving a teacup at us antagonistically.

"Oh, serve yourself, Bilbo," I hiss.

Cressida feigns shock. "Well, how rude!" she hisses, grabbing her mobile phone. "Y'know, ladies? I think it's time for our first official complaint."

I look to Fleur to calm things down, but by now her face has altered from calm composure to the crazed firecracker I know and love.

As Cressida punches in numbers on her phone, Fleur strides around the table and stands before the huge pomegranate and cream gateau, her nostrils flaring with anger.

"Oh, so you're going to complain, are you?" says Fleur.

Cressida just smirks and carries on dialing.

"Well, then!" says Fleur, grabbing the cake with both hands. "I'd better give you something to complain about!"

"Noooo, Fleur!" I scream. "Not the cake!"

"Fleeeeur!" implores Claude. "Cool as ice, remember?"

But this is soooo the opposite of cool.

"Gateau is served!" Fleur yells with evil glee, unceremoniously splatting the entire fruity, spongy creation all over Cressida Sleeth's head.

Oh my God!

"Spppllllgh pgghhhhgh!" splutters Cressida as cake drips all over her expensive dress.

"What do you think you're doing?" screams Panama.

And at this point, all hell breaks loose in the Windsmore Suite.

As Claude grabs two fresh cream scones and squishes them majestically into Panama's ears, pretty much destroying her Stella McCartney shift dress, I take leave of my senses, grab a plate of chocolate profiteroles and begin splatting them across the room at Abigail and Leeza. Cressida squeals about lawyers, legal fees and her lactose intolerance, while Panama grabs plates of jam tarts and attempts to fight back. Meanwhile Abigail and Leeza are screeching, chucking sandwiches and cream buns willy-nilly.

Within seconds the entire tea party has been reduced to a war zone of clotted cream, choux pastry and jam, and there's not a single morsel remaining on the table to chuck. All of our VIPs look like they've been in the gunk tank on a Saturday morning kids' show.

"You'll pay for this!" screams Panama, scooping clotted cream out of her ears.

"Whatever," says Fleur, brandishing the last remaining cream bun and taking aim at Panama's big forehead.

But at the same time, the door to the Windsmore Suite is creaking open, and to our horror Miss Scrumble appears, wearing her fake Harbinger grin.

"Good afternoon!" she coos. "Just a courtesy call to our new VIPs. How is everything—"

"Fleur, noooo!" I cry, but it's too late.

"Oh my Lord! What is hap—" Scrumble yells, just as trigger-happy Fleur Swan flings the final cream cake right across the suite, missing Panama, but knocking Scrumble's glasses off her snout and dripping raspberry jam and whipped cream all over her Harris Tweed jacket.

An eerie silence descends on the room.

"Fleur Swan," Scrumble says in a low venomous voice, removing the offending cake from her person, "go to the West

Turret immediately and clear your belongings. You are dismissed!"

Sacked

"Stop laughing!" Fleur is sniffling crossly into her mobile phone as she wanders around the West Turret, gathering handfuls of thongs, strappy sandals, mascaras and hair clips. "Stop it right now, you horrible man!"

"I don't think Fleur's dad is being too supportive about this," I whisper to Claude as we sit side by side on the sofa, totally shell-shocked.

"Oh, so you had a bet, did you?" Fleur snaps to the phone line. "Well, I'll have you know, Father, I've worked my butt off for almost a whole month, so tell that so-called mother of mine she owes you nothing!"

Fleur is storming about now, listening to Paddy's response, slamming things about angrily. "I can't believe this!" she is saying, clearly rising to his bait. "You're just as bad as that Scrumble! You think you know me, but you don't! Well, I've got news for you, Paddy Swan, I don't need you laughing at me and writing me off as a total numpty. In fact I don't need you at all! Got it? Good! Right. I'm hanging up now."

Fleur picks up a skirt from beside her bed and throws it into her case.

"Oh, and one other thing, Daddy," she sniffles more humbly. "You'll pick me up at the station, won't you? Oh, you will? Cool. See ya later."

183

Fleur puts her phone down on the coffee table and dries her eyes a little, turning to speak to us. "I can't believe this is happening, girls," she says mournfully. "I can't believe I've been sacked."

Claude and I look at Fleur sympathetically. We can totally believe Scrumble sacked Fleur. But we just can't believe she *didn't* sack us too. But saying that, she didn't catch us red-handed. Or cream-cake-handed, as it were.

"It's just so dramatic," Fleur sobs, grabbing another handful of tissues and blowing her nose. Two thick streams of blue mascara are cascading down Fleur's pretty face. Her nose is crimson from blubbing.

"What did I do to deserve this?" she whispers, shaking her head incredulously.

"Fleur," I say reasonably, "you assaulted one of the VIP guests with a pomegranate gateau. What did you expect? A gold star and promotion to a managerial position?"

"Hmmppgh, when you put it like that," sighs Fleur, shoving handfuls of eye pencils and lipsticks into her vanity case. "But I think you'll find I wasn't the only hooligan. What about Claude? She virtually perforated Panama's eardrum with a cream scone!"

"I know," sighs Claude, slouching back on the sofa and folding her arms. "And it felt so good!"

Fleur wanders miserably back into the bedroom and begins removing all her teensy little dresses off their hangers. She stands by the chart on our bedroom wall where the LBD has awarded ourselves points for every boy we've snogged. Obviously Fleur is yards ahead—she's even got the bonus prize for snogging a man over the age of thirty with a mustache, called Keith. Bleugh.

It feels like the party is well and truly over.

"Is Paddy angry?" I ask Fleur gently.

"Well, not really," sighs Fleur, folding up her fave It's a Girl's World halter-neck rah-rah dress into the size of pocket hankie. "He was pretty sarcastic. Y'know what he's like; he was laughing at me, saying he couldn't believe I'd lasted so long. Mum bet him I'd be back within a week."

Fleur looks sort of hurt.

"Mmm," I say. "Well, you did walk out of that job at Dunkin' Donuts after one hour because the overall shade clashed with your skin tone."

Fleur stops folding dresses and shakes her head at me exasperatedly. "Oh, who are you, exactly?" she tuts. "Mrs. Majiko the Memory Woman? Must you catalogue all my misdemeanors?"

"Sorry, Fleur," I mumble. I'm not making things much better, am I?

Fleur takes her framed LBD Triplet Day picture off the bedside cabinet. She looks at it for a little while. "I'm sorry I didn't win you the Demonboard Babe money, Claudey," she says sadly.

"Aw . . . hey," sighs Claude, feigning a smile. "It's not . . . I mean, it's . . . y'know . . . look, don't worry about all that."

But then Claude's voice trails to nothing.

There's no point in saying don't worry. With Fleur banished back home and Claude now looking even more likely to be moving to Mossington, this could very well be the last time the LBD hang out together for a long time. It feels like everything has been blown to smithereens.

Fleur packs her beloved photo into her case and closes the zip. She pulls her floppy sun hat over her blonde locks and paints hot-pink lipstick onto her lips, blotting it on a Harbinger Hall serviette.

"Okay, girls, I'm done," she says with a brave smile. "That's me."

"Oh God, Fleur," I say, walking across to her. "Give me a hug."

Fleur moves forward and whisks me up in her arms. She smells of Supermodel Eau de Parfum and strawberry lip gloss. Big salty tears begin to fall from my eyes and splosh down her T-shirt.

"C'mon, Ronnidge," Fleur says, hugging me. "Don't set me off again."

"But this sucks, man!" I sob. "I can't believe you're going. Psycho Killa and all the MTV people are checking in this week! I can't be a Demonboard Babe without you! And what about that beach barbecue down at Destiny Bay tonight? It's been in our diaries for weeks!"

Fleur lets me go. She hands me a pile of tissues. "Listen, Ronnie," she says. "Fact is, I've got to be out of the West Turret by 6 P.M. or Cressida Sleeth says she wants the police to investigate her assault."

At the mention of Cressida's name, Claude, who's been sitting with her face in her hands, deep in contemplation, leaps up and begins to pace about the apartment. "You can't go home," she says vehemently.

"But . . . ," begins Fleur.

"But nothing," says Claude. "Look, when I told you about Mossington that day on the beach, Fleur, I was about to give up. But you kept strong. You believed that we could overcome it."

"I know I did," smiles Fleur. "But now . . ."

"It's just the same," says Claude, folding her arms. "It's just another obstacle. We've got over worse than this!"

"But . . . ," says Fleur.

"Look, you've been psyched about Booty Quake for months," Claude says. "You've been doing salsa-cise and butt-blast classes for a fortnight for your appearance on MTV. We're not letting Squarepants, Bogwash or Slime ruin everything. It's time for the LBD to get devious!"

"But Claude, I'm homeless!" cries Fleur. "What can I do? Sleep on Misty Beach? Beg Paddy for cash so I can sleep eight to a room at the Banana Hostel? Scrumble doesn't want to see my face ever again!"

Fleur and Claude stand staring at each other, willing each other to think.

Suddenly, the solution thwacks me between the eyes. I know the most perfect Fleur Swan hiding hole.

I take a deep breath, knowing the can of worms I'm about to open.

"Well . . . maybe Scrumble doesn't have to see your face," I begin, peering up toward the trapdoor to Saul Parker's secret kingdom.

When I hooked up with Saul on the beach this morning, he said he'd be out for the rest of the day. (Well, if you want me to be specific, he actually said he'd be thinking about me 24/7 be-

187

cause I'm the hottest girl he's ever known. Gnnnnnngn . . . he is so lush!) But how would Saul feel about his squat being squatted?

"Maybe, Fleur," I say, slowly, "you could stay here, but be invisible, if you know what I mean."

"No," says Fleur, shaking her head. "You've lost me."

"That's two of us," says Claude.

"Okay," I say, taking a deep breath, praying my secret will be well received. "Now, no one freak out too much, but there's something I need to tell you about the West Turret."

exits

"Oooh, Fleur, these bags are soooo heavy," I complain in my loudest voice as Claude and I pack what appears to be all of Fleur's worldly goods into a taxi waiting at Harbinger Hall's back door. Miss Scrumble, who's watching Fleur's departure from the doorstep, gives us all a little wave before ticking something off on her clipboard. Little does Scrumble realize that Fleur's bags are actually stuffed with newspapers. The blonde bombshell hasn't the slightest intention of leaving Harbinger Hall.

A devious LBD plan is afoot.

As our taxi driver tuts and points at his watch, Fleur cranks up an Oscar-worthy performance, puffing, panting and tossing her hair about in dismay.

"I can't believe I have to go!" Fleur snivels, forcing out her best crocodile tears.

"I know, Fleur. It's so hard," I say, putting an arm around her shoulder. "But you must be strong."

Fleur opens the taxi door and pretends to take one last look at the West Turret. "Farewell, Harbinger!" she cries. "You were a good friend. Parting is such sweet sorrow!"

Then Fleur begins to fake-sob really hard, actually forcing snot down her nostrils. If she'd done this in the school play auditions last year, she might have got a bigger role than "third tree on the left."

"Shh, don't overdo it," whispers Claude, fighting to keep a straight face.

"We'll escort Fleur down to the railway station," Claude tells Scrumble. "She's very upset."

Scrumble nods, as if to say "very well." But then as we all hop into the taxi, myself in the front, Claude and Fleur in the back, Scrumble scurries across, commanding Fleur to roll down the window. For a crazy moment I think she's going to wish Fleur well for the future.

"Good riddance, Fleur Swan!" grumps Scrumble, hoisting her bosom with one arm as she talks. "You've brought this all upon yourself. I've no sympathy for you."

"Come on, driver," sighs Claude. "Destiny Bay station, please."

But Scrumble wants a final word. "Summer's over for you, Swan!" she cackles as the car pulls away. "Over!"

Fleur buries her face in her hands and gives a little moan. But then, as we pass through Harbinger Hall's main gates, Fleur sits up, chucks back her head and laughs before leaning forward to speak to the taxi driver. "Change of plan, driver," Fleur chortles. "We don't really want to go to the station. Could you take us to A Land Down Under on Destiny Bay beach, please?"

"And quick as you like," laughs Claude. "We've somebody important we need to meet!"

As we reach A Land Down Under at dusk, the barbecue is well under way. The sand outside the small bar is packed with surf dudes and bikini-clad girls flirting, dancing and giggling, or lining up for shrimp, chicken or pitchers of cocktails. All around the DJ booth, the crowd begins to sway and swell as Norris Noise, the resident DJ, cranks up an R&B set. Kids are already starting to jump up onto the podiums and chuck some shapes. One extremely happy young woman is boogying on the bar in a red bikini while the bartenders serve martinis around her silver stilettos.

Claude, Fleur and I must look highly overdressed as we fight our way through the crowds carrying suitcases and bags.

"Wait," laughs Fleur, stopping for a second to whip off her T-shirt, displaying a hot-pink bikini top. "So summer is over, is it? Huh! I reckon it's just taken a new lease on life!"

And that's when I see him, standing in the corner of A Land Down Under, surrounded by a posse of bedraggled-looking boys all dressed in shorts and Rip Curl T-shirts, each of them sporting trademark Destiny Bay shaggy surf hair.

Saul Parker looks totally incredible. He's wearing a tight black T-shirt, which shows off his pecs, with long camouflage shorts. Saul's hair is looking extra-specially, gloriously unkempt, like he's spent the day wrestling fifty-foot waves and alligators.

It seems like all the girls are trying to dance close to Saul's gang. I feel a tiny stab of jealousy just seeing girls near him. Ugh, I've got it bad! I pause for a second and watch as one tiny peroxide-blonde girl in a silver bikini and miniskirt tries desperately to chat in Saul's ear. As Saul rolls his eyes, then looks at his watch, peroxide girl resorts to dancing lewdly in front of him, wiggling her bum and jiggling her boobs. Saul just looks past her and checks the door again. Then he spots me. His face lights up.

"Veronica!" Saul whoops, running over to me. "You made it!"

"Just!" I laugh as he twirls me around. "Hey, I'm not, erm, interrupting anything, am I?"

Saul looks at me oddly; then he rolls his eyes and lets out a little snort. "What? You mean . . . her?" he smirks, nodding at his blonde admirer, who has resorted to doing weird star jumps beside him. "Are you serious?"

"Well," I blush, "I didn't know. I mean . . ."

"I've been watching that door for the best part of two hours," groans Saul. "The lads have been laughing their heads off at me."

Just then I look over Saul's shoulder and realize we've got quite an audience. There are about six lads all watching and laughing.

"Cooooooooo-ey, Saul!" waves one lad, before making a kissy-kissy sound with his mouth. Then they all begin cracking up.

"Aw, shut up!" moans Saul. "Hey, Veronica, I need to apologize about my friends. They can be a bit unruly."

"Don't worry about it," I smile. "Actually, that reminds me . . . you know I said on the phone before that I needed to tell you something important?"

"Sure," says Saul. "Is everything okay?"

"Well, the thing is . . . ," I begin.

Just then Fleur and Claude appear over either shoulder.

"Ah, hello, hello, we meet at last!" giggles Claude. "So you must be the mystery guest."

Saul looks at Claude and lets out a little groan of embarrassment.

"Claude," I say. "Can I introduce my er, *friend,* Saul Parker."

"Pleasure to meet you, Claude," grins Saul, holding out his hand.

"And I'm Fleur Swan," announces Fleur, eyeing Saul up and down. "Now, Saul, don't worry at all. We're going to get along just fine. I'm moving into your loft space from today onward. I'm your new roommate! Isn't that great?"

"Oooh . . . Erm, well, okay," stutters Saul. "I mean, I suppose, erm . . ."

"I'm psyched too!" yells Fleur as the music cranks up another notch. "And don't fret. 'Cos I'm a quiet little thing. You'll hardly even notice I'm there! Will he, girls?"

Saul is looking a little bewildered. I owe him a serious explanation here. But just as I try to begin, Fleur spots Saul's gang of surf buddies, who are all standing behind us, trying to catch my friends' eyes.

"Oooh, Saul, are these your friends?" beams Fleur, waving at them. "I must introduce myself. Hello, boys, I'm Fleur! Hey, do any of you guys like dancing?"

"I'm Stevo," chirps up one lad, not missing a chance. "I'll dance with you."

"Oooh, great," smiles Fleur. "Hey, Ronnie, watch my suit-cases!"

"And I'm Danny," says another, grabbing Claude's hand. "Let's dance to this track, then I'll buy you both a drink."

Within seconds Fleur and Claude have disappeared into the party, leaving Saul and I standing on the dance floor, sur-rounded by Fleur's luggage. I wrap my arms around Saul's waist and look up into his eyes.

Saul shakes his head and we both begin giggling. "Okay. Start from the beginning," he chuckles, kissing the top of my head.

arrivals

"That's odd," I say to Claude.

It's 8:45 A.M., three days later, and I'm peering out of the West Turret's lounge window down onto the gardens.

"What?" says Claude, fixing her hair into perfect asymmet-ric bunches.

"Mr. Greenhall," I say. "The gardener dude—he's mowing a big square into the Tatershall Memorial Lawn."

"Really?" says Claude distractedly. "Maybe Carbzilla and Three-Minute Egg are going to play cricket. They're unhinged enough."

Claude grabs her lip gloss and vanity mirror. She refuses to turn up for work looking anything less than perfect. "Hey! Are you ready?" she nags. "Scrumble wants us down there in ten minutes."

"Yeah, coming," I say, as a girl wearing a headset and carrying a clipboard hurries over the grass to Mr. Greenhall. She's shouting at him to make the square bigger.

"It looks like a landing pad," I mutter, shaking my head.

Claude stops preening abruptly. "A landing pad?" she repeats. "You know what that means!" she grins, hopping up and down.

"They're preparing for an alien visitation?" I suggest.

"Noooo! More exciting than that," Claude squeaks. "For helicopters!"

"Eh?" I say, being slow on the uptake.

"Psycho Killa!" grins Claude, jumping up and down. "Psycho Killa is coming! All the Booty Quake people must have started checking in!"

In a flurry of arms and legs, Claude runs for the door. "Gonna carve ya up! Gonna bury you!" Claude chants, singing Psycho Killa's international platinum-selling hit "Graveyard Time" from the Grammy Award–winning album *Body Bag Holiday.*

"Gonna hide yer body where they won't find ya!" hums Claude, disappearing out the door.

"Bag you up! Bag you up!" I sing, chasing Claude as fast as my feet will take me down the spiral staircase and into the hotel reception lobby.

Wow! Harbinger's lobby is in total chaos.

Everywhere you look there are huge scary hip-hop blokes clad in baseball caps, massive padded jackets, random wonky sports headbands, jeans so baggy they're probably a safety hazard, imported limited edition Reebok sneakers and oodles of bling. Everyone seems to be wearing a huge diamond cross or diamond-encrusted dog tags. Cartier watches and diamond-studded teeth are de rigueur as well.

"It's . . . it's the Mortuary Team! Psycho Killa's crew!" gasps Claude. "They're really here!"

"Unreal!" I say, turning to tell Fleur, then realizing she's not here. "But there's about a hundred of them!"

"Some of them must be Psycho Killa's staff," says Claude. "'Cos I know he travels with two chefs—a sushi chef and another guy who specializes in fried chicken. Oh, and he's got a braid technician who does his hair. And a hip-hop accountant on call 24/7 to talk him out of buying things like Lear jets and nightclubs!"

"I thought Fleur was high maintenance," I mutter.

Outside on the drive, streams of fabulous vehicles are arriving: Cadillac Escalades, Lamborghinis, Porsches and SUVs with blackened windows, as dozens more hip-hop dudes pour out, throwing their car keys to Cedric, Harbinger's geriatric car valet.

"Watch the rims, man!" shouts one hulking guy, dressed bizarrely in a customized orange prison jumpsuit, flipping Cedric a £50 tip. "Just had those twenty-inch babies fixed up."

"Man, can I get a coffee around here?" sighs his friend, an exhausted-looking, equally huge hip-hop man-mountain, wandering over and taking a seat on the lobby's leather couches.

"Ronnie! That's Freaky Death Squad and Detonator from the Mortuary Team!" says Claude, nudging me. "And, oh my God! Here's Knucklehead coming in now!"

Detonator appears to be wearing a jewel-encrusted bomber jacket made from an entire Friesian cow.

"They're even scarier than they look on MTV!" I say as the

195

three hulking hoods crouch around a coffee table in the lobby, clearly plotting a sinister gangland hit on a rival hip-hop syndicate.

In the midst of the chaos, poor overworked Precious the receptionist is attempting to allocate rooms to the hip-hop fraternity.

"Er, attention, please!" Precious yells, typing away furiously on the hotel reservation system. "Do we have a Mr., erm, Freaky Death Squad?"

"S'up!" says Freaky D, jumping up, his crisscross braids bouncing as he moves. "That's me, ma'am."

"Ah, good!" smiles Precious. "Now then, Mr. Death Squad, you prerequested a nonsmoking room with a garden view? But are you the gentleman who is allergic to goose down?"

"Sure am," says Freaky D bashfully. "Makes me itchy."

"Worry not, sir," smiles Precious. "Housekeeping has located you a man-made-fiber pillow for sensitive skin. Sign here, please. Now, Mr. Knucklehead and Mr. Detonator? You're sharing the deluxe twin room, aren't you?"

Claude and I look at each other and dissolve into giggles.

"Right, guys. Psycho Killa ETA in forty-five minutes!" shouts Kelsey, Psycho Killa's personal assistant, whom I saw in the garden this morning. "His helicopter has just left Canary Wharf in London. We'll be leaving for the sound check in one hour!"

As the Mortuary Team begin to disperse to their rooms, three more bodies arrive in reception: a small Japanese guy wearing vast dark glasses accompanied by a leggy, vacant-looking teenage lap-dancer type with her hair in ringlets carrying a small fluffy-faced Pekinese dog wearing a pink collar with a diamond-encrusted name tag, and behind them, a rotund bloke with a skinhead struggling with two large solid-steel record boxes.

"Claude, that's Warren Acapulco!" I say in my very, very worst stage whisper, managing to attract the attention of the whole trio.

"Oh, hi there," smiles Warren graciously, flipping his sunglasses up and giving me and Claude a big showbiz smile. Warren's girlfriend just rolls her eyes and begins shouting at Precious about dog-minding facilities.

"This is Trixiebelle Frou Frou!" the woman is shouting, pointing at the dog. "And she moves her bowels at 6 P.M. each day precisely. I'll need someone with a poop scoop who understands Pekinese behavior at my suite by 5:45. Is that a problem?"

"So anyway," Warren Acapulco continues, smiling at me and Claude, "how long have you been waiting to meet us?"

"Erm, oooh, well," I smile, flushing pink. "We weren't. We were waiting for Psycho Killa."

Warren's face remains poker straight. He produces a photo from his pocket and a pen, signing the picture,

Let the beat play on . . . Warren Acapulco xxx

before handing it to me and walking away.

"From now on," giggles Claude, "let me talk to the celebrities."

"But I didn't even ask for an autograph!" I laugh, staring at the cheesy publicity shot.

197

"Never mind," laughs Claude. "Stick it on eBay. Some fool will buy it."

This is turning out to be the best day ever!

But just then, a face in the crowd spoils my happy mood. "You girls!" shouts Scrumble. "Come here!"

"Quick, look busy!" says Claude as Scrumble storms toward us, ignoring us and grabbing at two Harbinger Hall cleaners pushing a trolley of mops, brooms and bleach through the lobby.

"Where are you going?" Scrumble shouts at the older of the two girls, clad in a green cleaner's pinafore.

"Er, we're, erm, going to clean the Edelweiss Suite," the girl stutters.

"Oh, really?" tuts Scrumble. "Can I see your ID cards?"

The girls begin to flap.

"I've lost mine!" claims the younger girl.

"Run for it!" shouts the older girl.

But now Scrumble has a walkie-talkie in her hand, barking orders. "Security! We have a situation here," she's flapping. "More intruders have infiltrated the building en route to God Created Man's suite!"

"We're not intruders!" squeals the older girl as her overall falls open to reveal a God Created Man tour T-shirt and a digital camera hanging from her neck.

"Tell that to the judge!" shouts Scrumble.

"Claude, God Created Man are here!" I gasp. "Phwooooar!"

"Oh my God, they are so lush," grins Claude.

"And they're right here in this hotel!" I laugh.

"Well, you can't snog any of them," winks Claude. "Don't think Saul would like that!"

"Hmmm, good point," I blush, thinking of the very lovely Saul Parker for the zillionth time that day. Blimey O'Reilly, I have totally lost my marbles over that boy. And he's not exactly remaining sane about me either. In fact, last night, after a moonlight walk down on the private beach, Saul even said he's been considering getting a little *V* tattooed on the bottom of his back so he'll always remember this summer. Serious stuff, eh?

Agh, I cannot stop thinking about Saul Parker! It's like a form of wonderful insanity. I'm like a different person ever since he came into my life. More confident. More alive.

"Ronnie, stop dreaming," says Claude, nudging me back to the real world as the two fake cleaners are marched past me by security personnel. "You keep drifting off. You've got it bad, you have."

"I soooo have not," I blush.

"But we only wanted an autograph," pleads one of the girls.

"Trespassers must be prosecuted," huffs Scrumble, looking very proud of herself indeed. And then her eyes rest upon Claude and me and she looks even smugger.

"Ah, Veronica and Claudette," she smiles. "And three become two."

"Good morning, Miss Scrumble," says Claude.

"It certainly is," she replies, "now that we've trimmed the deadwood from our waitressing workforce."

Claude and I say nothing. It's for the best.

"Miss Swan arrived home safely, I take it?" Scrumble says.

"I spoke to her this morning," says Claude. "She's fine."

"Good riddance to her," mumbles Scrumble under her breath. "I shall be forwarding her the dry-cleaning bill for my jacket."

At this point a small giggle tries to surface on my mouth. It happens every time I think of the satisfying *thwack* the cake made colliding with her forehead.

"Now," continues Scrumble, checking her clipboard, "I have it here that several weeks ago you both booked tomorrow off for this beach party affair." She wrinkles her nose as she says "beach party."

"That's correct," says Claude. "Is there a problem?"

"I'm not sure yet," goads Scrumble, waddling away. "Let's see how hard you work today."

room service

And work hard we do.

Delivering room service orders, running messages, serving cocktails and clearing away plates. Scrumble tries to break our spirit with a mind-boggling list of demands, but she can't. We're on cloud nine. Behind every Harbinger Hall hotel room door lies another pop star, rapper or MTV presenter! Standing there live in the flesh!

In Room 307 MTV presenter Lonny Larson begs for hot lemon and honey after he's been up all night partying with God Created Man and feels like hell. Lonny still looks totally gorgeous with his huge green eyes and rich Belfast accent. He signs

Claude's and my order books and even lets us snap camera-phone pics of him in his fluffy terry-cloth bathrobe!

Upstairs in Room 404, the Mortuary Team's Freaky Death Squad calls up requesting Harbinger Hall stationery, pens and vanilla ice cream with extra chocolate sauce, as the calm ambience of the hotel, the regency antiques and the regal chandeliers have inspired him to finish his new track, "Gonna Chop You Up, Sucka!"

Our next delivery, at the newly painted Barclay Suite, is for Dita Murray from the Scandal Children, who flew in at 3 A.M. from Singapore. Dita is a tiny little thing with blonde braids and a white pale complexion, much frailer than she looks in her videos. When we arrive with her herbal teas, Dita is with some flouncy guy in a pirate-inspired outfit who is holding up swaths of fabric to her face and muttering "fabulous" and "bella" again and again while a dozen personal assistants flurry around, asking her if the room is ivory enough for her. Weird.

But probably the best job of the day comes from the Edelweiss Suite. Cathy, long-suffering personal assistant to internationally successful boy band God Created Man, calls up begging Rosco to whip up some late brunch for her three pop stars. Siegmund asks if we want to deliver it. Try to stop us!

After a lot of swearing on Rosco's part, Claude and I set off to the Edelweiss Suite with a trolley laden with eggs Benedict, coffee and croissants, only to be met at the door by the one, the only, international sex god Jenson Carter! He's wearing nothing but a cheeky smile and small hand towel covering his dangly bits.

Gnnnnnnngnnnn! Claude and I nearly faint with glee.

"Come in! Come in, ladies!" Jenson smiles, beckoning us into the suite.

Claude just stands there opening and closing her gob. "But . . . but . . . you're nak—" she burbles.

"Move it, sister!" I hiss, dragging Claude into the suite.

The band checked into Harbinger Hall only at 1 A.M. that morning, but the place already looks like a herd of wildebeest stampeded through it. The place smells of feet, farts and pot noodles—the smell of all boys' bedrooms since the beginning of time. Everywhere you look there are clothes, shoes, plates, discarded bottles of booze and dirty glasses.

"Sorry 'bout the mess, girls," apologizes Jenson. "Me, Lonny Larson and the boys had a little poker game going last night. Things got a little wild."

Next door in the main master bedroom, lying zonked out on his front, in the middle of a four-poster bed, is a totally unconscious Sebastian Porlock, the second gorgeous member of the shirt-phobic triumvirate.

This really throws me. I almost burst into tears with happiness. I've had a poster of Sebastian on my bedroom wall since I was fourteen. I mean, okay, he's not as swoonsome as Spike Saunders, Duke of Pop, but he's still a tasty dish all the same. My mother once caught me crying inconsolably into my pillow one night because I'd finally figured out Sebastian would never be mine.

I've grown up a lot since then.

To our amazement, Sebastian Porlock is also totally and utterly stark naked. His small, pert tanned bottom cheeks greet us as we tumble into the bedroom to serve his eggs Benedict.

Sigh. It's such a perfectly formed, soft and blemish-free bottom, I want to bite it.

"Oooh! Er . . . aaaagh!" stutters Claude, covering her eyes.

"Good morning, er, afternoon . . . Mr. Porlock!" I shout. "We've brought breakfast."

"Sppghhhllgh," snores Sebastian, stretching a little before turning over on his back to reveal . . . well, to reveal more than I really wanted to see.

Euuuuuuugh!

"Oh, please!" squeals Claude as Sebastian snores like a trooper, legs akimbo. "My eyes! My eyes are burning! Cover him up! Aaaagggggh!"

But neither of us can pull the cover up for laughing.

"And a snorer too?" tuts Claude. "I can't stand that! So inconsiderate."

"Yes, Claude," I say, drying my eyes. "*So inconsiderate.* Hey, have you got your phone?" I chortle. "Let's send Fleur a picture!"

"Let's hope she's finished lunch," Claude laughs, snapping away.

Of course there are some guests Claude and I aren't exactly over the moon to see. Downstairs in the indoor tropical spa area, Cressida Sleeth and Panama Goodyear are relaxing by the pool in their teensy-tiniest bikinis. Neither of them has a single lump, bump or ounce of spare flab, and both are a gorgeous honey color from head to toe and all over their disconcertingly plentiful cleavages.

"Claude," I groan, as we approach with their drinks order, "have you noticed something different about Cress—"

"The boobs, right?" says Claude.

"Uh-huh," I say.

"It's not just Cressida," Claude says. "They've all gone up three cup sizes at least."

"Have they had surgery?" I whisper.

"Dunno," says Claude, furrowing her brow. "I shall have to investigate."

"How are you going to—" I begin, but then Cressida spots us.

"Oh, wonderful," she says through gritted teeth. "It's the phantom flan flingers. Still slaving away, I see, girls? Well done, Claude; you'll stay off the streets yet."

Claude narrows her eyes, then serves Cressida her elderflower infusion.

"Tsk. Ignore them, Cressida," Panama sneers. "It's so totally déclassé to chitchat with staff. My mother won't even make eye contact with our cleaner."

Yards away, Abigail and Leeza are splashing about in the whirlpool, Leeza's ginormous boobs acting as her own flotation system. At a nearby table a group of MTV producers are holding an impromptu meeting to discuss tomorrow's Booty Quake.

"Oh, Abigail," Panama yells across the spa, intentionally loud enough for everyone to hear, "being surrounded by all these music industry types really takes me back. It puts me in mind of when we almost signed that recording contract."

Abigail cringes a little. Panama, Abigail and Leeza did once have an amateur pop band. Catwalk, they were called. It was the closest thing you could get to audible excrement.

"Well, it was more of a hobby," blushes Abigail. "We weren't very good."

"Rubbish!" squawks Panama. "We were far hotter than half of these losers playing tomorrow."

Several of the MTV crew and assorted Mortuary Team members stop what they are doing and stare crossly over at Panama.

"Shh, Panama," hushes Cressida, visibly shrinking into her lounger. "Everybody will hear!"

"I want them to hear!" storms Panama. "I happen to know that I've got star quality. If you're hanging with me, you better fasten your seat belt, because I'm going places fast. I'm going to be a famous singer one day, mark my words. Listen!"

Panama clears her throat, then scrunches her face up and begins to sing. *"Oooooh, I'm floating in the sky!"* she squeals. *"Like a big love pie! I'm running to your love. Oh meeeee! Oh my!"*

Panama sounds like she has her bottom caught in a paper shredder. She's using that excruciating singing technique bad singers always use, taking a perfectly normal song, then making it last fifty-five minutes longer by doing wibbly-wobbly key changes on every note. The MTV staff are actually running out of the room clutching their ears.

"They're off to call their managers," says Panama, nudging Cressida proudly. "Tell them there's a new star in town."

them upstairs

At 8 P.M. I stagger back to the West Turret, through the crowds of pop stars, journalists and assorted hangers-on in the hotel lobby, feeling utterly exhausted. There's no way Scrumble can stop us from going to Booty Quake tomorrow. We've worked our butts off.

In the flurry of orders I managed to lose Claude entirely. I last saw her chatting with a journalist from the *The Mirror* in the day spa area. He was giving her his card in case she had any inside scoops. Then, when it was time for us to clock off, Gene and Leon told me Claude had been sent by Scrumble to the Windsmore Suite to clear dirty plates away from Panama and Co.'s rooms.

I am a little worried about her, actually. It sucks facing that lot alone.

The second I enter our apartment, I grab a dining chair, pull down the trapdoor and climb up into the loft, where Fleur is sitting on a blanket on the dusty floor surrounded by swaths of material, glitter and sequins.

"Hurray, you're back," she smiles. "How's it going?"

"Veronica!" smiles Saul, who is lying on his sleeping bag on the other side of the loft about twenty meters away. Saul chucks down his *Ripboard Monthly* magazine, rushes across and proceeds to wrap his arms around my waist and give me a big snog.

"Eeeuuuuuuh, get a room," groans Fleur, covering her eyes.

"Ha! Sorry," I laugh, pushing Saul away gently. "So what have you two layabouts been doing all day?"

"Well, when the coast was clear downstairs," Fleur says, "Saul crept down and went off surfing. Apparently he's got some surf thingy to do tomorrow . . ."

"Fleur," I tut, "Saul's one of the Demonboard Surf contestants tomorrow."

"What? Are you?" coughs Fleur, looking at Saul. "Oh!

That's what you were wibbling on about. I heard something about, y'know, surfboards or something, then I sort of switched off. Sorry, Saul."

We can't help laughing at her.

"Anyway, back to me," Fleur says. "So once Saul had gone, I spent the day preparing. Y'know, having a bath, exfoliating, pedicure, manicure, eyelash tint, that sort of thing."

"And then I got back from the beach," Saul interrupts. "And I thought I'd been followed."

"So we thought we'd better hide," says Fleur, who's loving her new "Secret Squirrel" lifestyle, "which gave me time to make this!"

Fleur proudly holds up a black halter-neck bikini with small silver stars and pink bows on it. The bottom section has tiny little pink ties.

"That's amazing!" I say. "You did that yourself?"

"Not just a pretty face, huh?" she smiles.

"You'll look great in that tomorrow," I nod enthusiastically.

"No, I won't," Fleur says. "I'm wearing my fabulous cerise polka-dot bikini from It's a Girl's World. *You're* wearing this one!"

"Oh . . . hmmm," I groan, staring at the bikini, which now appears to have shrunk to the size of a snowflake. "Wonderful."

"Ronnie, you're not flaking out on me, are you now?" says Fleur.

"No, I'm not. It's just . . . ," I mutter.

"Saul, tell her," commands Fleur.

"I don't need to tell her," says Saul, wrapping his arms around me again and nuzzling my neck. "She knows she's a babe."

"Yak!" sneers Fleur, looking physically sick. "Not like that!"

Saul and I both start blushing.

"Now then, Ronnie Ripperton," says Fleur, "this is the eleventh hour. I know I'm going to try my hardest to win that money tomorrow. And you are too. All you need to do is smile, prance about a bit and don't say anything nincompoopish when the cameras start rolling."

Fleur pauses. She shakes her head.

"Okay, scrap that," she says. "Just don't fall over or insult any of the judges."

"Gotcha," I nod.

Just then we hear movement downstairs. We all freeze.

"It's just meeeeeeeeeeee," shouts Claude. The trapdoor opens and Claude's face appears through the hole. "I'm coming up."

After a small struggle, Claude Cassiera is up in the loft, looking around in amazement.

"Wow! It's soooo much nicer up here now," says Claude, wrinkling her nose playfully at Saul. "That terrible smell of underpants has gone."

"Oh, don't start," groans Saul. "Look, I didn't ask you three to invade my penthouse. This was my home, can I remind you?"

"Saul, Saul, Saul," sighs Claude, shaking her head. "Don't even start me on the legal impossibility of that. Now, anyway, everyone be quiet, because I need to tell you about my afternoon."

"Go on," I say.

"Well, after I left you, I had the pleasure of taking Warren Acapulco's dog Trixiebelle Frou Frou for a whoopsie in the garden."

"Euuuuuh, gross," sniffs Fleur.

"And I got a hundred-pound tip for my trouble," says Claude.

"Hot dang," chuckles Saul, shaking his head. "It'll need a dump tomorrow too, won't it? Can I take it?"

"No way," laughs Claude. "That dog is the gift that keeps on giving. I'm going to pop up later and give it extra dinner. Oh, and listen to this: guess who just saw Psycho Killa, in the flesh, right in front of her eyes?"

Claude pauses dramatically, then points at herself. "Meeee!" she giggles.

"What does he look like?" I ask.

"Mmm, to be honest, small and quite camp," says Claude, shaking her head. "He was wearing this blue Lycra jumpsuit with silver buttons. Actually, he put me in mind of your aunty Susan's godson."

"Oh," I say, feeling slightly disappointed. I half expected him to be holding a severed human head, just like on the cover of *Body Bag Holiday.*

"And finally," says Claude, looking rather mischievous, "I've just been up to the Windsmore Suite. I was sent to collect all of Panama and Cressida's filthy plates and cups. And let their putrid bathwater out. Yuk. They don't call them filthy rich for nothing."

"Oh dear. Are you okay?" I say. "Were they being nasty?"

"No," says Claude. "They weren't there. They'd gone into Destiny Bay. They were having dinner with some pro surfers— well, according to hotel gossip."

A small crafty smirk sweeps across Claude's face. "So I had a little snoop around in their vanity cases," she says.

"Naughty," I giggle.

"And," she says, slowly, "I think I've got to the bottom of their collective boob growth."

"Spill it!" I gasp, moving closer.

"It's so gross," says Claude. "They've been taking some weird hormone boob-grow pills. And far too many of them, by the looks of it."

"What?" gasps Fleur. "Noooo! There's no such thing! You can't take pills to make your boobs swell up four cup sizes. I should know—I asked my doctor about it when I was thirteen."

"She's right," I say sensibly. "You can't get a hold of such a thing."

"You can if your father is head of chemical research at a major pharmaceutical firm," Claude says. "You can get a hold of whatever you want. Tested or untested."

"Noooo," squeals Fleur. "That's terrible! It's illegal. And dangerous too!"

The LBD stand looking at each other in total shock.

"Well, thank God they didn't catch you snooping," I say eventually. "That was lucky."

"Lucky for me," Claude says, but then under her breath she mutters, "but for them, rather unfortunate."

Chapter 8

booty quake

It's the day the LBD has been dreaming about for months.

Saturday, August 14th!

The Big Beach Booty Quake!

Destiny Bay, which is hectic at the best of times, is absolute bedlam. Kids are flocking in from miles around, pouring off trains and jumping off buses, road-blocking the surrounding streets with their cars, each one reverberating with pumping bass lines and loud hip-hop. It's 11 A.M. and the sun's already blazing down. There isn't a single cloud in the sky, nor on the horizon, which means most of the kids flooding down onto the sand are already in states of undress, revealing their skimpiest bikinis and pumped abs.

Down on Misty Beach several huge outside broadcast vehicles and dozens of stressed-out staff are working away on today's live TV show, which is beaming out on MTV, the Extreme Sports Channel and Entertainment News Europe. Everywhere you look, hairy, sweaty technicians are fiddling with TV cameras, speakers and lighting rigs or congregating around the various marquees and soundstages, checking clipboards and barking into walkie-talkies. Meanwhile researchers are dispensing green VIP wristbands to various important bods as they enter the front gate.

In the midst of this chaos, Claude and I are running as fast as we can, apologizing to Fleur on my phone for being so very, very late.

"But you were meant to be here two hours ago! The Demonboard competition has started," Fleur screeches into her mobile phone. "You've missed Round One! Saul's just paddling out for his second now."

"It's not our fault! Scrumble made us do breakfast!" I cry, feeling terribly guilty as we battle our way through the crowd. "Then we hitched a lift from Harbinger Hall with Raw-T, Psycho Killa's sushi chef. But one of the tires blew coming down the coast road. We've had to run the last mile!"

"Well, you're here now anyway, so just . . . hurry up . . . ," shouts Fleur, suddenly sounding rather distracted. "Oooh . . . oh noooo . . . Oh, bad luck, Saul! Never mind."

"What's happening?" I gasp.

"Errr . . . it doesn't matter," Fleur shouts. "Just get down here now! The Extreme Channel cameras keep floating past, filming crowd shots. Paddy has just called. He says he's already spotted me on Channel 214 wearing next to nothing and chatting up surfers! He says if I don't put a cardigan on immediately, he's going to drive down and take me home. Ha ha ha!"

"We're coming!" we yell.

Eventually, among the melee of oily bodies we spot Fleur's fuchsia sun hat, blonde locks and huge aviator sunglasses. She looks totally radiant in an emerald bikini top and black hot pants, standing beside the Demonboard Surf Championship judges' marquee. Her ruby lip gloss is glinting in the sun.

"Fleuuuur," we shout. "We're here!"

"Hurray!" she smiles.

"Where's Saul?" I say. "How's he doing?"

"He's over there in the competitors' enclosure," says Fleur. "Those gorillas dressed as security guards over there say I've not got a green VIP wristband to get in."

Over in the enclosure, I can just about make out Saul Parker's crazy brown dreads among the nine other competitors. Saul looks really unhappy. Almost like he might cry.

Just then, rapturous applause sweeps through the crowd as Finn Talbot, a blond shaved-headed guy with huge pecs from New Zealand catches a perfect wave and begins ripping along it, right on the end of his board for well over twenty seconds. Saul's shoulders slump farther.

Right at that moment, I'm filled with an urge to run across the sand, hug Saul and tell him that this whole daft surf contest just doesn't matter, but I know that would go down like a cup of cold vomit. Surf gods must look macho at all times, you see. There's a lot of testosterone splashing about among these extreme sports guys. I mean, some of them are even having arm-wrestling competitions while waiting for their round.

Sad, I know.

"Okay, so things aren't so good," Fleur says. "Santiago Marre, the Argentinian dude, is in the lead—he's surfed two great waves. Then Finn Talbot, that blond guy with the shaved head, is in second place. And y'see that dark-haired lad over there with the ponytail and the huge shark bite on his back? He's in third."

"And Saul?" I ask.

"Sixth," winces Fleur. "His first wave was pretty good, but on the second he wiped out after about five seconds."

Saul looks rather awkward as we all stare silently toward the enclosure. All the other competitors look totally at home there. They all have more expensive surfboards than Saul and high-tech wet suits with their sponsors' names splashed across the chests. None of them look like they've spent a month living in a loft, existing on stolen biscuits.

Inside the competitors' enclosure, a gaggle of beautiful models in tiny bikinis with huge boobs are frothing around, fawning over the surfers. "Oh, good luck, Sandybago darling!" shouts one plummy-mouthed brunette girl. "You can do it!"

"Accchhhoooo," sneezes another of the girls. "Will somebody fetch me a parasol, please? This direct sunlight is making me sneeze. I'm a photophobic, don't you know."

Ugh! I don't believe it. Cressida, Panama and the other witches are in the competitors' enclosure.

"Noooo!" I groan. "It's them! They've got green wristbands."

"Oh God," sighs Fleur. "The Argentinians must have sorted them out with VIP passes. That's who they must have been having dinner with last night."

Claude says nothing. She just rolls her eyes, then ignores them.

"That's totally unfair," tuts Fleur, as Panama purrs and bats her eyelashes at Santiago and he struts around in front of her like a caveman flexing his muscles. They make a hilarious couple. "I've been giving Santiago the full Fleur Swan flirty-flirt treatment for more than two weeks now," she moans. "And I've got nowhere! It's illogical!"

As Saul paces around, nervously watching the other surfers' performances, he spots me in the crowd. He nods toward the scoreboards and looks sort of embarrassed.

"You can still do it," I mouth.

"Thanks, babe," Saul mouths back, looking rather unconvinced.

"Hang on. I've been thinking: This isn't as bad as it looks," announces Claude, pointing at the scores. "Quite a few of the contestants have had a terrible third round so far. So if Santiago really messes up his last wave, and Saul can pull off something special, then logically Saul can still take third position."

"And there's prize money for third, isn't there?" says Fleur.

"Yeah," I say, as the announcer calls for Santiago Marre to come down for Round Three.

Santiago Marre, who looks as conceited as a human face would physically allow, quickly begins paddling out for his third and final wave. Once he's out, floating where the set waves are crashing down, the Argie heartthrob bobs around for a while searching for the perfect break. On the shore, the Windsmore Suite witches are leading the encouragement.

"Oh, get on with it, Sarabongo!" shouts Panama helpfully.

"Oh, this is so boring," moans Cressida. "Is it time to get ready for the beauty contest yet?"

But then things began to go awry for Santiago. The surf appears to be dying down dramatically. In fact, for the next long five minutes, dozens of little ripple waves proceed to wash past him, doing nothing except sweep the surf god back to the shore. And with the pressure growing to perform, the Argentinian appears to be losing his nerve.

Eventually, Santiago springs to life, catches a wave and jumps up . . . before losing his footing and crashing back into the water headfirst.

Santiago Marre has wiped out after two seconds!

"Oh, bad luck," says Fleur as Santiago grabs his board and staggers sulkily back to the shore, swearing loudly at anyone who commiserates with him. Panama immediately runs up and wraps herself around his salty torso like a giant limpet, trying to nibble his shoulder.

"Does that kick Santiago off first place?" mutters Fleur.

"I'm not sure," I say, squinting at the scoreboard and trying to do the math. I look for Claude to help me, but she's vanished.

"Next up, third round, is Saul Parker," announces the compere.

I can barely bring myself to watch.

"Oh, come on, Saul!" I will him, half covering my eyes as Saul walks to the water looking terrified. What's up with him? I know he's more than capable of beating any of these surfers. Only last night, I'd slipped down to the private beach and watched him tackle far bigger, crazier waves than these. I know he's more than capable of impressing the judges. I mean, sure, Saul may be of no fixed abode, with no firm plans for the future, no qualifications, and in fact may be as wild as wild can be, but the one absolute certainty about him is that he can surf like a professional.

If only he can do that now.

As Saul paddles out, the waves are whipping up again, crashing hard and fast around him. Without time to hesitate, Saul chooses a wave and goes with it, quickly leaping up onto his board with total confidence.

"Yessssssss! Come on, Saul!" I shout, beginning to roar loudly.

Quick as a flash, Saul is ripping along the crest of the wave, stepping right to the end of his board and hanging ten toes over the edge. As the crowd goes wild, the surf judges begin scribbling furiously on their pads.

"That's my friend's boyfriend!" Fleur is shouting proudly to anyone who will listen. "I know him! My best friend Ronnie is his girlfriend!"

"Fleur!" I blush as Saul wades proudly back up onto the beach, giving me a big wave. "He's not my boyfriend."

"Pardon?" laughs Fleur. "Well, he certainly thinks he is."

"He does?" I gasp, tingles rushing all over my body.

"Totally!" chuckles Fleur. "He never stops talking about you. I've spent the last few days in a flipping attic with him. I felt like putting cotton wool in my ears!"

"Ooooh!" I grin, going gooier by the second. "Really? He really thinks he's going out with me?"

"Yes!" splutters Fleur, shaking her head. "You total berk."

Down on the beach Finn Talbot is heading down to the water's edge to surf the final wave of the contest. I'm a little distracted now, though. I'm thinking about being Saul's girlfriend and what that actually means. My stomach is doing backward somersaults. I know I'm meant to be deliriously happy, and I am, but it's accompanied by all sorts of little anxieties. You see, I've started to think about Saul Parker all the time lately. Day and night. Night and day. And I feel like puking every time I see him, which appears to be the requisite side effect of finding someone you really fancy.

"Aw, just go with the flow, Ronnie. Have some fun!" laughs Fleur as we watch Finn jump up onto his board and rip along for about ten seconds to wild applause. As Finn washes up on the shore, the judges begin totting up their final scores.

"But I didn't plan to get another boyfriend so soon," I say. "Or feel this way so quickly. I mean, I hardly know him and—"

"Look, the main thing," interrupts Fleur, "is that you're soooo over Jimi Steele. How cool is that? You're dating again. You never have to cry about that pigeon-toed, dog-breath buttmunch ever again!"

Fleur has a point here. A smile sweeps across my face.

"Hey!" I grin, flapping my hands. "That's true. I've not even thought once about Jimi and Suzette Laws for over a fortnight. I'm cured!"

"Hosannah in the highest!" cries Fleur, flapping her hands in the air.

"Jesus saves!" I cheer.

"Alan is good!" cries Fleur.

"You mean Allah," I correct her.

"Praise him too!" laughs Fleur.

And suddenly a massive cheer erupts.

"Look! Look!" shouts Fleur, pointing at the scoreboards.

"There are the final scores. Saul's got third! He's come in third! That's excellent! He wins ten thousand pounds!"

I watch proudly as Saul staggers up the beach, spots the scoreboard and lets out a huge yelp. Then things get a little crazy. Finn Talbot, the winner, jumps on Saul and begins hugging him while jumping up and down. Nearby, Santiago Marre, who has ended up in second place, begins flipping out and threatening to kill the judges.

Suddenly, the crowd around the enclosure surges forward, knocking down the flimsy wooden barriers, as all the TV crews, sponsors and well-wishers clamor to be near the surfers. As security tries to lead away Santiago, who's in the midst of surf rage, people are popping corks on bottles of champagne and spraying it over Saul and Finn while the TV cameras beam the pictures out live on the Extreme Sports Channel and MTV.

Then Saul spots me, breaks free of the huddle and runs in my direction. "Veronica!" he shouts. "Ten thousand pounds! Not bad for a wildcard entry, eh?"

"I knew you'd do it!" I laugh, hugging him. Saul whisks me up and swings me around and around.

"Excuse me, Saul Parker," butts in a man, thrusting a microphone under both of our noses. A full TV camera crew is now surrounding us.

"You're live on Extreme Sports Channel!" says the man. "Now, Saul Parker, you were an unknown wildcard in the Demonboard contest and you've managed to grab third place and a hefty check. You must be ecstatic!"

Saul hugs me tight into his chest. "I'm stoked, man!" he tells the interviewer. "And can I just say I couldn't have done it without my girl, Veronica Ripperton! She put a roof over my head for the last few weeks while I was in training. She's a total star."

I try to look cool, but all I can do is grin and give a big involuntary "thumbs-up" to the camera. Uggghhh! That does it: I'm cutting my thumbs off as soon as I get home. It's not as if I ever hitchhike anywhere. They have to go.

"That was Saul Parker, viewers," says the presenter to the camera. "A sure surf star of the future."

"Saul? Can we interview you for a moment?" shouts MTV's Chloe Kissimy, whisking Saul away to the press enclosure.

As the camera crew follows him, Fleur grabs my arm. "Hey, Miss TV Star," she laughs. "Have you seen Claude?"

"Not for ages," I say, looking at my watch, suddenly remembering what we'd promised to do this afternoon.

"It's time to get ready for Miss Demonboard Babe," says Fleur, clearly relishing the horror.

"Okay, okay," I say, feeling nervous again. "Let's go and win Claude some money."

"That's the plan," says Fleur as we make our way toward the Demonboard Babe marquee where the dressing rooms are. "Hey, and that reminds me, what's Saul going to do with his ten thousand pounds? Is he going to buy you something nice? Diamonds? A new bass guitar?"

"Oh, that cash is all spoken for," I smile, proudly thinking of my surf-hero "boyfriend."

But then I stop dead in my tracks remembering what Saul is really spending his money on.

He's going to Australia.

game on

"Okay, ladies, can I have your attention, please?" begins Candice, the Miss Demonboard Babe organizer, shouting above the brewing girly chaos. In the backstage dressing room, fifteen girls are attempting to share two wall mirrors, two electrical sockets and one loo. You need extremely sharp elbows and a warrior instinct if you want some mirror time with your lipstick.

"Don't touch my hair straighteners!" Leeza Palmer is yelling at Tina, a drippy Icelandic chick who has mistakenly picked them up. "I'll have you prosecuted for theft."

"Girls, girls!" shouts Candice. "This is supposed to be a fun competition. There are no prizes for being a bitch."

"Nonsense," tuts Panama Goodyear, examining her manicured talons. "There's always a prize for that."

As Tina ducks out of the way, looking rather wobbly lipped, Panama's friend Abigail adjusts the straps on her gold Miu Miu frock, wearing a rather perturbed expression. Elsewhere, in the far left corner of the room, Svetlana Varninka from Vladivostok is buttoning up her tiny black silk shift dress, muttering something crossly under her breath. Even when Svetlana's content, she looks just on the brink of killing someone with a Bruce Lee one-inch punch.

"Are you okay over there, Miss Varninka?" shouts Candice. "Happy?"

"Extremely happy," scowls Svetlana.

"Excellent," says Candice. "So, ladies, the show will be

broadcasting live on MTV and Extreme Sports. Has everybody signed their legal waivers to say they agree to be on TV?"

"I have!" Fleur yells happily, rubbing light-reflecting moisturizer into her brown legs.

"Fleur, you look amazing!" I say as Fleur stands up, then spins around, showing off her hot-pink halter-neck Latino-style dress, whooshing her hair about with her hands.

"Cheers, Ronnidge!" Fleur laughs, pausing to help me zip up my favorite lucky strappy black dress. There's something about the way this dress hangs on my body that always gives me extra confidence. This dress has seen so many fabulous LBD nights out.

But as Fleur and I chat and giggle, Panama and Cressida are glowering at us both across the room. "Oh, hello there, Ronnie," Panama yells across, pointing at my dress. "I see we're going down the old tried-and-tested route, are we?"

I put my head down, pretending to be deaf.

"Awww, I love that old dress," coos Cressida, who's clutching a bunch of tissues in her hand. Her voice sounds croaky.

"I never get tired of seeing it," snipes Panama.

"Right, ladies," interrupts Candice. "The plan is really straightforward. Round One will be judged by the clap-o-meter. That's where five of you will be eliminated. Next round, we move on to swimwear, where the judges will vote off another five ladies. Then the remaining five girls will come back in daywear—that is, jeans, T-shirts, whatever you like—and have a little talk to Lonny Larson about why they're the perfect Demonboard Babe . . . blah blah blah . . . and then the judges vote. All clear?"

"Yes!" we yell.

"And I'm sure you know," smiles Candice, "that first prize is twenty thousand pounds in cash? Well, I can also say that the check is available to take away today as soon as the winner is announced."

Claude takes a sharp intake of breath.

"Second prize is a holiday for two in Barbados," continues Candice, "and third prize is a five-thousand-pound shopping expedition to It's a Girl's World at Emerald Park Shopping City."

The LBD look at each other nervously. We have to get first prize. Nothing less will do.

"Any questions?" asks Candice.

"Me!" says Panama, looking slightly drag-queenish in her purple Dolce and Gabbana dress. "When I win, can I get the money transferred directly into my account? Because I don't handle money."

"Let's cross that bridge when we come to it," sighs Candice. "Any other questions?"

"Is anyone in the bathroom right now?" blurts out Abigail before walking briskly to the loo, clenching her bum cheeks together, slamming the door behind her.

"Anything else?" asks Candice.

"Acccccchhhhooooooo! I've gotsh a queshtion?" sniffs Cressida, whose eyes are now becoming rather red-rimmed. "Doesh anyone have a pet in here? I've already taken two antihistamine pills, and I still feel very sneezy! I have a pet hair allergy, you see, and . . ."

Everybody just ignores her and carries on getting ready.

"Okay, eight minutes till showtime!" shouts Candice. "Good luck, ladies."

At the side of the room, Claude sits quietly in front of a mirror, looking totally exquisite in her favorite black vintage dress with silver strappy sandals and a fake-diamond necklace. When Fleur and I had reached the dressing room, we'd found Claude already there, practically ready to rock. She told us she knew how busy it was going to be, so she'd got down here early.

As Claude sits there, painting on a layer of lip gloss, she looks rather distracted. I know she spoke to her mum earlier today and Gloria felt sure they had a buyer for Lister House. A young couple had looked around just that morning remarking that "with a lot of work" the flat would be their "perfect starter home."

"*A lot of work?*" Claude had repeated to me crossly, imagining all her Lister House memories being torn out and wallpapered over by a pair of newly marrieds. "But that place is perfect! It's my home. What are they going to do to it?"

I look across at Claude. We have to keep the faith that one of us can win this thing. We have to stay strong.

"Four minutes," shouts Candice as the entire room erupts into a frenzy of last-minute titivation. "Start making your way to the stage wings now."

"Hey, Ronnie, is that your phone ringing?" yells Fleur, spraying her hair and pointing at my makeup bag, which is vibrating and playing a tune.

"Yeah!" I shout, trying to fix a rose hair clip into place. "Have I got time?"

"Hurry up. We're going!" shouts Fleur.

"Got it," I yell, grabbing the handset. It has to be Saul wishing me good luck.

"Hellooooo!" I yell above the girly din.

"Ronnie?" shouts the voice. "Are you there, Ronnie?"

"Mum!" I yell. "Is that you?"

"Yes, it's me. The woman time forgot!" Mum chuckles, sounding much more like her old feisty self. "Hang on, speak to your brother for a second." There's a muffled sound and then a soft squelchy raspberry noise on the line that sounds like "Wonnnnnopghhhl."

My heart melts. Suddenly it hits me how much I have missed them all.

"Hear that?" laughs Mum, bringing the phone back to her. "That was poor Little Lord Fauntleroy asking why he's been abandoned."

"Aw, tell him I'm sorry. I've been busy!" I shout, dearly hoping that my voice is drowning out a heated exchange between Svetlana and Leeza over a tube of false eyelash glue.

"Anyway, Ronnie, Paddy Swan just called me," shouts Mum. "He says you're going to be on telly or something? Fleur told him to watch MTV this afternoon!"

"Erm, well, oooh," I cringe. This is totally the opposite of what I wanted!

"This sounds very exciting!" says Mum. "Are you being interviewed about Destiny Bay?"

"Well, erm . . . something like that," I mumble.

"'Cos I'm out today, you see. I'm at the wholesaler's," shouts

Mum. "So I've rung Aunty Susan and Aunty Cath and Gloria Cassiera and they're going to tape it for me. And I've just seen Mr. McGraw in the post office, so I told him to watch out for it too. And your dad says he'll put it on the wide-screen in the pub downstairs."

"Well, you don't have to go to all that bother . . . ," I mumble, beginning to feel bilious.

"Oooh, my little girl, eh?" shouts Mum. "A TV travel expert? I'm going to be so proud!"

"Er, I don't think so," I mumble, feeling faint.

"Break a leg, darling!" yells Mum.

"Thanks, Mum," I say, hanging up, not knowing whether she'll see the funny side of this one within the next decade.

"Girls, I need you outside now!" shouts Candice. "There must be at least two thousand people waiting for you, and they're getting impatient!"

"C'mon, Ronnie," Claude shouts, grabbing my arm and whisking me out of the dressing room. "Let's go and smile nicely for the judges."

"Hey, who are the judges, by the way?" asks Fleur, tagging along behind, taking one last look in the mirror. "That was the one thing I could never find out."

"Oh, I can tell you that," says Candice, who's chivvying us all along. "There are four. There's Finn Talbot, the guy who won Demonboards. Then Freaky Death Squad from the Mortuary Team, Sebastian Porlock from God Created Man . . . and finally . . . ," Candice checks her clipboard again. "We've got local dignitary Lord Vanderloo, owner of Harbinger Hall. No, hang on, he canceled at the last minute with a golfing injury . . . so we've got another head honcho from Harbinger Hall. Helga, erm, Scrumble? That name ring any bells?"

"Oh yes," the LBD say, marching intrepidly toward the stage. "Ding dong."

~~~~~~~~~~~~~~~~~~~~~~~~~~~~~~

♪howtime

It's 3 P.M. and the sun is blazing down on the Demonboard Babe marquee as Warren Acapulco plays out a loud mix of R & B and hip-hop to the hectic party crowd marauding all over the entire beach. As far as the eye can see, thousands of kids are winding their waists and quaking their booties, trying to get their faces in front of the MTV cameras.

Meanwhile, waiting in the wings of the stage stand the Demonboard Babes. Well, everyone aside from Abigail Munro, who's mysteriously vanished.

"Oh, where is she?" tuts Panama, her face suggesting she's not overly bothered.

"Shhhpgh, she's in the toilet," sniffles Cressida, mopping her dripping nostrils.

Eventually, after a lot of banging on the cubicle door by Candice, Abigail appears, stepping precariously toward the stage with a highly contorted face. It's as if she's concentrating really hard on carrying a ten-pence piece between her butt cheeks or something.

Then, as she draws parallel with Claude and I, she pauses and throws both perfectly manicured hands over her mouth. A loud rumble erupts from her tummy, followed by a high-pitched squeakity-squeak of the bottom variety!

Did I just hear what I think I heard?

"Claude," I hiss, shooing away a growing stench. "I don't think Abigail's feeling very well!"

"Hmmm," smiles Claude, wearing a highly angelic expression as she cups her arm around my waist and pulls me close to her. "Well, Ronnie, I'd advise you to keep your eye on Abigail Munro. She may have inadvertently swallowed laxatives, mistaking them for boob-grow pills."

"What?" I gasp. "How?"

"Oh, it's just a little joke," smiles Claude, repeating Abigail's phrase from the Windsmore Suite tea party. "I mean, can't she take a joke?"

"Hello, Destiny Bay!" screams Lonny Larson as the crowd goes crazy, whistling, clapping and letting off Klaxon horns. "I wanna hear you make some noise for the one, the only, the legendary, Miss Demonboard Babe contest!"

As Fleur, Claude and I stand nervously awaiting our cue, the judges are taking their seats. We can see Freaky D from the Mortuary Team, wearing a green plastic body bag with armholes slashed in each side and a wonky Gucci headband, flipping peace-out signs at the TV camera. Next to him sit Finn Talbot and Sebastian Porlock, both looking dangerously snoggable. Then beside them, not looking in the slightest bit snoggable—in fact, more slappable—sits Helga Scrumble, who is a vision of frumpiness in her horn-rimmed glasses and stiff Harris Tweed.

Scrumble is staring directly at me, so I give her my best amiable grin, which she reciprocates with her trademark Scrumble death glare. It's at this point that I remember Saul announcing to the whole of Europe on live TV that I gave him "a roof over his head" for the past month. Oh no. Busted!

And just when I think Scrumble can't look any more irate, she spots Fleur Swan, pirouetting about beside me giddily in a pink dress. Yes, the very same Fleur Swan I promised I'd loaded aboard the 4:38 P.M. train out of Destiny Bay more than a week ago. Scrumble whips off her specs and polishes them furiously, quite clearly hoping she's seeing things.

"And now, with no further ado, can we get a big cheer for the Demonboard Babes?" yells Lonny. "Bring on the girls!"

Aaaaaghhh! There's no going back now!

Panama Bogwash goes first, sashaying onto the stage with a smug smile, throwing kisses to her awaiting public, with Cressida trotting behind her sneezing and coughing with every step, followed by Leeza, then Svetlana, then me, Claude, Fleur, Tina and then six other girls. As the crowd spots us all, the roar almost knocks me off my feet. And to my utmost pleasure, there seems to be a crowd of gorgeous surf dudes right on the front, hanging over the safety barrier, wolf-whistling and yelling my name!

"Veronnnnnnica!" yells Saul, as we all take our first circuit around the stage before lining up along the back wall. "Hey, lads, that's her! That's my woman!"

Okay, normally I'd be totally opposed to any bloke saying I was his possession. But darn it, when Saul Parker says it, it sounds kind of primitive mannish and cool. I am Saul's woman!

"Oh, where's Abigail gone to now, Leeza?" tuts Panama. "I thought she was with us."

"I'm here, don't worry," says Abigail, appearing from the

wings, walking very slowly with her knees locked together, clearly determined to make an appearance. However, as she crosses the stage, passing the judges' table, Freaky D's nose wrinkles. He turns to Finn Talbot and raises an eyebrow.

"Man, did you squeeze cheese?" Freaky D laughs, nudging Finn with his elbow.

"What?" laughs Finn, shaking his head, then pointing at Sebastian. "Nah, not me! It must have been Mr. Boy Band here."

By this point Sebastian has his nose cupped in his hands, looking like the toxic fumes are poisoning him. "Not guilty!" moans Sebastian. "But whoever let that one go better get themselves to a doctor. They're clearly unwell."

As the male judges roar with laughter, Scrumble takes a small bottle of smelling salts out of her bag and inhales deeply. Meanwhile Abigail carries on with her promenade of the stage, walking like she's fractured her bottom.

"What's up with you?" hisses Panama. "Stop walking like a freak!"

"I can't help it," mumbles Abigail. "I've got a bad stomach."

With all fifteen contestants now lined up at the back of the stage, the MTV cameras sweep up and down the line, filming us. I try to do my best noncheesy smile and wave, knowing that everyone at the Fantastic Voyage is watching. Claude does a dainty wave, while Fleur begins pulling rock 'n' roll devil horns with both hands and doing a fancy "jump and wind" dance move. Okay, she looks pretty daft, but at least she's happy.

"Aren't they all gorgeous?" yells Lonny. "But sadly, now it's time to eliminate some lovelies. So let's make some noise for the Demonboard Babe clap-o-meter machine!"

"Good luck, girls," shouts Fleur, crossing her fingers and jumping up and down even more.

"You're bound to be safe, Ronnie," whispers Claude, nudging me and pointing down at Saul's gang, who are whistling and cheering. "Your fan club has been going wild down on the front row."

"Yeah, Ron," laughs Fleur, "you'll walk away with this one!"

But just as I begin to beam with joy, I spot the clap-o-meter. Or the *crap-o-meter*, as it should have been called. It's not a scientific noise-level meter at all—in fact it's just a rubbish box with "clap-o-meter" written on the side in red crayon, and some milk-bottle tops and old egg cartons stuck on to it by a crowd of preschoolers. My heart groans as Lonny walks along the line shouting names out and pointing at us, with the crowd cheering equally wildly every time. Suddenly I realize that the first round is a complete joke—anyone can be kicked out.

After a few minutes of total bedlam, Lonny fiddles with his earpiece and calls for silence.

"I have the results!" Lonny shouts. "And that was a really tough one to decide, but I can tell you now that the five girls we're saying good-bye to in Round One are Amy Harding, Tatiana Winehouse, Gail Winters . . ."

"What!?" huffs Amy Harding, a tiny slip of a girl in a dress so indecent she's clearly wearing it only for legal reasons. "You're getting rid of me? Are you insane? I'm the only one you'd even look twice at in the street."

"But . . . I . . . I . . . ooooooooooh!" begins Tatiana Winehouse, dissolving into tears as her friend Gail Winters wraps an arm around her shoulder and blubs in unison.

Meanwhile, poor Lonny is trying to continue with the list. "Also leaving in this round," he shouts, "is Abigail Munro!"

"Now there's a shock," says Panama, holding her nose and elbowing Abigail, who is standing beside her. Abigail simply shrugs in acceptance as some security guards elbow past us all, trying to remove Amy Harding, who is up at the judges' desk squaring up to Freaky D and calling him a "blinkered fool."

"And, erm, finally this round," shouts Lonny above the racket. "We're saying good-bye to . . . Fleur Swan! Give them all a big hand now, everyone!"

Oh my God! Fleur is out!

Our trump card has been eliminated.

Claude and I glare at each other in total horror.

This is terrible, but worse still, Fleur clearly hasn't heard that her name has been called. As Candice begins to chivvy all of us girls off the stage, back to the dressing rooms, our blonde friend is still clapping and smiling, blissfully ignorant of her fate.

"Fleur!" shouts Claude. "Fleur, come here."

Fleur looks directly at Claude, stopping clapping for a second to give us both a big thumbs-up.

"Oh no," Claude groans, sidling over to Fleur and whispering something discreetly into her ear.

Fleur looks at her curiously, then asks her to say it again, which Claude does. Then Fleur's face crumples. I feel a sting in the back of my throat.

"C'mon, Fleur," whispers Claude, taking Fleur's hand and walking her off the stage, back toward the dressing room. "Don't take it personally. That clap-o-meter thing is a piece of garbage. It was totally random! You should have won. You're beautiful."

232

"Yeah," I say quietly, walking behind them, realizing that while Fleur is now history as a Demonboard Babe, Panama Goodyear, Cressida Sleeth and Leeza Palmer have all lived to fight another round.

Right, I think. This is war.

judgment day

Back in the dressing room, the atmosphere has turned decidedly belligerent.

"Oh, stop sniveling, Abigail," growls Panama, looking annoyingly sublime in a purple Gucci bikini with gold clasps. "I'll have the prize money in my hands within half an hour. We'll grab Sandybongo and the other Argies and go out and buy some bubbly to celebrate."

Abigail lets out a little sniffle.

"Look, keep on being a pain in the butt," Panama warns Abigail, "and I'll send you back to the Windsmore Suite."

Meanwhile, beside them, Leeza is beginning to boil over. "Right, who's got my bikini top?" she snarls, rifling through her Louis Vuitton carryall. "Hey you! Fake blonde with the bedraggled mop! Precious, is it? Where's my top?"

"Who, me?" whimpers Precious. "I've not touched your bag."

As Claude and I change into our swimwear, trying to ignore the fuss, Leeza becomes noisier and more personal.

"Somebody in here has stolen my bikini top! I can find the bottoms, but not the top!" Leeza fumes, her huge boobs juddering under her dressing gown. "Hey, Ruskie!"

"*Ja?*" replies Svetlana Varninka, throwing an icy glare.

"I know you've got it," Leeza bitches. "I mean, that bikini top would keep your peasant clan back home in potato vodka for a year."

"What did she say?" gasps Svetlana, pulling herself up at least two inches taller than I remembered her. "She called my family *what*?"

As the rest of the room winces, waiting for the inevitable bloodbath, Abigail begins to weep even louder. "Oh, borrow mine, Leeza!" Abigail cries, throwing her bikini top at her friend. "I won't need it now anyway."

"Cuh, that won't fit," tuts Leeza. "I had to preorder a double-D cup from Gucci in New York. It was the biggest one available! I packed it into my carryall to bring here last night. And now it's gone!"

Leeza simmers silently for a second before swiveling around to where Fleur is sitting sadly with her face in her hands, totally devastated about her Round One ejection.

"Oi, Swan!" shouts Leeza. "Want to give me my bikini top back? Now. Or else."

Fleur glares at Leeza with total revulsion in her eyes before throwing her head back, somehow finding the energy to defend herself. "Oh, my turn now, is it?" she yells. "Well, I've not touched your bikini top! In fact, what would I do with it anyway? Throw it over my dad's car in cold weather, you mega-boobed mutant?"

"Well said!" shouts Precious.

"Oh, shut it, thunderhips," snarls Panama, jabbing Precious in the chest and sending her flying backward into her makeup bag.

"Achhhhhooooooo!" splutters Cressida, standing meekly in her magenta bikini, rifling through her Miu Miu vanity case. Cressida's eyes are puffed up like golf balls. She's getting sneezier by the second.

"Leave Precious alone," roars Svetlana, waving her finger menacingly at Leeza, "or I'll paint you all over that wall!"

And with that, a tremendous fight erupts between Svetlana, Panama, Fleur, Leeza, Precious and almost every other female in the room. Makeup brushes are hurled, girls are shoving each other, all sorts of insults and accusations are being thrown. And all the while, one little Miss Claude Cassiera is calmly painting strawberry lip gloss onto her full lips and adjusting the straps on her camouflage bikini.

"Claude," I whisper as Svetlana begins to drag Leeza around the room with her hands gripping each of her earlobes, replicating some sort of World Wrestling Entertainment tackle, "what exactly have you done with Leeza's bikini?"

"I beg your pardon?" says Claude innocently, with just a soupçon of minx in her voice. "I've no idea what you're talking about."

"Claude," I say, shaking my head slowly, trying not to smirk. "The truth, now."

"Look, Ronnie," says Claude quietly. "If Leeza packed the bikini into her bag last night, then surely it must be there. Well, unless somebody went in her suite and moved it."

"Claude!" I gasp, looking around the room at the growing carnage. "And . . . and . . . what about Cressida? Is that your work too?"

"Who?" says Claude mischievously, powdering her nose.

"Cressida Sleeth," I repeat.

"Oh, *her*. Well, you know what Cressida's like," smiles Claude. "The slightest thing sets her off, doesn't it? Dust, detergents, dog hair. She's so fortunate that she doesn't need to work near them every day. Like I do."

Claude pauses for a second to stare across at the one-woman snot mountain. Cressida is waving something in the air that looks like a necklace while simultaneously shouting and sneezing.

"But then," continues Claude, looking at me and winking, "Cressida's so blessed her mother isn't dependent on her for money."

But by this point Claude's voice is being drowned out by Cressida's wailing. "Who is Trixiebelle Frou Frou? Is it a dog?" she squeals, standing beside her vanity case, waving what we can now see is a pink dog collar with a diamond-encrusted name tag. "Why is there a dog collar in my vanity case? Achooooooo! This is an outrage! I'm very, very highly allergic, you know!"

Just that moment Candice appears.

"Girls?" she yells. "What's going on? I could hear the shouting down the hallway. Is everything okay?"

"I'm unwell," bleats Cressida, brandishing the dog collar.

"Oh dear," says Candice. "Well, would you like to give Round Two a miss?"

"Yes," sniffs Cressida pitifully. "There's terrible negative energy around here. The marquee needs to be cleansed of its heavy aura. Do you have a shaman on staff?"

"Listen, Candice," butts in Leeza, "some thieving scumbag

236

has stolen my bikini top from my bag. I'm going to have to go out topless. Okay?"

"Noooo!" howls Candice. "It's not that sort of contest."

"Tsk," tuts Claude, watching the brewing chaos. "All that money. No class."

"Well, this is just wonderful!" shouts Leeza, pointing at Fleur, Claude and me. "Just because I'm in a different league of beauty from these ugly hounds, someone's sabotaged my chances of winning."

Candice rolls her eyes and looks at her wristwatch. "So Leeza, are you telling me you're not competing in the swimwear round? Because I need you to be ready, right now."

"I'm ready," smiles Panama, checking her perfect reflection in the mirror and heading for the door. "I was born ready. Catch you later, losers."

"Well, I'm ready too then," quacks Leeza. "Abigail, give me that bikini top. I'm wearing it in this round."

"But I thought it was too small," Abigail says.

"Shut up," huffs Leeza, flinging off her dressing gown and beginning to wrestle herself into the groaning top. Leeza's boobs look like they're being strangled to death. The left one keeps making a bid for escape, but Leeza keeps pushing it back in while nagging Abigail to tie the clasps tighter around the back. If that bikini top manages to survive one whole round without exploding, it will be miraculous.

"See?" says Leeza, checking herself in the mirror. "Not too shoddy, huh?"

"No, Leeza," winces Abigail. "You look great!"

"Oh, and incidentally," says Leeza, as she heads toward the door, "good luck, everyone. Especially you, Ronnie—you're going to need it." Leeza nods at my less ample cleavage with a little smirk. "Huh! No prizes for guessing what you'd spend your prize money on."

But as Leeza passes by, I spot something very, very wonderful indeed. Unbeknown to her, there's a large patch of brown goo smeared all over the back of her bikini bottom. It smells exactly like chocolate, but it looks like something very, very different.

"Oh my God," Fleur gasps. "Look! Look at Leeza's bikini briefs!"

"Ugh," I howl, laughing till tears ran down my face. "That's chocolate sauce, right?"

"Right," winks Claude, with a small self-satisfied grin.

So, okay, "Round Two: Swimwear" is a bit embarrassing.

But not a fraction as embarrassing as it is for Leeza.

Because with the entire crowd cheering and the TV cameras rolling, Leeza trots out onto the stage, sucking in her cheeks like a supermodel, with one hand on her hip and her nose aloft, totally oblivious to the large chocolate stain all over her cream bikini bottoms. As Leeza reaches the photo pit at the front of the stage, where snappers from the *Daily Mirror, The Sun, The Star* and *NME* are all gathered, they begin to snigger and point. Rapidly, the news spreads throughout the crowd. Then a slow handclap starts and some comedians begin to shout some rather uncharitable stuff.

"Hey, lady," yells one lad, as the entire crowd cracks up, "maybe that chicken vindaloo last night was a mistake!"

Leeza blows him an extra-special kiss.

"Hoo hoo!" squeals another girl. "Don't think your whites would pass any doorstep challenge. Think you need a better detergent!"

"Ha!" beams Leeza, turning to Panama, who's frantically signaling to her to get the heck off the stage. "See? They love me!"

"Keep the cameras rolling! This is priceless!" yells the MTV director to his cameraman as Leeza proceeds to strut to the front of the stage. She turns around and wiggles her bum suggestively at the camera, sending the crowd wild with glee. But suddenly, Miss Scrumble, who's been watching this whole pantomime with a thunderous expression, can't bear the agony a moment longer. She leaps up from behind the judges' table, whips off her Harris Tweed jacket and scurries toward Leeza, intending to wrap it around the offending chocolate stain.

"Unhand me, you mad old hag!" Leeza squeals, batting her away. Then, somehow in the ensuing tussle, Scrumble manages to garble something into Leeza's ear, making her stop dead in her tracks. Leeza slowly turns and examines her rear end with a look of growing horror.

The entire crowd falls silent, waiting for Leeza's reaction. Eventually a deafening scream pierces the air.

"Nooooooo," Leeza bawls. "Nooooooo! It's not what it looks like! It can't be!"

And with the crowd now in fits of hysterics, there's nothing left for Leeza to do but turn and leg it, trying to cover her bum with both hands as she runs.

After Leeza's humiliation, walking about in a bikini is a piece of cake by comparison. Claude and I simply throw our shoulders back and laugh our way through the whole thing. And when the judges' scores come back, Leeza and her chocolate bum have been eliminated . . . and me, Claude and Panama Goodyear have made it through to the final five.

little miss personality

It's crunch time.

The final "Interview" round.

First up with Lonny is Harbinger Hall's very own Precious, who, although sickeningly pretty and bodily perfect, is a tad, well, dull. Precious's interests seem to consist of aerobics, aqua-aerobics, yoga, going to the hairdresser's and most riveting of all, "collecting teapots." Thank God someone has a Klaxon horn in the crowd or else we'd all have fallen asleep.

"That was Precious, everyone, give her a big hand!" shouts Lonny, rubbing his eyes. "And next up, let's hear it for Claude!"

Claude is a different matter entirely, waltzing onto the stage in black hipsters and a hot-pink boob tube, shaking things up by announcing that one day she fully intends to be Claudette Cassiera: prime minister. The crowd really loves that. Especially when Claude announces her parliamentary manifesto, which includes banning balding men from combing their last hairs horizontally across the bald patch; government grants for sparkly lip gloss and nail extensions; and last but not least banning family

240

members over the age of thirty from disco dancing or playing air guitar at weddings!

"Wooooooo! I hear you, sister!" yells one girl while the crowd roars with delight. As Claude totters offstage, we all know she's made a huge hit.

Next along is Tina from Iceland, who floats onstage in a Hessian smock, carrying some sort of piccolo under her arm, only to tell Lonny that her Demonboard Babe prize money would be donated to War Moggy, a charity that rescues kittens with sore paws from war zones. Tina then grabs the microphone and starts singing "a song for peace" called "Whiskers Across the World." It isn't very good. Despite Freaky D and Sebastian Porlock trying to clap their hands supportively, the crowd appears to be turning on her.

"Look out, Tina!" yells Claude as something whizzes a fraction of a millimeter past Tina's ear and splats all over the stage.

I didn't realize people could be so accurate when flinging plastic cups of beer. I hope it was beer anyhow.

As Tina shuffles off, Lonny announces the next contestant, Panama Goodyear, who strides onto the stage snapping the straps of her purple bikini, then doing a little pirouette, wiggling her bottom, all to rapturous applause. Even some of Saul's gang on the front row are cheering wildly.

But that's the thing with Panama Goodyear—until she opens her big nasty mouth, you never know the hideousness that lies within.

"Hello, Panama," says Lonny. "And can I just say, you look gorgeous today."

"Yes, I do, don't I?" agrees Panama matter-of-factly.

241

Lonny starts giggling. He thinks she's being kooky.

"Now, there's some big prize money up for grabs," continues Lonny. "What will you do if you win the money?"

"Oh, well," Panama says, looking slightly distracted. "Don't know really. How much is it again?"

"It's twenty thousand pounds," Lonny reminds her.

"Oh. Not that much then," shrugs Panama. "I'll probably pay off my AmEx with it. It took quite a battering last month when Leeza and I did lunch, then hit Bond Street."

"Ha ha!" laughs Lonny, trying to cup Panama's waist. "Isn't she great? Such a dry sense of humor!"

"I don't like being touched," says Panama, picking Lonny's hands off her.

While most of the boys in the crowd are giggling, the girls are simply staring at her, not quite believing she's real.

"Anyway, Panama, you're a big hit with the lads today," says Lonny. "I just wonder, if a normal, everyday boy in the crowd wanted to ask you out, what chat-up line would win your heart?"

Panama looks at Lonny like he's berserk.

"A normal everyday boy," repeats Panama. "You're joking, yeah?"

"Er, no, not really," stutters Lonny.

"You know who I go out with, right?" coughs Panama. "I'm with Santiago Marre, the international king of pro surfing. I've got a green VIP wristband, for God's sake. I'm a VIP!"

"Oh, whoopie do!" jeers a female voice in the crowd.

"Hey, Panama," yells a male voice in the front row. "I'm a VIP too! Look!"

When we all look down, all we can see is a pair of bum cheeks mooning Panama from the front row. They appear to belong to Saul's friend Danny.

"Ugh!" squeaks Panama. "Put that away, you horrible, unwashed pig! See, Lonny, that's why I don't mix with commoners."

And with that Panama turns on her heel and storms offstage, winning the most rapturous applause of the day.

"Just relax, Ronnie," Fleur tells me as I wait nervously in the wings. "Deep breaths, in through the nose, out through the mouth."

"I'm fine," I lie, as the crowd cheers and my name is called. "I'll just be myself, eh?"

"Erm, yeah," yells Fleur. "Just, y'know, not too much. Good luck!"

Five seconds later, I'm back out onstage, in front of the crowd, as well as millions of people worldwide, with a TV camera almost stuck up my nose.

"Well, hello there, Miss Ronnie Ripperton," smiles Lonny, wrapping his arm around my waist.

"Ooooh, er, howdy!" I laugh, doing a weird military salute.

Noooo! My evil hand, which seeks to destroy me, is coming to life again!

"Having a good time today?" Lonny asks.

"Everything's just wonderful, thanks!" I beam, my thumb twitching to be held aloft beside my face in a wacky manner.

It *won't* get the better of me.

"So, Ronnie," says Lonny. "What do you do in your spare time? Any hobbies? Sports?"

Hobbies or sports? Errrrrrrm. My mind suddenly goes blank. I used to play a bit of swingball with my dad when I was seven. Noooo! Don't say that! What do I do in my spare time? Think, Ronnie, think.

"Oooh . . . erm," I mutter, examining my fingernails. "I've not got . . . I mean . . . er . . ."

"She surfs!" shouts a lad's voice in the front row. It's Saul! I look down, and all I can see is his crazy brown hair and impish eyes waving back at me.

"Oooh yeah, I go surfing!" I smile, suddenly finding my tongue. "And I play bass guitar. And I love hip-hop and metal. I try to get to a lot of gigs. And I'm into partying and just having a laugh really. Y'know?"

"Wow, Ronnie," tuts Lonny, "you sound like the perfect woman. You'll be telling us your dad owns a pub next!"

"Er, he does, actually," I reply, feeling slightly confused.

"And can I ask what you'd do if you won the Demonboard Babe money?" asks Lonny.

That's easy. I know that one. "I'm giving it all to my best friend," I tell him.

"Ha ha! Good one," laughs Lonny, throwing his head back with a chuckle. The crowd laughs along politely at my little joke.

"No, seriously," Lonny smirks. "What would you blow it on?"

"I am being serious," I say, feeling a little indignant. "I'll give it to my best friend. 'Cos . . . well, she sort of really needs it right now."

I look to the wings of the stage where Claude and Fleur are standing. Claude winks at me. She looks a little bit emotional.

"Blimey," says Lonny. "You must be the world's best mate."

"Well, I try my best," I say, feeling a bit puzzled again. "I mean, isn't that what friends are for? To help each other out when there's a crisis?"

The crowd isn't cheering now, though. They're sort of mumbling among themselves. They obviously think I'm some sort of freak.

I've totally blown it.

As I walk off stage, Scrumble, Freaky D and the rest of the judges are in a huddle, arguing furiously. I even hear my name being mentioned a few times, mostly by Scrumble, who doesn't exactly sound like she's my biggest cheerleader. She's obviously telling them what a dishonest, work-shy employee I am, just for good measure.

Eventually, after what seems like forever, Candice passes a gold envelope with the results to Lonny Larson. "And we're back!" shouts Lonny, signaling to the sound deck to turn down the music. All the original Demonboard contestants are gathered on stage now, Cressida, Abigail and Leeza included.

As Fleur wraps her arms around Claude and my shoulders, my heart's beginning to thump harder and faster. "Get on with it!" I mutter as Lonny stalls for time, pretending to be having trouble with the envelope.

Finally, he begins to read. "And in third place, winning the It's a Girl's World voucher worth five thousand pounds is . . . Precious Elton!"

Precious lets out a huge eardrum-piercing scream, clearly imagining blowing £5000 on Lycra aerobics thongs.

Claude and I look at each other fearfully.

"And in second place," reads Lonny, "winning a fabulous holiday for two to Barbados is . . . Tina Gunttersdorf!"

What? Miss Save the Kittens has won second place?

As Tina bursts into tears and begins to crank up a song of thanks on her piccolo, Panama swivels around and looks at the LBD with a large grin.

She's won and everyone knows it. It's Panama Goodyear, for crying out loud. As if I ever had a chance against her.

"And the Demonboard Babe first prize goes to . . . ," says Lonny, "with a three-versus-one judge decision . . . *Ronnie Ripperton!*"

Pardon?

Have we heard that right?

Suddenly everything seems to move in slow motion. Fleur is jumping on me, hugging me and squawking. Panama is jabbing Lonny in the chest and demanding to see his "superior." Claude is standing by herself in the middle of the stage sobbing. The crowd is cheering and dancing to Warren Acapulco, who's stuck on his hit track "Undercover Lover" and cranked up the volume on the decks. And somehow in all the bedlam, I've ended up clutching a vast five-foot-long cardboard check made out for £20,000.

"Here, Cassiera," I smile, walking over to my friend and placing it in her arms. Claude looks at me; her face is stained with happy tears. She slowly shakes her head, like she can't believe what's happening.

"Thank you, Ronnie," she says. "Thank you so much."

"Hey," I smile. "Told you we wouldn't let you down."

party time

It's time to celebrate!

With Psycho Killa and the entire Mortuary Team just about to hit the stage for a live performance, Saul, Finn Talbot, Claude, Fleur, a dozen of Saul's surfer buddies and I are trying to exit the Demonboard Babe marquee and follow the crowd to the main soundstage. As our little gang makes its way through the throng, kids are stopping me, wanting their picture taken, hugging me and asking me to record voice-mail messages on their mobile phones. I sign an autograph for some girls from Wales while Claude scoots off to give an "exclusive" to her journalist friend from *The Mirror* whom she met at the pool yesterday. Apparently, he wants the LBD lowdown on our fight to stop her move to Mossington.

We reach the main stage area, and it's absolute bedlam, with thousands of kids jumping and yelling to the familiar opening bars of Psycho Killa's "Graveyard Time." As some loud samples of machine-gun fire boom out, the entire crowd begins chanting Psycho Killa's catchphrase "Bag you up! Bag you up!" while the rest of the Mortuary Team leaps onto the stage, clutching mikes and shouting all sorts of hilarious nonsense.

We reach the outer fringes of the main crowds, and I turn to make sure Fleur is still with us. Behind me, my blonde chum is standing looking rather perplexed, examining a small white piece of cardboard in her hand.

"You okay, Fleur?" I shout above the din.

"Yeah, think so," Fleur replies, looking at the card again before passing it to me.

The card reads

CATRIONA LEESON

BOOKER, NEW FACES DIVISION
MILLION DOLLAR MODELS (LONDON)
TELEPHONE: 020 7 323 766665

"Where did you get this?" I shout.

"This girl came up to me backstage, when I was waiting for you guys," yells Fleur. "She asked me to stand in front of the dressing room door, with a white background behind me, snapped a Polaroid of me and then gave me this. Says I've got to ring her."

"Fleur!" I laugh. "That's amazing!"

"Is it?" asks Fleur, looking a little puzzled. "I mean, does that mean I've been, like, scouted? 'Cos I thought it would be more, y'know, official . . . or something."

Fleur stands for a few more seconds, reexamining the card with a small look of growing excitement on her face.

"Yes!" I scream, almost drowning out Freaky D, who appears to be throwing around a vial of fake blood and doing a little war dance with an ax. "That's what happens when you've been scouted, you great nork!"

Fleur's mouth falls open as I throw myself upon her for a hug. "I knew it!" she chortles, folding up the card and sticking it into her jeans pocket before dancing off into the crowd. "I knew it, Ronnie! My time has come!"

"C'mon, Veronica," yells Saul, taking my hand and trying to pull me farther into the crowd where all the rest of our group are standing. But in my jeans pocket, I can feel my phone vibrating. Probably Mum, I think, wanting to congratulate me. I gesture to Saul to give me five, before wandering off outside the marquee.

"Helloooo?" I shout, sticking my finger in my other ear, battling my way through the crowd.

"Ronnie?" says a male voice.

"That's me," I say. "Who's this?"

"It's Jimi," he says. "Jimi Steele."

I freeze.

I feel like you must four seconds after jumping from an airplane.

"Errrr . . . what . . . erm . . . what do you want, Jimi?" I say, wandering behind a hot-dog stand where it's quieter.

"I just called to say hi," he says in an odd voice I barely recognize. "My mate Naz rang, says he saw you on TV this morning, with your, erm, friend."

"Oh," I say, feeling a little winded.

There's an awkward silence. What am I supposed to say now?

"So, how . . . er, are you?" I ask.

"Not so good," he says drably. "It's been one pretty lame summer. As I'm sure you'll agree."

No, I don't agree, actually. It has been the best summer of my entire life.

Something in Jimi's voice sounds like he's inviting a deep, heavy conversation. The same one I ached for when I sat on his

249

garden wall all those months ago feeling sick with heartache. But now that it's available, it just seems futile. I'm cured.

"So, Jimi, how's Suzette?" I say, allowing a soupçon of bitterness to creep into my voice.

"Er . . . oh," stutters Jimi, sounding put on the spot. "That sort of fizzled out. She's been training loads for this charity half marathon with Miles Boon, y'know . . . they've been spending weekends together while I was working at Wacky Warehouse and . . ."

Jimi's voice trails off. A small grin creeps across my face. "She dumped you for Miles Boon," I say plainly.

"No! I wasn't dumped," argues Jimi. "It's more that—"

"She dumped you for Miles Boon," I repeat. Then I throw my head back and laugh, rather more cruelly than my normal persona would allow, but heck, this feels so good.

"I'm glad I amuse you, Ronnie," Jimi mumbles crossly.

I want to tell him exactly why this is so amusing, but it really is time for me to go. In the distance, I can see Saul's silhouette at the door of the marquee, beckoning for me to hurry up and watch Psycho Killa's final track.

"Look, Jimi, what did you call for?" I say rather brusquely. "Was there a point?"

"Oh . . . erm," he stutters, floundering for words. "Okay. Well, I called because I've been thinking about me and you."

"Thinking what exactly?" I say.

"Thinking about what *we* threw away," Jimi says, without a hint of irony. "'Cos, y'know, we really loved each other, didn't we, Ronnie? And, well, I just think we could work through this rough patch. I mean, all those annoying things you do, I can turn a blind eye to them. 'Cos that's what love's about, isn't it?"

By this point, I can't really think of a fitting, succinct reply to Jimi that would communicate how I feel about that last remark. And besides, he's wasted too much of my time already.

"Jimi, I'm putting the phone down now," I tell him calmly. "Will you do me a huge favor?"

"Anything," Jimi says.

"I'd like you to erase my number from your phone," I say, "and never call me again. Ever."

"But Ronnie, I—" he begins to yell as I turn off my phone and place it into the pocket of my jeans. I think this could be what writers talk about in those serious *Cosmopolitan* magazine relationship articles when they talk about "having closure."

"You're a total one-off, you are," Saul tells me as we stand on the sand right at the back of the crowd, watching Dita Murray and the Scandal Children's set. It's dusk and the Booty Quake crowd is growing even larger as people finish work and flock down to join the beach party.

"What do you mean?" I ask, blushing slightly.

"I've never met anyone like you," he tells me. "You get your heart set on something and you just do it. Y'know, all that business with Claude? And learning to surf? And taking a chance on me when you found me in your attic? You've just got spirit, y'know?"

I look at Saul. Not only is he utterly gorgeous, but stuff drops out of his mouth quite naturally that no one has ever said to me before but I've always dreamed of.

He really is the most perfect creature I've ever met.

And he's moving to the total opposite side of the hemisphere.

I take a deep breath and decide to say what's really on my mind. "Look, can I ask you a serious question?" I say.

"Go on," he says.

I pause for a while, wanting to wimp out.

"Do you think we can stay in touch when you go to Australia?" I ask. This is me being very brave. I know full well that "being free" is Saul Parker's life philosophy. It's risky to make any demands.

Saul is silent for a while. Then he sighs and looks down at his feet. "Long-distance relationships suck, Veronica," he says quietly.

"Mmm, yeah, I know," I nod, doing my best unbothered face.

Then Saul turns and looks at me oddly. He smooths his hand over my hair and looks me right in the eyes.

"Look, Veronica," he says, "I've got a ten-thousand-pound check here in my pocket. It's the most money I'm ever likely to have in my entire life. All I want to do is buy a ticket to Australia, then buy a VW camper. Then I'm going to roam about the world surfing and going to beach parties."

"Yeah," I smile, feeling a tiny lump growing in my throat. "I always knew that. Don't worry."

It sounds like a marvelous plan. I can't begrudge him for not wanting to get involved.

Saul grabs my hand and wraps his fingers around it tightly. "So come with me?" he asks.

Chapter 9

the morning after

The following morning at 8 A.M. prompt, after a thorough search of the West Turret by Miss Scrumble and assorted flunkies with stepladders and flashlights, the LBD are sacked from Harbinger Hall. Oddly enough, Scrumble didn't appreciate Claude's and my ingenuity in using the loft space to harbor Saul and Fleur, or "the debris of society," as she referred to them. Instead, Scrumble bars us and any subsequent generation of our families from Harbinger Hall and all other Vanderloo Hotels sister properties "for the duration of our dismal lives."

It's the first place I've ever been barred from. And my first official sacking too. I feel inexplicably proud.

"And don't dare ask me for a reference!" crows Scrumble, pinballing around the West Turret, throwing about handfuls of our clothes and shoes, threatening to have everything burned by the gardener if we're not off the property by 10 A.M.

To be honest, this suits us just fine.

It's almost September and we're ready to leave anyhow. Claude especially is dying to see her mum. She already phoned

Gloria Cassiera and explained all about the money and how we plotted to stop Flat 27, Lister House, from being sold. Apparently Gloria broke down in tears. She just couldn't believe what we'd done for them both.

"It took me a while to convince her I hadn't gone crazy," smiles Claude. "Then she kept accusing me of being drunk and warning me of the slippery slope of alcohol abuse."

"But she believes you now?" I ask, sitting on my suitcase in an attempt to close it.

"Yeah, she does now," nods Claude. "She says she can't thank you enough. Oh, and incidentally, you're all going to heaven. And she's promised to take the house off the market right now. And cancel my place at Mossington High."

Claude pauses for a second to look at Fleur and me, then gives a little shake of her head in disbelief. "You two are unreal, y'know?" she smiles. "As long as I live, I'll never forget this. It's all just . . ."

As Claude's voice became a little misty again, Fleur picks up her suitcase and looks at her watch. "Now, now, Miss Cassiera," she grins. "No slushiness. It's time for our offical drumming off the premises. And I, for one, can't wait."

Fleur turns to where Saul is lying on the sofa with a cushion over his face, trying to grab ten minutes of extra sleep. "Right, Saul Parker," Fleur yells, "who's going to carry some ladies' suitcases down a hundred and eighty-eight stairs? Any volunteers?"

As we clamber into the mini cab outside the main entrance, Siegmund, Rosco, Gene and Leon all wander out of the staff entrance to wave good-bye.

"Girls, girls," sighs Siegmund, with a small, almost proud grin. "I tried my best to save you. But you *really* did it this time."

"Never mind, Sieg. Thanks anyway," I smile, as the striking vision of Carbzilla strolls into view wearing a large white terrycloth dressing gown, clearly on her way to the day spa.

"Hey, Mrs. Fontague!" shouts Fleur. "We have to say goodbye now. We're being ejected from the grounds!"

Carbzilla turns and looks at us, her face a picture of disappointment.

"Ejected?" she cries. "No! Who'll bring my banana daiquiris now? You were the best waitresses this place has ever seen. That Scrumble character is a horse's ass. A horse's ass, I tell you!"

We all try not to laugh, but we just can't help ourselves.

"Godspeed, girls!" shouts Carbzilla, trundling away.

And with our stuff packed into the car and Saul's surfboard tied on the roof rack, we set off for Destiny Bay station.

departures

"Right, the next train to Gatwick Airport leaves in twenty minutes," says Saul, scanning the timetable on the platform before turning to me.

"Ours is just about to arrive," Fleur announces, pointing at the arrivals screen above us. "In about three minutes' time."

"Okay," I say softly, linking Saul's arm.

Claude and Fleur, sensing a "moment," make excuses and wander to the other end of the platform.

I've decided to get the train home with Claude and Fleur. I

can't go to Australia. I think Saul understands. All those things that Saul rated about me—my spirit, my loyalty, my brains—well, they don't quite fit in with jacking my entire life in and ditching my A-levels and the LBD for a lad I've known just longer than five minutes.

Do they? Even if he is totally beautiful?

Ninety-nine percent of me knows this is the right decision.

"Here we are then, kiddo," he says, nodding toward the train, which is approaching Platform 1.

"Yep," I sigh, going up on tiptoes and kissing his forehead. His dreads smell of sea salt and wax. I inhale the smell discreetly.

"Now, you have a good time at school," he sort of laughs, as if the idea is totally absurd.

"Yeah, I will," I smile, wrapping my arms around him. "And you enjoy Australia."

Then we have one last snog, which would have been nicer but for the fact that my heart is literally hurting and tears are dribbling down my face, sploshing all over his Rip Curl hoodie, as Claude and Fleur bundle my stuff onto the train, yelling at the guard to give us five more seconds.

As the train pulls away, I look out the window at Saul. He's sitting alone on a cold metal bench, beside his surfboard. All his worldly belongings are packed in an army surplus rucksack beside him. The train picks up speed, and the breeze plays with his brown dreadlocks, lifting them slightly. Saul pulls the hood up on his jacket and slumps forward slightly, resting his face on his hands.

As I take my seat, I catch his eye one final time.

He gives me a wink, and then he's gone.

"Come on, Ronnie," says Fleur, as the train hurtles through mile upon mile of countryside. "Look, I bought you the new *Red Hot Celebs* mag! And some Ribena. And some Chocky Wocky Doo-Dahs for you and a Twix for me."

Fleur's clearly trying to distract me.

I open my chocolates, unwrap one and stick it in my mouth. "Pssst . . . save the silver foils," Fleur says, doing a bad stage whisper. "Then when Claude starts to snore, we can play throwing them in her mouth."

"It's a deal," I stage-whisper back.

"Very funny," groans Claude, who's reading today's *Mirror* very closely. "Oh, dear me," she says. "This is a shame—listen to this: Apparently, there's a terrible scandal going on at Farquar, Lime and Young Pharmaceuticals. Apparently one of the chiefs there, a Mr. Alan Sleeth, has been fired for selling untested pills. The newspaper must have had a tip-off from someone. They've done a huge exposé on him!"

We all stare at page six of *The Mirror*. It's all there in black and white. *The Mirror* had the exclusive.

"Does that mean the Sleeths will have to leave town?" I ask.

"Probably," smiles Claude, turning to the celebrity gossip page.

"Oh, dear," says Fleur. "What a big fat shame."

~~~~~~~~~~~~~~~~~~~~

ʃo anyway

Back at the Fantastic Voyage, our welcome-home party is in full swing far before Fleur, Claude and I even get off the train. Our parents don't need much excuse for a knees-up at the best of times.

As I walk into the pub, the first person I spot is my mum, standing behind the bar, looking rather more robust than the last time I saw her. She's wearing red lipstick and yelling abuse at my dad about not taking out the trash quickly enough, while the customers duck for cover. It feels like normal services post-Nan are being resumed. I give Mum a huge hug, which feels marvelous. Absence really does makes the heart grow fonder. In fact, it's a full twenty minutes before she finds a comb and starts trying to detangle my "surf-chick" hair, claiming my bunches are "a haven to fleas." Charming.

There seem to have been a few changes at the pub while I've been away gallivanting. Above the bar, on the blackboard, I notice all sorts of Thai and Malaysian dishes I've never seen before on the pub food menu. Over in the corner, Toothless Bert is slurping a kare lomen noodle dish with a look of contentment. And at the bottom of the blackboard, written under "Puddings," Mum has scribbled:

Fresh homemade scones, served Thunder and Lightning style, 2 for £1

"They're selling like hotcakes," Mum says. "Pardon the pun."

I think of Nan and smile. She'd have been totally proud of both of us.

Just then Dad appears with my little brother, Seth, who must have grown at least three inches since I last saw him.

"Beeeeaaaaaaaabllll!" squeals Seth when he spots me.

"He says hello," explains Dad, giving me a huge kiss. "Hey, and nice booty-quaking yesterday, Ronnie!"

"Oh well . . . y'know," I blush as Seth flaps around in Dad's arms demanding to be put down. Once placed upon the floor, he stumbles about ten steps before smashing headfirst into Gloria Cassiera's handbag. Gloria scoops him up, dusts him down and passes him back to me.

"Ronnie," she says quietly, "I don't know how to even begin to thank you."

"Aw . . . don't worry about it," I blush.

It's worth every penny to see her and Claude sitting there together in the pub looking so happy.

"Loz!" Paddy Swan shouts across at my dad. "Let's make a night of this! Shall we get the karaoke going later? I'll do my Rat Pack medley."

"Not tonight, Paddy, please," sighs Saskia, Fleur's mum.

"Good idea, Paddy," agrees Dad. "And I'll do my Marvin Gaye!"

It feels great to be home. Among all the people who know and understand you.

"I'm so happy you saved me from Mossington School," sighs Claude as the LBD sit around a pub table nattering about all the super-cool things we're going to do in Year 12. Excitingly, Fleur turns seventeen next month and Paddy has just hinted that he has his eye on an old Mini for her to pass her driving test in.

"The bambino buggy!" says Fleur. "We should spray it pink!"

"Hey, we can drive down to It's a Girl's World at Emerald Park Shopping City," says Claude. *"Together,* this time, that is."

Fleur groans in embarrassment.

"Hey, sorry to break up the party, girls," says Dad, "but I've just had a weird phone call from a Mr. McGraw."

"Mr. McGraw, our headmaster?" I ask.

"Yeah, sounded like him. Sounded a bit, y'know, depressed," Dad grins. "He said he'd heard through the grapevine that you were all back home after your summer job. He was waffling on about his poodles. Have you girls made some sort of arrangement?"

"Oh . . . oh no," grimaces Fleur, hanging on to the pub table.

"So anyway," continues Dad, "the message is 'Anytime early evening tonight is fine.' Oooh yeah, and he's bought special shampoo."

By this point Claude and I are in hysterics.

"Noooo!" pleads Fleur. "Not tonight. Not any night! Let's pretend we're not here. Let's say we've been abducted . . . by aliens?"

"Fleur Swan, a deal is a deal," laughs Claude. "Let's go over and do it now. We can be back in time for karaoke. Pull yourself together, Blondie!"

"Bleeeeeugh," retches Fleur, just thinking about the task. "Oh God. Oh . . . okay then. But just promise me something—I'm just in charge of the front ends. Teeth and ears. Not the bums. Not the poo-encrusted bums!"

Claude and I are laughing so hard now, we can hardly speak.

"Anything but that!" Fleur pleads, walking very slowly toward the door. "Girls, say you'll do those bits, pleeeease?"

"Okay, Fleur," I laugh as we both link her arms and pull her along.

"After all," chuckles Claude, "what are friends for?"